OF
BITTER
THORN

ALSO BY KAY L MOODY

The Fae of Bitter Thorn
Heir of Bitter Thorn
Court of Bitter Thorn
Castle of Bitter Thorn
Crown of Bitter Thorn
Queen of Bitter Thorn

The Elements of Kamdaria
The Elements of the Crown
The Elements of the Gate
The Elements of the Storm

Truth Seer Trilogy
Truth Seer
Healer
Truth Changer

Visit kaylmoody.com/bitter to read the prequel novella,
***Heir of Bitter Thorn*, for free**

CASTLE

OF

BITTER

THORN

KAY L MOODY

THE FAE OF BITTER THORN

2

Castle of Bitter Thorn
The Fae of Bitter Thorn 2
By Kay L Moody

Published by Marten Press
3731 W 10400 S Ste 102, #205
South Jordan, UT 84009

www.MartenPress.com

Cover by Angel Leya
Edited by Justin Greer

ISBN: 978-1-954335-00-4

CHAPTER

1

Magic, enchantment, and… danger. With all of Faerie's delights came a host of troubles. Troubles that could maim, destroy, or even kill. *So, why am I so desperate to stay?*

Elora's toe met the mossy stone floor of her bedroom in a flurry of taps.

She had promised Prince Brannick she would stay and help him win the testing to become High King of Faerie. But then what? Was she really just going to go home like the prince insisted? Could she really return to the mortal realm to care for her two sisters while knowing Faerie existed? Could she live knowing it was just out of her reach?

When an ache split through her ankle from how often she tapped her toe, she jumped off her bed.

If she *had* to leave after the testing, then she also had a *duty* to explore Faerie before leaving it forever.

Her eyes flicked toward the open window of her bedroom.

Exploration took more effort these days. A forest breeze fluttered inside, ruffling the leaves on the tree in the middle of her room.

While the breeze could move freely in and out of her window, she could not. The brooding prince of Bitter Thorn had placed an enchantment over her window, preventing her from reaching even a finger through it.

He claimed the spell would protect her. At the first phase of testing, she had played a harp for High King Romany and hundreds of fae had heard her remarkable skill. Supposedly, other fae would now stop at nothing to snatch her away from Bitter Thorn.

Yet, the enchantment still seemed like an excuse to keep her trapped.

Sneaking out the window was out of the question. Her door, on the other hand, had no such enchantment. She could sneak into her hallway with no effort at all—sneaking anywhere interesting would take more skill.

Pulling on the leather strap of her door, she peeked into the hallway. Empty. Just as she suspected. Rising up to tiptoes, she started down it. The dark solitude provided the perfect backdrop for a memory she kept trying to ignore.

The first phase of testing.

During the revel that night, she had been forced to kiss Prince Brannick just to prove to a particularly nasty fae that no one could claim her as a pet. Apparently, the stupid kiss hadn't been enough to keep her safe.

Everything had gone wrong that night. They managed to kill the king of Dustdune before he could inflict deadly shards on half the fae in Faerie. But stopping him had come at a cost.

Prince Brannick had been weakened when he destroyed some of the shards. There had been a fight. An ogre. And the kiss.

Now the prince insisted she have an escort everywhere she went, and her window was enchanted every night to lock her inside.

Too bad for the prince, she had perfected the art of sneaking out by the age of thirteen. She only needed a destination, quiet feet, and a good excuse if she got caught. Her excuse tonight would be a nightmare. Or sleepwalking. Or maybe both.

She'd figure it out on the spot if she had to. She just had to get out and experience the wonders of Faerie while she still could. Before Prince Brannick won the testing to become High King and forced her to return to the mortal realm.

Vines of green leaves stretched across the stone ceiling of the hallway. A light wind fluttered through the leaves, making just enough noise to mask her steps. Black thorns twisted through the greenery. They creaked in the breeze, covering her sounds even more.

Her fingers trailed across the mossy wall at her side. Just as she neared the end of the corridor, the cool, rocky texture of stone vanished.

She jerked her head sharply to the side and sucked in a breath. Where did the wall go?

To her eyes, the stone wall looked the same as it always did. The sight of it curled her gut into a knot. Reaching out with one hand, she waved her hand through the air in the exact spot that the wall appeared. And yet, no wall met her fingertips.

At least now she had a name for the trickery. *Glamour*. The fae could use magic to make things look different from how they really appeared.

Using both hands to sweep the area in front of her, she found that the empty space was the exact size of a hallway opening. Her heart thumped in her chest at the thought. With tingling fingers, she leaned forward.

What would happen when she tried to push her head through the glamour that looked like a wall? Her hands hadn't met any resistance, so why should the rest of her?

Despite those thoughts, a part of her still held back. At one time, nothing could have stopped her curiosity. She would have charged forward without a thought. But that was before she discovered Faerie. Before she betrayed a prince and conspired with a king. Before she had ever kissed anyone.

Now she knew the dangers of Faerie were just as real as its magic. Her body hovered at the hidden doorway. What if she couldn't find her way back? What if a treacherous creature lurked beyond the glamour?

When a whiff of decay met her nose, she stumbled backward. Her feet slapped against the stone floor, letting out a noise that rang down the hallway on both ends. The thumping in her chest shook harder than before. The tingles in her fingertips suddenly felt like needles.

She whipped away from the wall that wasn't really a wall. Why did she have to explore that hallway right then, anyway? Another day would be better. Besides, she still wanted to sneak into the forest to gather some purple berries for her brownie, Fifer.

Footsteps neared from an adjoining corridor. Based on the sound of them, she only had a moment to dash away before getting caught.

Using the light feet she usually reserved for dancing, Elora slipped into a new hallway. Luckily, it was as deserted as her own. She prioritized speed over silence as she moved. Even if someone heard her footsteps, hopefully she could get away before they arrived.

Crisp forest air trickled through the castle hallways thanks to large, open windows. Still, nothing compared to meeting the air outside. When Elora finally stepped outside the castle and entered the forest surrounding it, she took in a deep breath.

More footsteps sounded behind her. She scurried around the nearest castle turret. A stone staircase covered in moss and twigs was tucked in between the turret and the black castle wall at its side. It sat at a strange angle, which was probably why she had never noticed it before.

Without a good excuse for being out, she welcomed the chance to hide as quickly as possible. Spongy moss gave off the scent of wet earth as she trailed down the staircase. A black door with a leather strap for a handle stood at the bottom. She didn't think twice before pushing it open.

Briars and thorns creaked all through the room. Their black vines twisted over the walls and around the plush furniture. A tree stood in one corner, but the black thorns twisted so tight around its trunk and around every branch that the poor tree had died. A strong stench wafted all around, but it wasn't unpleasant exactly. It was just... different.

In fact, everything in the room felt different, though she couldn't explain how. Her theories came to a halt when a cold voice cut across the room.

"What are you doing here, mortal?" Prince Brannick slouched in a chair made from leather and bundles of thin branches. His black hair hung down to his shoulders—as glossy as ever but limper than usual too. Even when he shook out his shoulders and ran a hand through his hair, it didn't bounce as it usually did.

"Prince Brannick." She curtsied before him, but the tone of her voice was mocking.

He could tell.

His nose twitched. The chill in his voice transferred to his limbs. Tension rocked through him as he leaned forward with a glare. "Get out now." Each of his words came out like its own sentence. Each felt like a knife to the gut.

One kiss. They had only shared one kiss, and it was even a fake one only meant to convince the fae, Ansel, to leave Elora alone. But that one kiss had changed everything.

She didn't know what Brannick hated more, the fact that he had been forced to explain his past to her or the fact that he revealed his feelings for her. Either way, the combination had turned him even colder than she had ever seen.

Then again, love had destroyed his life once before. He had given his heart to Queen Alessandra of Fairfrost. He made a bargain with her and promised to follow every order she ever gave him. He also promised he would never touch anyone besides Alessandra if he had romantic feelings for that being in his heart.

That was the most frightening thing about fae bargains. They *couldn't* be broken. When he and Elora shared that one kiss, even though it had been a fake one, he still almost vanished from existence. Despite how he tried to deny it, Brannick had strong enough feelings for her that the bargain tried to destroy him when he touched her.

At first, Elora foolishly believed the truth would bring them closer together. She thought the prince might turn to her for advice or even comfort. Instead, he seemed intent on avoiding her altogether.

Before he could repeat his command, she raised herself up to the balls of her feet. "You promised to get me a new sheath for my sword. You said you would put a glamour on it that would make it invisible so I can carry my sword with me everywhere."

His nose twitched again. As he moved his hand upward to pinch the bridge of his nose, a pair of black ears appeared from behind his woody throne.

A snout soon followed and then the wolf's entire body could be seen. Only a moment later, he bounded forward and nuzzled into Elora's leg.

"Hello, Blaz." She grinned as she dug her fingers into his soft black fur. At least the wolf had missed her. Her knees dropped to the earthy woven rug under her feet, so she could more easily scratch behind Blaz's ears.

Her eyes turned to the prince as she knelt. For the briefest moment, a soft smile adorned his face while he watched her with his wolf. The expression melted away so quickly, she almost thought she imagined it.

The thorns twisting around Brannick's chair creaked as he let out a huff. "It is too dangerous for you to leave your room at night. Do I need to put an enchantment on your doorway as well as your window?"

She left a soft pat on top of Blaz's head before glaring up at the prince. "Am I a prisoner?"

The words tumbled from her lips, as if they'd had this argument many times. The ease with which they quarreled came as naturally as it had between her own parents. With that thought, she felt her mouth twist up into a knot.

A matching snarl filled Brannick's face. "You are not a prisoner. And do you think I actually care for your safety? It is your sword skill I need. My life will be much easier if you do not get injured or kidnapped before the final phase of testing."

This was the first time she had seen the prince since he told her everything about his past with Alessandra.

So why did everything feel different?

Blaz padded across the woven rug to stand at the prince's side. Brannick arched his hand over the arm of his chair to reach for the wolf's head. At least two more vines of black briars had covered the arm since Elora entered the room.

That was part of the curse on the prince's court of Bitter Thorn. Thorns followed him everywhere he went in his court. But was the curse getting worse? She had never seen the thorns grow around him so quickly.

Smoothing out the wrinkles in her purple skirt, Elora kept her gaze away from the prince. "Shouldn't we begin training again then? It's been days since we were in Dustdune and destroyed the shards, but I haven't done any sword training with you at all. Aren't we running out of time?"

The chuckle that left Brannick's lips held no humor. "There is no *time* in Faerie. High King Romany will not announce the next phase until we are ready."

It seemed like the perfect moment to roll her eyes. Knowing it would bother Brannick, she flopped herself onto the nearest chair. "Are we just going to forget the testing then? If you never prepare for it, then it will never happen. Is that your plan?"

As she lifted her eyes to roll them again, an unexpected sight met them.

A chandelier.

The sparkly crystals caught the light, showering the upper walls of the room with a rainbow of light. But it wasn't just the crystals that caught her eye. Soft light glowed from the spot where candles should have been. The light was mostly white with a hint of pink, but it definitely wasn't fire. Even more intriguing, it wasn't green.

She glanced around the top of the room another time, finally recognizing why the room looked different. In every part of Faerie that she had ever been, small glowing green lights always floated up above. She now knew the glowing lights were actually sprites who sent messages throughout Faerie. She had even befriended a small sprite named Tansy.

But this room had no sprites. Instead, the only light source in the room came from the chandelier. It must have been from magic she hadn't seen before.

When she finally turned back to the prince again, he glared even harder than before. With a wave of one hand, a swirling tunnel appeared at his side. Brown, green, and black smudges twirled around each other down the length of the tunnel. A cool and gentle breeze floated through the tunnel, bringing along with it the scent of wet earth, moss, and rain.

Just when the slightest hint of wild berries filled the air, Brannick cleared his throat. "That door will take you back to your room."

Elora pouted as she leaned back into her chair. "But I don't want to go back to my room. Once the testing is over, I have to return to the mortal realm. I'm anxious to explore Faerie and enjoy it as much as I can before I go."

His shoulders stiffened as he sat taller in his chair. "Then explore it during the day and with an escort. At night, you must stay in your room."

Glancing toward the door that led to the forest, she sat up straighter. "But I don't have an offering for Fifer. I must leave him an offering, or he won't bring me anything to eat in—"

As she spoke, the prince whirled one hand in a circle. A clump of purple wildflowers appeared at Elora's feet by the time he finished. The flowers would make a perfect offering for her brownie.

She snatched them off the ground as she stood from her chair. Another night, she would have argued more. She would have reminded him again about the sheath he promised. But truthfully, she was getting tired and the thought of her warm bed was too nice to ignore.

Just for fun, she snarled at the prince as she moved toward his swirling tunnel.

He met her expression with a clenched jaw. "You should be safe inside the castle, but do not leave its walls again unless you have an escort. Your skills are too valuable in Faerie. You are not safe."

She mostly ignored his words as she stomped toward his Faerie door. He could order her around as much as he liked, but she didn't have to follow. She had learned something since being in Faerie, and that was how to take her life into her own hands.

He couldn't stop her from enjoying Faerie. No matter how hard he tried.

CHAPTER 2

Even with air as her only opponent, Elora loved practicing her sword skill. Her blade swished and sliced, glinting in the light of her room. Only after she'd been practicing for a while did a thin bead of sweat break out over her forehead.

After completing a difficult set of exercises, she finally let her arms drop to her sides. The leather hilt of her sword fit perfectly in her palm like it always had.

A twinkling noise accompanied a glowing green light that flew down from the ceiling. Pink sparkles glittered against the green. Only a moment later, Tansy flopped onto Elora's shoulder. The sprite's velvety hair bounced as she landed.

"I have traveled everywhere in Faerie many times, but I have never seen anyone with sword skill such as yours."

The compliment turned Elora's lips up. She lifted the soft mattress of her bed and hid the sword underneath it. Now she turned to the sprite. "Should I be worried that you know about my sword skill? Brannick insists I must keep it secret. You won't tell other fae will you?"

With a glistening snort, the sprite clutched her belly. "Sprites do not speak to other fae, except to deliver messages."

Elora raised an eyebrow. "But you speak to me?"

Tansy gave a casual shrug as she ran a hand over her spiked-up hair. "I'm not supposed to. But you did prevent us from delivering shards that would have killed half the fae in Faerie." She shrugged. "We like you."

At those words, the sprite flew off Elora's shoulder. Her glowing green wings flapped hard, but she moved with the elegance of a hummingbird. Seeing the sprite fly brought Elora's thoughts to the wings on her own back.

Brannick had given her wings in exchange for her help with sword skill, yet she had hardly used them at all. Fear was the biggest reason. But Tansy could fly, and she liked Elora. Would the sprite be willing to share her knowledge of flying?

Elora bent to test the strength of the ribbon around her ankle. The red ribbon had come from her sister, Chloe, and it acted as a ward against fae enchantments. Luckily, the knot remained as tight as ever.

When Elora stood, she tilted her head toward the sprite in front of her. "Is that the only reason you speak to me? Because you like me?" Elora had learned early on that everyone in Faerie had devious intentions. As much as she liked the sprite, she didn't expect anything different from her.

The sprite's wings glowed brighter as she turned in a loop. Soon, she was hovering right in front of Elora's face. "Hundreds of my brothers and sisters are still trapped by Queen Alessandra in Fairfrost Court. We are trying to devise a plan to free them, and that plan might include you."

"I thought it might be something like that." Elora chuckled, but she didn't mind the feeling of being needed.

A moment later, the captain of the guard arrived to escort her to the council room. Tansy immediately disappeared among the sea of sprites near the ceiling while Elora entered the hallway with Soren.

The stocky gnome uttered gruff complaints as he led her down the hall. Once the council room was in sight, he left to perform one last duty as captain of the guard before he would return to the council room again.

Twelve trees grew inside the room, shading the long wooden table at the center of it. The sight always took Elora's breath away, but just then, something else caught her attention.

Blaz dipped his black-furred head, almost as if telling her to stop where she stood. Only then did she notice the two people already standing in the council room. Prince Brannick stood at the head of the table speaking to the dryad, Kaia. Her flowing emerald hair ruffled in the light breeze going through the room. Brannick's head bent while he glared.

Neither of them had noticed Elora's presence.

She glanced at the wolf again. This time, he tipped his nose upward at the two beside him. Did he want her to listen?

Kaia traced circles over her palm, mixing together some sort of powder and liquid. She frowned at the sight of it. "Your essence is still suffering since the battle in Dustdune."

"I know." Brannick folded his arms over his chest as he glared at the ground. "I can feel it. I thought seeing Queen Alessandra again had caused it, but I think it might be related to..." His voice trailed off for a moment as his nose twitched. "...something else."

The dryad shook her head, still staring at her palm. "It hasn't been the same since you escaped from Fairfrost."

Brannick's voice raised in pitch. "You said it was getting better."

Letting out a sigh, Kaia reached into her pocket for a white cloth. "It was, but then…"

Her voice stopped as she wiped the mixture off her palm. The movement caused her head to turn just enough to see Elora standing in the doorway of the room.

The slightest twinge of pink colored the prince's cheeks before he clenched his teeth together. "Where is Soren?"

Elora flipped a portion of hair over one shoulder. "He said he had to check on a squad before the meeting."

That answer only brought an even angrier snarl to the prince's lips. He hissed as he dropped himself onto the throne that merged stone and tree together at the head of the council room table. After snapping away the twisting black thorns that covered the arms of the throne, he shot an angry huff toward Elora.

The dryad took a seat at the table. She smoothed her emerald hair and glanced at the prince. "That attitude will not help you. Strong emotion could be making it worse."

He let out another huff. "How am I supposed to control my emotion with such an infuriating presence nearby?" He punctuated his question by jabbing his thumb in Elora's direction. "Why must she go around listening to private conversations?"

A nearly inaudible snicker escaped the dryad's lips before she smothered it with the clearing of her throat.

Several pairs of footsteps sounded in the nearby hallway, which ended the conversation immediately. Brannick's other council members, Vesper, Quintus, and Lyren, entered the room one after the other.

Lyren's eyes flitted around, looking at nothing in particular. She touched a hand to her seashell necklace several times, as if her thoughts were far from that moment. In her other hand, she held a long, shimmery-blue javelin.

The other two fae were much more animated. Quintus shook his head, which rustled his neatly parted black hair. His eyes were wide when he spoke to Vesper. "You angered a giant in Mistmount by accidentally sleeping on it and then you decided to fight with it?"

Vesper slid a hand through his brown curls before giving a casual shrug. "I would have opened a door and left, but you know how I love a good fight." He chuckled as he sat down at the table. "Anyway, the giant swung his blade, which was longer than most of the trees in Mistmount, I might add. I managed to avoid it, but a nearby home wasn't as lucky. The giant's sword smashed all the way through it."

As Lyren took a seat at the table, she bit her bottom lip. Still, she stared off at nothing in particular.

Vesper sat forward in his chair, his blue and gray eyes bright. "Naturally, I summoned fire, which scared the giant away. Unfortunately, the fire also caught onto the broken home. I thought nothing of it until a dwarf child came running out of the house screaming about his parents."

At those words, Quintus pulled a pad of paper and pencil from his pocket. He began sketching the scene before nodding at Vesper to continue.

Now Vesper smiled. "I ran into the burning home next. I did not care for the lives of the child's parents." His mouth tilted in a grin. "But I could not refuse the adventure. Obviously, I survived, but the entire dwarf family did too. It was one of my most memorable travels."

Widened eyes and shocked gasps accompanied the end of the tale, but the words only gnarled Elora's insides. Her stomach churned as memories of a different fire filled her mind. She couldn't help notice the irony of the fae's story. He saved the dwarf family with his desire for adventure. But it was only when Elora accepted her arranged marriage—and lack of adventure—that her own parents were killed in a fire.

The thoughts twisted inside her, writhing so fast that tears pooled in her eyes before she had even taken a breath. Her throat ached as she tried to blink the tears away. Her fingers curled into tight fists as she forced herself to take deep breaths.

Those memories were too painful. She couldn't face them, especially not in the middle of a council meeting. If Brannick saw her weakness, he would surely find a way to exploit it. And who enjoyed pain anyway?

When the prince stood from his throne and began talking about their plans, Elora shoved the memories away and forced herself to focus on nothing but his words. No one needed the distraction more than she did.

"We have two phases left in the testing." Brannick's voice seemed different than it had when she first entered the room. Now it seemed stronger. Surer. He stood taller too. "Lyren, Soren, and I are working on the speeches. My speech is the most important, but High King Romany might ask any of you to give a short speech on my behalf."

Elora sucked in a breath before quiet words escaped from her mouth. "Even me?"

From across the table, Vesper tapped his chin. "Elora has done her part, has she not? Can we not return her to the mortal realm now?"

The slightest flinch went through Brannick's shoulders before he answered. "Because she helped with the first phase of testing, High King Romany will consider her a member of my council until the testing is over."

Though pain from her past had churned in her stomach only moments earlier, fear completely crushed it now. Her every thought was chained to the current conversation. "But I'm just a mortal. I don't know how to give a speech. What if I say something wrong?"

She had already broken many Faerie rules and all of them came with consequences.

"Hush." Brannick threw her a sharp look before standing straight again. "You have adventure in your blood. You will be fine."

Fear probably would have clutched her tighter, except Vesper jerked his head toward the prince with eyes so wide the light of the room filled them. A moment later, Vesper turned to glance at Elora. When he looked to the prince again, a weight rested in his eyes that hadn't been there before.

Brannick stood even taller, but it didn't hide his hard swallow. He gave a brief glance toward Elora. "Lyren will write your speech. You only have to give it." Now he cleared his throat. "The winner of the speech gets to choose the weapon that will be used in the final phase of the testing, the tournament."

Now Elora's eyes went wide. "The winner of the speech *chooses* the weapon for the tournament?"

Lyren glanced toward the doorway of the room. Her lips parted as if to respond, but she merely stared at the entrance instead. Was she waiting for something?

When silence filled the room for another moment, Brannick took the opportunity to fill it. He was careful to avoid Elora's eyes no matter how she tried to catch his.

Still her stomach churned. The prince's entire plan for the tournament rested on him using a sword. That was the whole reason she had been brought to Faerie in the first place. To teach him a weapon no fae would ever guess he could use. And the plan would only work if he first won the speech phase of the testing.

While she continued to attempt to catch the prince's eye, a sprite flew into the room and hovered in front of Lyren. It spoke with a shrill but quiet voice. "Lyren of Swiftsea, I have a message for you from Queen Noelani of Swiftsea."

Lyren jumped up from her chair. She barely had enough time to say "Excuse me" before she left the room and entered the nearby hallway. She took her javelin with her.

Brannick gave no reaction to her exit. He simply turned to Quintus, who was still sketching the story of the giant and the fire. After clearing his throat, the prince asked, "Are you almost finished with…" He raised both eyebrows instead of completing the sentence.

In response, Quintus nodded swiftly. "It will not take me much longer."

Now the prince turned to Kaia. "Prepare the elixir we discussed. I will take it this evening."

Bark-like striations had broken out across Kaia's brown skin. Her emerald hair grew stringy, almost like thin, green tree branches. "Yes, my prince. I must return to my tree at once, but I will bring it to you as soon as I can."

As the dryad left the room, Lyren entered it once again. "Did I miss anything?"

"No." Brannick shook his head and then waved toward Elora. "Would you return the mortal to her room for me? I must speak to Vesper."

Lyren's eyes went alight at the sound of those words. "Certainly." The quality of her voice had changed. It spoke of deviousness, and even more concerning, desperation.

The fae beckoned as she moved toward the doorway. "I would be happy to take her to her room."

Even though Elora followed, her knees shook with each step. But that was part of exploring Faerie. Sometimes it meant walking into danger.

CHAPTER 3

Anticipation coursed inside Elora as she stepped into the hallway. Once no other fae could be seen, she glanced toward her companion.

Lyren's dark skin was practically glowing in the green light from the sprites above. Her dark curls were looser than usual today, but they still bounced at the slightest movement. "Elora."

Though the fae's voice held lightness, Elora could sense something else along with it. The shimmer in Lyren's brown and silver eyes gave the secondary emotion away.

Fear.

After a single blink, a devious smile stretched across Lyren's face. "How would you like to visit Swiftsea?"

A rush of excitement leapt through Elora's stomach. Almost immediately, it dropped as she considered how quickly a simple visit could turn into something darker. She thought of Lyren as a friend, but she knew better than to trust the fae. In Faerie, it was better to not trust anyone.

Taking a step away, Elora narrowed one eye. "Is it safe?"

"Of course." Lyren reached for the seashell hanging from a silver chain around her neck. Her lips pursed together tight, but it didn't stop a sputtering cough from erupting a moment later. After several hard coughs, she managed to take in just enough air to squeeze out a few quiet words. "It is not. Of course it is not."

Smirking, Elora rested one hand on her hip. "Is that what happens when fae try to lie?"

But the fae did not return the amused expression. Instead, focus flashed in her brown and silver eyes. Lyren grasped her seashell even tighter. "I need your help."

Elora's smirk fell. The spark of fear in the fae's eyes seeped into the room around them, thickening the air. When she tried to speak, even her voice felt tight. "What's wrong?"

"I will protect you if you come with me." Lyren dropped her hand to her side. She paced the width of the hallway. "I cannot guarantee your safety, but I have my javelin. I am not as good as some, but I am more than proficient."

As if to illustrate her point, the fae snatched her shimmery-blue javelin from where it leaned against one wall. She spun it around so fast it made a whooshing sound.

"But why do you need me?" Elora reached into her hair, drawing her fingers over the two feathers tied there. She had one from Soren that would protect her from accidental danger. She had another from Brannick that would enhance any skills she had. But she didn't even have her sword with her. Neither of the feathers seemed particularly useful at the moment. "How could I possibly help you?"

The silver in Lyren's eyes burst with light. "I just need a story. You can even tell the same story you told me when you first arrived in Faerie, the one about your parents when they lived in the castle in the mortal realm."

Flips turned in Elora's stomach as she drew her eyebrows together. "A story? What's going on?"

Lyren shook her head side to side, faster each time. "I just received word from Queen Noelani about…" She gulped. "Perhaps it is time for you to see anyway."

The twinkling of the sprites above became easier to hear when no other sound filled the room. Elora gulped.

"Please." Lyren flinched the moment the word left her lips.

Elora remembered when she had said *thank you* to Lyren after the fae had given Elora a special shell. Saying such words required a gift be given in return. Did Faerie have similar rules for when someone said *please?*

Lyren stepped forward, now grasping both of the shells hanging from her neck. "I will owe you a debt if you agree, but *please*. Help me."

Whether a good idea or not, Elora wasn't about to sit around and waste her time while she was in a magical realm. Not when she had so much left to explore. With a stiff nod, she agreed.

No sooner had she made the gesture than Lyren waved her hand through the air. Her Faerie door swirled with waves of foamy white and bright blue. The smell of salt and sand drifted through it. Even stepping through it felt like walking over a sandy ocean shore.

Elora expected a similar sight to meet her on the other side. It didn't.

Instead, decaying palm trees rotted from the inside out. The sand beneath their feet had hardened like textured glass. An ocean with too-thick water bubbled before them. Salty air ruffled around them, but the salt was too strong. Too heavy. It brought the bitter taste of sickness to rest on her tongue.

Though Elora curled up her lip at the sight, Lyren grimaced. Her shoulders shook. With each breath, she brought one hand closer to her neck until it wrapped around it. Her head jerked with several shakes. She turned to Elora, desperation etched onto every feature.

Pointing to the crusty and hard ground, Lyren opened her mouth. "This is the very spot where I used to meet my mermaid friend, Waverly."

At the mention of the name, the water rippled and shook. Soon, a magnificent mane of blue and green hair broke over the surface. The body that followed had dark skin tinged with blue. Her black and green eyes sunk deep into her head with dark circles beneath them.

"You must go, my friend," the mermaid said to Lyren. "We have tried every story we can think of against this decay. It will not back down."

Lyren reached for the mermaid's hand, clasping her own around it tight. "I brought a new story."

With that, Lyren turned to Elora. She didn't say another word. She just gave an expectant nod.

Swallowing, Elora reached both arms over her stomach. "I don't understand. How can a story help?"

"Please."

The mermaid flinched when Lyren spoke. Ignoring her, the fae stepped away from the water and closer to Elora. "Please just tell your story. It will be stronger coming from someone who has lived it."

The words to the story swam in Elora's mind. Her parents had told the story so many times in her life, she probably could have spoken about it in her sleep. Her father and mother lived at the castle. Both of them worked for the king, her father as a swordsmith, her mother as a musician. They fell in love. But her mother feared what castle life would be like for their future children. Her mother dreamed of a life different from what they had experienced in the castle. So, they moved away to the country and raised their family there. Her parents had always told the story like it was the most romantic thing in the world.

Maybe it was because Elora had never found that story particularly romantic, or maybe Faerie itself knew that story wasn't the one, but a different story entered her mind now.

Without thinking about it, she stepped forward and began the tale. "When I was a young girl, only five years old, my mother's belly grew bigger than a bucket. She was going to have another baby. My father hoped it would be a boy. My mother hoped it would be a boy. My younger sister, Chloe, claimed she *knew* it was a boy. If it wasn't a boy, it would be much more difficult for our father to provide for us. My mother was very sick. They knew it would be their last child. So, everyone hoped and wished and prayed that it would be a boy."

At some point, Elora had dropped her hands to her side. She pinched the fabric of her skirt on either side of her, almost as if she was about to lift it to curtsy. "But I didn't want it to be a boy."

Without any warning at all, a lump filled Elora's throat. As she touched the skirt her mother had given her, the memory of her parents' death did everything it could to push its way to the front of her mind. After a hard swallow, she shoved it back again. She used the story to smother it.

"When the baby was born, everyone held their breaths. My mother's sickness nearly took her life, but she survived. The baby was healthy and strong and cried with the lilt of a nightingale. And she wasn't a boy. My baby sister, Grace, stole all our hearts. But my heart was happiest of all because I knew something no one else wanted to admit. Now my father would teach me the things I had been begging to learn. Things that only boys were supposed to know. Now that my father knew he'd never have a son, he'd finally stop waiting, and he'd teach me."

The enchantments Prince Brannick had placed on Elora were still in place, which prevented her from talking about her sword skill in any way. She had been prepared for it. The end of the story came out vague, but she still managed to tell it. Emotion burned in her chest while the memory sparked like a fire within.

It hurt. Her sisters were still in the mortal realm, but at least they had the fancy dresses and opulent jewelry from Faerie. And Brannick had promised he could return Elora to the exact same time and day she had left the mortal realm.

Her sisters were safe. They had money in case they needed it. They wouldn't even miss Elora no matter how long she stayed in Faerie. But it didn't stop her from missing them.

She swallowed again.

A single tear slipped down her cheek. When the tear splashed onto the crusty sand, purple steam bloomed above it in the shape of wildflowers. A gentle breeze dispersed the steam, sending it over the sand and over the water.

Everything the steam touched glowed with a bright light. So much light filled the area around them that it became difficult to see. When the light began to dim, an entirely different view lay before them.

Lush palm trees fluttered in a gentle wind. Clear, sparkly water waved in the dusky night sky. The sand had turned brown and soft. Even Waverly's eyes looked less sunken than before.

The brown in Lyren's eyes shimmered with silver as she smiled. "You did it," she whispered.

But loud shouts erupted from a nearby rocky cove. They sounded as pleasant as dripping blood.

Lunging forward, Lyren grabbed Elora's wrist. "We need to get out of here."

CHAPTER

4

Elora had just enough time to glance over her shoulder. She regretted the action at once. A group of at least eight fae charged toward her and Lyren. The fae wore heavy white coats with silvery threads woven throughout. Just looking at the coats made the warm Swiftsea air seem even warmer.

Lyren yanked Elora forward, pulling her down the sandy beach. The sea fae gestured toward a narrow path just beyond a thick clump of palm trees. "This way. And hurry."

Hiking up her skirt, Elora ran. Part of her wanted to glance over her shoulder again, but she feared what she would see. Instead, she turned to her side while sucking in gulps of air. "Why can't we open a door back to Bitter Thorn?"

Lyren hissed as she tripped over a rock hiding amongst the sand. It didn't take her long to regain her balance. "It is not safe. These fae have magic that can keep Faerie doors open indefinitely. If I open a door, they will simply follow us through."

After jumping over a large boulder covered in seaweed, Lyren twisted her body in another direction. She yanked on Elora's hand to keep them both moving the same way. Only with Lyren's help did Elora notice a rocky path to the side. The sea fae moved onto it with expert precision. Again, she turned in a direction that didn't seem to have any path along with it. But of course, a path appeared just in time.

Soon, they both huddled inside a hidden cove that overlooked the sea. Lyren peeked her head around one wall, looking back at the area they had only recently left. "Just as I thought." When she pulled her head back into the cove, she began combing through her brown curls with her fingers. "Those were Fairfrost guards."

As if on cue, a strange whipping sound filled the air. When Lyren glanced up, Elora followed her gaze.

A gasp escaped Elora's lips before she could stop it. Her hand clutched tight against her chest. "Is that a dragon? They're *real?*"

Sneering, Lyren shook her head. "You need not fear the dragon. It is the rider who brings destruction."

Now Elora was the one peering over the side of the cove. She didn't have a great angle, but she just managed to catch a glimpse of the fae on top of the dragon. One look at the heavily beaded white crown was all she needed to hide back in the cove once again. "It's Queen Alessandra."

Lyren nodded before glancing away.

"That's who brought the decay?"

"No." Moving to the other side of the cove, Lyren ran a hand over the rocky surface. "At least we do not think so. But she does take advantage of it. Queen Alessandra's greatest magic is in emotion. When stories create renewal magic like yours did, she can steal the emotion out of it. The process makes her stronger and Swiftsea weaker."

At her sides, Elora's fingers twitched. She ached to reach for a sword, but of course she didn't have hers with her. No one in Faerie was supposed to know about her sword skill except for Brannick and his two advisors, Kaia and Soren. But even without the weapon, she still longed to fight.

Her teeth clenched as she raised an eyebrow. "So, you're just going to let Alessandra take the magic?"

Snapping her head to the side, Lyren glared. "Of course not. Every fae in Swiftsea is skilled with the javelin. We know how to fight out of necessity, and we do it very well."

As she spoke, she raised one hand into the air. The moment the last word left her lips, she clicked her tongue three times. A glowing sprite from above fluttered down until it landed on Lyren's palm. The sea fae reached into her pocket and pulled out a tiny, gray pebble. "I have a message for Queen Noelani and her guards. They should be near."

The sprite's wings glowed a brighter green as he nodded.

Lyren quickly gave a message for the sprite to deliver, which gave the exact location and size of the Fairfrost queen's guard. While the sprite flew away, Lyren's curls bounced with a nod. "That should do it." Now her gaze turned to Elora's. "It is time to take you back to Bitter Thorn."

The urge to fight still bubbled in Elora's gut. If anything, it only churned with greater desire. "Have you gone to High King

Romany? Does he know how Queen Alessandra is terrorizing your court? Surely, he could send people to help you."

With a tinkling laugh, Lyren waved her hand through the air. "You do not understand how things work in Faerie. Queen Alessandra breaks no Faerie rules by stealing emotion from our renewal magic. It is her duty to help her court, and the renewal magic does just that. If we Swiftsea fae cannot protect our own court from stronger fae like Queen Alessandra, that is our own failing. Fae have no duty to choose peace over power."

Grumbling under her breath, Elora kicked away a pebble. "It still seems like a horrible thing to do."

Lyren laughed again. "Oh, it certainly is. Queen Alessandra's actions have made the decay far worse than it would have been on its own, but no other court will save us from her." She waved one hand, bringing forth her door once again. This time, the smell of salt and sand wafting out from the door was indiscernible when paired with the smell of Swiftsea all around them.

The door led them straight to the hallway leading to Elora's room inside Bitter Thorn Castle. Heat surged across Elora's brow as reality sank in. Her fists clenched while she considered the injustices Swiftsea had endured at the hand of the Fairfrost queen.

Of course, they weren't the only ones to endure misfortune because of Queen Alessandra. Prince Brannick himself had fallen in love with the fae before he even knew her true identity. The bargain he made with her lost him his freedom both in action and in love. He only knew safety because the queen's memory had been altered until she had forgotten Brannick completely.

But it wouldn't last.

Even now, she was starting to remember him. At any time, she could give him an order, and he would be forced to follow it.

Shoving the thoughts out of her mind, Elora focused on the first thing she could. She turned to Lyren. "Where did that decay come from? You said it wasn't caused by Queen Alessandra. Is it a curse like the curse on Bitter Thorn?"

Eyeing the Faerie door at her side that led back to Swiftsea, Lyren let out a sigh. "If it is a curse, we do not know who placed it."

"Is it because you don't have enough stories?" Elora touched the toe of her boot to her other ankle where a bright red ribbon was tied. Her heart immediately dropped. If her sister, Chloe, were here, she probably could have healed Swiftsea on her own with all the stories she knew.

That thought only brought another wave of pain.

Lyren tapped her toe as she glanced toward the Faerie door again. "It is not because of that. Stories help heal our court and stop the spread of the decay, but they are unrelated to the cause. We have checked many times."

Elora's heart continued to drop as she remembered her sisters. But they were safe. If remembering them only brought pain, maybe it was better to put them from her mind altogether. For now. She dropped her foot back to the ground, doing her best to ignore the ribbon around her ankle. "So, you have no idea what causes the decay?"

With a sigh, Lyren tucked a springy curl behind one ear. It settled neatly behind the white sea flower also sitting there. "Queen Noelani believes Faerie itself is rebelling against the fae. She believes the land is punishing us for keeping Prince Brannick from his rightful place as High King. My queen believes everything will heal once Prince Brannick wins the testing."

It wasn't the words as much as the way they were spoken, but Elora knew better than to just accept that explanation. She raised an eyebrow. "And what do you believe?"

With that question, the silver in Lyren's eyes burst into sparkles. "I believe there is more to it than that." Her jaw clenched. "But I know the decay is worse because of Queen Alessandra. Much worse." A shudder jerked through Lyren's shoulders so hard that the sea flower behind her ear fluttered to the ground. Her voice darkened. "She is far worse than you know."

A chill entered the room, almost as if Faerie were emulating the cold of the Fairfrost queen. Thoughts of Brannick's bargain filled Elora's mind once again. How long would he be safe? How long until Alessandra gave him an order he physically couldn't refuse?

After plucking her flower off the ground and tucking it behind her ear once again, Lyren stepped toward her door. "I must go back to Swiftsea and help fight the Fairfrost guards." She gripped her javelin tight. "I promised I would take you to your room, and now I have. You will be safe as long as you stay within Bitter Thorn Castle. I owe you a debt for your help. Go back to your room quickly."

She gave a curt nod before stepping through her twirling, foamy blue door. It vanished as soon as she disappeared through it.

The hallway was empty now, but Elora felt empty too. Or alone? Something inside her longed for a friend. Perhaps being surrounded by fae she couldn't trust had done more to her than she realized. Or maybe she just wanted the attention of a particular fae and not getting it had hurt her more than she wanted to admit.

Shoving that thought to the darkest recesses of her mind, she turned on her heel and stomped toward her room. Prince Brannick needed her to train him in sword skill. He couldn't avoid her forever.

But though he had fallen for her, she would *not* give her heart to him.

She knew better than to be that foolish.

CHAPTER

5

The remains of a delicious berry scone were still on Elora's lips when a knock sounded on her door the next morning. Even before answering, she knew the knock belonged to Soren. His knuckles always hit the wood with unique aggression.

She checked the red ribbon around her ankle before joining the gnome in the castle hallway. His bug-like eyes glanced back into her room. "Get your sword."

Her heart skipped as she ran back to retrieve her sword from its hiding spot under her mattress.

When they began walking down the hallway, the gnome stroked his pointed white beard. "Can you hide it with your skirts? I don't want any fae to see it accidentally."

It only took a moment to wrap the blade between the folds of her purple skirt. She held it in place with her hand, careful to make it seem like she was only lifting her skirt to walk.

Soren nodded, his soft leather boots padding against the stone floor. His cheeks puffed with his every exhale. It made the pointed hat on top of his head jiggle.

The sight of it caused a grin, which Elora simply could not help. And he hadn't made a single complaint, which was remarkable on its own. Smirking, she raised an eyebrow at the gnome. "You look well today."

His gruff exterior fell away as his eyebrows flew up to his forehead. She could see him forming the word *me* as his hand touched his chest. But before the word could escape his mouth, he let out a grunt. "I would probably look better if my forces had polished the arrowheads like they were supposed to. And there are still enchantments that need to be placed on our weapons. We will need to hunt for more feathers to adorn our spears."

Elora's step faltered. "Do your forces always spend this much time with weapons?" Her eyes narrowed. "Or are you preparing for a battle of some sort?"

Whatever hint of friendliness he had on his face quickly fell away. His beard bunched up as he glared at the hallway ahead. "These are Faerie matters. You need not worry."

She heard the unspoken message in his words. *No more questions.*

They continued in silence until he ushered her into a room she knew well. Brannick and his wolf stood at the back of the room. The mossy wall at their backs blended into the green vines hanging from the ceiling.

Blaz's ears immediately perked at the sight of her. He pawed the stone floor while his eyes softened with delight. The prince ignored her completely.

After a quick wave to the wolf, she turned her nose up at Brannick. But the prince had already turned away from her. He reached for the vine that opened the door to the armory. When he stepped through, he did not look her way. Only Blaz turned back to glance at her.

She let out a huff as she stomped in after the pair of them. Brannick continued to ignore her. Maybe this was why Soren was so grumpy all the time. If so, she couldn't blame him.

On the other side of the room, Brannick waved his hand to open the compartment where her sword had once hidden. From it, the prince pulled out his own sword as well as a sheath Elora had never seen before.

The sheath had a golden tip with designs of trees and vines swirling over it. It was attached to a leather belt which had the same vine and tree design embossed on it.

Brannick set his sword on top of a nearby clay pot that held bundles of arrows. With it secured, he handed the remarkable sheath to Elora. His eyes remained rooted to one corner of the room as he spoke. "See if your sword will fit inside."

Her fingers tingled as she took the sheath. For a moment, she could do nothing but trace a finger over the designs in the belt. After letting out a gasp of awe, she finally slid her sword inside the glinting metal.

"It fits perfectly. It's like this sheath was made for my sword." Wrapping the leather belt around her waist, she found that it too fit perfectly. Her eyes narrowed. "Where did you get this?"

Brannick removed a piece of lint from his soft leather coat before answering. "Quintus crafted it for me."

Her thumb ran over the metal that formed the main section of the sheath. It was smooth, but it didn't have the same strength as the sheaths her father always made. "This metal is strange." The words came out before she could stop them.

He shrugged, as if unsurprised by her comment. "It is a Faerie alloy."

"Fae have special alloys?" All at once, she dropped the sheath, causing it to tug on the belt that held it around her waist. Her mouth had dropped. "You told Quintus about my sword skill?"

"No." Brannick raised one eyebrow, which did not help Elora focus at all. "I told Quintus I acquired a sword that had once belonged to the great mortal, Theobald. I said it could make an impressive gift for Ansel, one that should convince him to stop asking if he can have you."

Her hand shot toward her new sword hilt, gripping it hard. "Ansel knows about my father too?" Just like that, her mind spun until pieces of conversations clicked into place. "Is Ansel the fae my father made a bargain with?"

Brannick swallowed before answering. "Yes. When your father defeated Ansel in a sword fight, the bargain required Ansel to give your father strength against his enemies and protection from all fae until after he had lived a happy life."

An icy shiver trailed down Elora's spine. Even when she tried to shake it out, the chill persisted. If she had known all that, she might have glared a little harder at Ansel when she met him in the Dustdune ballroom. A deeper shiver shook inside her. She turned to the prince while nausea curdled her stomach. "You just said that to Quintus so he wouldn't suspect I have sword skill though, right? Ansel hasn't really been asking if he can have me." She gulped. "Right?"

The prince only stared back at her. At his side, Blaz covered his nose with both paws and stared at the ground. Brannick brushed the end of his coat. His voice came out lower, with a warning attached. "As long as you do not leave the castle without an escort, you will be safe. Even your sprite friend can act as an escort. She has enough magic. Just do not go anywhere alone."

The ice had spread from Elora's spine and up into her throat. She tried to swallow down the cold lump, but it wouldn't budge. Ansel had once tried to claim her father, and now he wanted to claim her too. And that was only because of her harp skill. He didn't even know about her sword skill.

While her thoughts spun, Brannick nodded to his wolf. Blaz's black fur flounced as he padded over to one corner of the room. While the wolf moved, Brannick removed his coat and lifted his sword.

The sight of his bare chest was just enough to thaw the ice in her throat. Or maybe she was simply too distracted to notice it anymore. When he ran his hands through his hair, something tangled in her heart. But the tangle felt like rapture, not entrapment.

Breathing had become a problem though. How was she supposed to breathe when he just stood there looking so beautiful? Good thing she had firmly decided *not* to fall in love with him. He'd have far too much power over her if she did.

"Give me your sheath. I need to put a glamour on it that will make it and your sword both invisible."

Her fingers stumbled over the buckle, but at least she had managed to suck in a few breaths. When she handed it to him, she had to place her hands on one side to be sure their fingers didn't touch.

He grasped the sheath tight with one hand and then waved his other hand over top of it. His dark lips opened and closed as he muttered hushed words. Perhaps if she'd been listening more carefully she could have deciphered them, but every bit of her attention had moved to his eyes.

They burst with light and color, yet they appeared colorless at the same time. The pulsing between color and light had mesmerized her several times before, but something felt different this time. Now that he focused on creating the glamour, his expression turned like she had never seen it before. It wasn't as heavy. It wasn't as cold.

He held so much weight in his eyes and in his shoulders too. Had it worsened since she first met him? Was it because his essence was suffering, like Kaia had said?

She didn't notice when he finished working, but she did notice when he caught her staring at him. Heat surged through her face as she hurriedly glanced away.

With the sheath in one hand, he stepped closer to her. Too close. They didn't touch, but she could feel his breath when it left his lips. Dipping his head, he reached for the part of her sword where the hilt met the blade.

His thumb traced a circle over the cross guard. With each rotation, his skin came dangerously close to brushing against hers. But she knew what would happen if they touched. She had seen it twice already. He would vanish, cease to exist.

Holding her breath didn't make his thumb any farther away from hers, but she did it anyway. Controlling her breath made it easier to control her hand too. At least he couldn't read her mind because then he'd know how her fingers itched to reach out. How they longed to brush against his.

After tracing the same spot several times, Brannick now held his thumb in place. He closed his eyes and dipped his head down a little more. It forced her to move back or else their foreheads would have collided.

He opened his eyes. They flashed bright and strong, even more enchanting than before. They were frustratingly gorgeous. He pointed to the sword in the spot he had just been touching. "Your sheath is now glamoured to appear invisible to all, including yourself."

Did it mean something that she hadn't even noticed when her sheath went invisible?

Brannick continued as he pointed to the spot on her sword once again. "There is one exception. When you touch this spot on your sword, you will be able to see the sheath. Once the sword touches the sheath, the sword will also appear invisible."

Had he taken off his coat just to bewitch her? Because the words from his lips could only barely hold enough interest to keep her from staring at his bare chest. Even then, she kept stealing glances.

In a panic, she slammed her eyes shut and backed into the wall of spears behind her. Only once the spears dangled at her back did she finally open her eyes. Luckily, Brannick had stayed in place. Her fingers fumbled as she attempted to buckle the sheath around her waist once again. It took longer than it should have, but she eventually managed.

Clearing her throat, she cut her sword across the empty air. "Perfect. Now it's time to train."

CHAPTER

6

Thinking came easier with a sword in hand. It didn't matter if Elora's opponent had rippling muscles or captivating eyes. She could ignore everything and focus only on the slices and strikes of her blade.

After a few introductory moves, she quickly determined Brannick was ready for more complicated maneuvers. Maybe he had faster reflexes, more strength, and better eyesight than a mortal, but she still assumed responsibility for his quick learning.

Some of it had to be due to her teaching skills.

From the corner of the room, Blaz pawed at a feather and leather string that hung from a nearby spear. His ears perked every time Elora or the prince breathed harder than usual. Though the wolf didn't interact with them during their practice, his presence still provided a surprising amount of comfort.

Elora taught the prince two different sequences of sword moves, which they then practiced several times. The more complicated moves caused them both to breathe heavier, but apparently fae had greater endurance than mortals too.

At least she still had something the prince didn't have, and that was expert sword skill. She jabbed and parried with finesse, blocking his blows with ease. When he got increasingly frustrated by how quickly she beat him, his sword came crashing down harder.

He fueled his swings with desperation. That only made it easier to beat him. He had grown skilled enough that she only had to hold back a little. But his increased frustration led to an unintentional slice.

The tip of her blade skittered across Brannick's shoulder, leaving behind tiny spots of blood. It was the sort of injury that would heal in a few days and not affect muscle movement. At least that's what it should have been.

But a sizzle of steam erupted from the prince's shoulder. Elora squeezed her sword with a gasp and jumped forward. His bare shoulder still had puffs of steam swirling out from the tiny scratch. She reached for it without thinking, desperate to help.

Brannick stepped back, baring his teeth. "Do not touch me."

Jerking her hand away, she immediately clapped it against her mouth. "Right." She shook her head, but her eyes landed on the scratch again. The sizzling had died away. "Should I go get Kaia, or…" It was only a tiny scratch. Why had the skin around the wound turned red like an infection? It shouldn't have been so bad.

The prince waved her off before reaching into his pocket. "I will be fine. I knew this might happen."

That didn't answer any of her questions. But the prince was too busy smothering the scratch with a gritty green ointment. He pulled a white feather from his pocket next. It fluttered as he brushed the end of it over the ointment and scratch.

Elora opened her mouth to ask how the feather would help. The moment her lips parted, the prince shot her a glare.

She turned on her heel, squeezing her hilt even tighter than before. If she couldn't ask questions, what was she supposed to do? Her feet carried her over to Blaz before another thought could enter her mind. She knelt at his side, running her fingers through his soft fur.

At least the wolf's eyes shimmered with as much concern as she felt. On the other hand, Brannick only acted inconvenienced. What did he mean *I knew this might happen?* How could he know her sword might make his skin sizzle?

Blaz buried his head in her lap while they both watched the prince work. After brushing the feather over his wound, he muttered words under his breath. When that was finished, he pulled a white cloth from his pocket to wipe away the gritty ointment.

Once wiped away, Brannick's skin looked good as new. His light brown skin showed no hint of the scratch, as if it had never existed. His face still twisted in pain as he shoved the cloth and other items back into his pocket.

Maybe the injury had been dealt with, but she wasn't about to lift her sword yet. "What happened? Why did—"

Brannick raised a hand into the air, stopping her midsentence.

She huffed and glanced down at her lap instead. While scratching behind Blaz's ears, another question came to mind. This one, the prince might answer. "Why did Ansel even try to defeat my father in a sword fight anyway? I've never seen any fae use a sword."

Rubbing a thumb over the shoulder that had been scratched, the prince let out a slow breath. "The fae in the Court of Mistmount use swords and daggers as weapons."

"And Ansel is from Mistmount?"

"Yes." Brannick's eyes fell closed as he rubbed deeper into his shoulder.

She chewed on her bottom lip as he kneaded the area. In her years of sword training, she had sustained many mild injuries and even a few serious ones. But none of them ever made her skin sizzle with steam.

Twirling a finger around a clump of Blaz's fur, she glanced up at the prince again. "Why did that shard kill King Huron? You said it would only work if a fae offered it."

Brannick winced as he dropped his hand to his side. "I *did* offer the shard to King Huron. I held it out and told him to hurt me the way he supposed I intended to hurt others."

Her gut twisted every time the prince gave another wince. "And that counts? Just by holding it out to him, that counted as offering it to him?"

Breathing out slowly, Brannick nodded.

Her eyes found the wolf again. "But that means the shard wouldn't have injured you even if King Huron pierced you with it. Because he never offered the shard to you."

Brannick's breaths came out evenly now. He shook out his shoulders, showing off his impressive muscles once again. "I offered King Huron the shard and told him to use it against me. By doing so, I essentially offered it to myself. Faerie rules are complicated." He chuckled to himself. "And they are not always consistent."

At some point, her hands had left Blaz's fur. Now they played with a piece of her own hair while her mouth dropped slightly. His stupid eyes had caught her attention again. No matter how she tried, she couldn't look away.

When he glanced toward her, a grin fell across his lips. He knew exactly the effect he was having. Even more infuriating, he liked it.

Her mouth clamped shut as she jerked her head away. Heat speckled across her cheeks, burning hot under her skin. He could probably see it, but she tried to hide it by patting Blaz's head and getting to her feet.

By the time she stood again, at least some of the heat had cooled.

He plucked his sword from the ground and twirled it in a circle. "Shall we continue?"

In moments like these, Elora was eternally grateful for how her mother had worked so hard to teach her how to appear dignified. Rolling her shoulders back, Elora raised her own sword with the grace of a delicate harpist. "Yes. This time, we won't use a pre-planned sequence as we did before. Just use what you have learned and try to block my blows."

She didn't mention that she'd go a *lot* easier on him this time. She didn't want any more steam sizzling off another scratch.

He threw the first strike. Her arm tensed as she blocked his blade. The tip jabbed toward his heart, but even if he didn't stop it, her sword was too far away to actually touch him. Still, he clashed his blade against hers, causing them both to swing toward the ground.

The victory sent a light into his eyes. They pulsed between color and colorless. He stepped forward with another blow.

Not wanting to injure him again, she took two steps back. Even when her sword swung, she stepped backward once again.

A wicked grin curled on his lips. He jabbed his own sword at her heart now. Though she blocked the blow, she paired it with another two steps back.

But he kept moving forward, taking advantage of the ground he gained. Soon, her backward steps pressed her against the wall of the armory.

His smile grew as he held his sword across her neck. He held it far enough away to keep her from danger, but it still pinned her against the wall. It wasn't lost on her that she had pinned him against a wall in exactly the same position not so long ago.

He raised one eyebrow, perhaps about to reference that fateful day.

Instead, she gave a pointed glance straight into his eyes. "You'll find any excuse to be close to me, won't you?"

For a moment, he froze as the words sank in. With a sharp intake of breath, he took a single step back. His sword clattered to the ground. "No. Why would I want to be close to you?"

She couldn't help the smirk that broke onto her face. "I know you care for me. What did your bargain with Alessandra say? You promised you would never touch another creature with romantic feelings in your heart. If you didn't care for me, you'd be able to touch me."

He flashed his teeth. When he stepped close to her again, she held her ground. He raised one hand, turning it so his knuckles were only a breath away from her cheek. "Perhaps you are not as dangerous to me as you believe."

His hand hovered in place, near enough to her skin that she could feel it. She stared at him, but he stared at his hand. Hovering. Deciding.

If his other arm hadn't been touching the wall on her other side, she would have stepped away. But he had her pinned in place. Exactly like he wanted.

His nose wrinkled as he looked into her eyes. She'd never seen hate so perfectly etched into someone's expression. Only then did his knuckles trail down her cheek, touching her.

For a moment, nothing changed. He stood as sure and as angry as before. Elora sucked in a breath, regretting her accusation about his feelings.

But then it happened. He flickered. His entire being vanished for a flash of a moment. He flickered again. She shoved him away and took several steps to the side. Her chest heaved as she tried to suck in calming breaths. She had to settle for shaky ones instead.

Glaring at his hand, she gripped her sword tight. "That was stupid."

His hand flexed as he turned away from her. "No, stupid was falling in love with Queen Alessandra. Falling for *you* is merely an inconvenience."

The words stabbed her, giving her the urge to run her sword through his heart. "An inconvenience?"

He shrugged her off, glancing anywhere but into her eyes. "There is nothing you can do to me. You are going home after the testing anyway. And then I will never have to look at you again."

The anger boiling inside her she could handle. But the tears stinging in her throat? Even clenching her jaw as tight as she could, her chin still quivered. She threw him her darkest glare.

"You're lucky I like it here in Faerie because I'd never stay if it was only for *you*."

If he reacted to her words, she didn't know, because she had turned her back on him. She reached for the vine that opened the door to the armory. She shoved her sword into the glamoured sheath just before throwing open the door that led to the hallway.

Her hands burned as she curled them into fists. She stomped toward her room, leaving as much noise in her wake as she possibly could.

Maybe the prince liked her, but he hated himself for it. It was clear now that it would never change. She blinked away every tear that tried to escape from her eyes.

At least she hadn't fallen in love with him. At least she wasn't *that* stupid.

Her wooden door flew open when she pushed it. But the writhing anger had something to temper it now. Brannick could force her to leave Faerie, but maybe that didn't matter.

Not if she could take a piece of Faerie with her when she left.

She glanced up at the glowing lights near the ceiling while hope for a new idea sprang to life inside. Grinning, she uttered a single word.

"Tansy?"

CHAPTER

7

Elora's palm buzzed with excitement as she held out her hand, giving the sprite a place to land. The tiny creature's limbs were strong as her soft green shoes landed on the palm. Her sparkly pink dress gave a soft bounce. Expectancy filled her pink and green eyes.

The buzzing in her hand trailed up Elora's entire arm and now consumed her whole being. When she spoke, she could barely contain the feeling. Her eyebrow tipped up. "You have wings."

The sprite put her hands on her hips. "Yes."

Reaching for one of the feathers tied in her hair, Elora took a deep breath. "I want you to teach me how to fly."

Tansy let out a soft chuckle. "I wondered how long it would take you to ask." She dropped down and folded her legs crisscross on Elora's palm. Now the sprite curled her hands into fists and propped them under her chin. "Fae do not generally offer help without something in return."

A yank twisted inside Elora's gut. "I'm not making a bargain." Her shoulders shook involuntarily as the memory of her bargains with both Brannick and King Huron haunted her. Squeezing the feather tight between her finger and thumb, she tried to push the thoughts away. "You said you might need my help in the future, right?"

Tansy's wings glowed bright green as she nodded.

Faerie must have been getting to her because Elora flashed a devious smile. "Then it benefits you to help me now because then I will be more likely to help you in the future."

With a chuckle, the sprite flapped her wings until she hovered in the air. "Now you're starting to talk like a fae."

The sprite tugged on Elora's finger and used her own chin to point toward the window. Sucking in a breath, Elora released the wings from her back. As Brannick had promised in his bargain, the wings could be retracted or called forth at will. Feeling them flutter behind her still filled her with an indescribable sense of wonder.

When the sprite tugged her finger again, she allowed the wings at her back to lift her off the ground. Tansy led the way out of her window and down to the forest floor just outside Bitter Thorn Castle.

Elora remembered how tangible the dream of freedom had been when Brannick offered her the wings. Even when she thought it was nothing more than make believe, she couldn't bring herself to refuse such a thrilling gift.

She landed on the mossy forest floor with lush trees all around. Nothing could have soured her mood in that moment. Nothing. Because now she'd learn to fly as well as a sprite could.

Once the sprite hovered in front of her again, Elora raised an eyebrow. "What first?"

Tansy smoothed her sparkly pink skirt. "First, fly up in a straight line as high as you can."

Not wanting to upset her teacher, Elora forced an even expression onto her face. "Don't you think we should start with something less basic? I just flew out here from my room."

The sprite snorted. "I was helping you just now."

Elora's eyebrows flew up to her forehead. "Were you?" Now she shook her head even more sure than before. "What about when I flew to the Balance Cliffs to retrieve that shard?"

Another chuckle escaped Tansy's lips as she raised an eyebrow. "I was helping you then too. And if you could fly better when you first got the wings, it was because Prince Brannick's creation magic was still inside you. Trust me. Start by flying up as straight as you can."

Wanting to reject the idea that she couldn't fly at all, Elora gladly set her wings beating. The moment her feet lifted off the ground, her body jerked backward so fast her hair flew into her face.

She snapped her arms down at her sides, slapping one against the hidden sword and sheath. Gritting her teeth, she flapped her wings harder. Immediately, her body jerked forward. When she attempted to move upward, her wings slammed her down onto the ground instead.

Wet dirt sprayed upward when her hand slapped against the ground. She had to spit out the crumbs of it that landed in her mouth.

Tinkling laughter filled the air as Tansy zoomed down to eye level. She clutched her belly as the laughs erupted. "This is going to take more work than I thought."

Dusting the damp earth off her palms, Elora stood up determined. Maybe flying would be harder than she expected, but it was the only thing about Faerie that she could take with her when she returned to the mortal realm. She wasn't about to give up.

This wasn't the first time she had attempted a new skill. Thinking back on her first days of sword fighting, an idea came to mind. With swords, it was important to start by learning stances. Practice could begin even before a sword ever touched the hand. Surely flying had a similar equivalent.

"What if I practice flapping my wings first? Can I figure out how to move them correctly without lifting off the ground?" Elora pinched her skirt, hoping the question didn't come across too desperate.

"No." Tansy gave an apologetic shrug. "Flapping your wings will lift you off the ground. The only way to learn how to fly is just to fly. You have to learn by doing."

Elora allowed herself one huff before she accepted the words. "Fine. I'll try again."

The second attempt did lift her higher off the ground. It also proved she had even less control than she thought. After only a moment, the wings slammed Elora into the trunk of a nearby tree. The hit forced a cough out of her.

The sprite zoomed in close, hovering right in front of Elora's nose. "Are you injured?"

Letting out another cough, Elora shook her head and forced herself to her feet. "I'm fine." She brushed the dirt from her skirt, glaring at the ground while she did.

The moment she stood, Tansy let out a giggle. "Good because…" The giggle grew. It burst into a thunderous laugh. "I have never seen such a pitiful flying attempt."

Her body rolled in flips and twists as she continued to giggle. "You have no idea how flying is supposed to feel. You keep trying to move as you would on the ground."

Folding her arms over her chest, Elora took a defensive pose. "How do I fix it then?"

Tansy rubbed her forehead with a wide grin. "Climb a tree and jump from its highest branches."

Though she could see merit in the idea, Elora still held back. "What if I can't fly well enough to keep from plunging to the ground?"

Twirling her pink dress out around her knees, Tansy shrugged. "Maybe the threat of injury is exactly what you need."

Elora climbed the nearest tree before she could think too much about the idea. Her limbs shook every time she moved higher. She had climbed hundreds of trees in her lifetime, and it never scared her. But she had never climbed a tree with the intention of hurling herself off it either.

By the time she climbed halfway up, her limbs were shaking too badly to continue. For the first time in her life, she looked down at the ground as a place to fall instead of a place to escape.

Gulping, she tried to steady her knees just enough to jump. Her fingers tensed around the nearest branch. Suddenly, the bottom of the tree looked so much farther away.

She swallowed again. Before fear could take over, she threw herself off the tree.

Elation hit the moment her feet left the branch. Everything around her stood still as she took in a breath. Nothing held onto her in that one moment. Nothing grounded her. In the truest sense of the word, she was free.

Grasping that feeling, she willed her wings to beat. Would they catch the air with the same sense of freedom she held in her heart?

The answer came too soon. With a sharp jerk, her body plunged downward. She flapped harder, but it only sent her body to the side at an abrupt angle. Her body did indeed slam against the ground as she had feared. Instead of just the force of the fall behind it, she now had the force of her beating wings contributing as well.

Her shoulder and hip groaned where they'd hit the ground. She could already feel the bruises forming even before she attempted to stand again. The defeat hurt more than she wanted to admit. The sting of oncoming tears burned in her throat.

Tansy's tinkling laughter filled the air once again. Each giggle dropped a heavier weight in Elora's stomach.

Dusting off her dress, Elora stood. She had to purse her lips to keep from frowning. When she glanced up, she found that Tansy wasn't the only one who had witnessed her embarrassing failure.

Brannick leaned against a nearby tree with a smirk tilting his lips. Maybe it was the angle, but his long hair hung perfectly against his shoulders. He flipped it back when he caught her eye, letting out a chuckle of his own.

He was probably on his way to see Kaia in her tree after getting that sizzling injury from Elora's sword. But *why* did he have to walk by at that exact moment?

The burn in her throat thickened into a lump that she quickly swallowed down. Shaking out her arms, she retracted the wings until they hid inside her back once again. Shrugging away every semblance of pain, Elora turned back to the sprite. "I suppose I'm not made for flying." Now she forced out a chuckle. "Oh well. I've gone my whole life without flying, why would I need to now?"

Tansy accompanied her as Elora moved back toward the castle, walking this time. They laughed together at the failed attempts. Never once did she give any indication of the disappointment that pricked against her every nerve.

It was about more than just flying. She had spent so much time clinging to the magic and wonder of Faerie, but maybe it was time to let it go.

After all, she had two sisters in the mortal realm. She had no intention of abandoning them just because Faerie was wonderful. Maybe she needed to stop trying to find ways to stay in Faerie.

Maybe it was time to say goodbye.

CHAPTER

8

Elora woke with a jolt. The soft green blanket covering her slid to the ground. While her heart pounded, she touched a hand to her forehead. When that revealed nothing, she pressed a hand to her chest.

Never before had she woken in such a rush. No nightmare had plagued her, no noise sounded anywhere nearby.

With tension sinking into her shoulders, she jumped off her bed to look out the window of her room. Fresh moss and green vines adorned the window like always. Just outside, a gentle forest breeze rustled in and through her hair.

The dusky light of a Faerie night still hung in the sky, which meant morning hadn't woken her.

What then?

Fear.

Sucking in a breath, she reached a finger toward the window. Just before her hand would have stretched outside, a flash of golden light rippled over the window. The light sent her finger springing backward toward her body.

The enchantment over her window was still in place then. Questions lingered in her mind, but they didn't last.

A spark lit deep inside her gut. It didn't hurt or cause more fear, but it did force her to act. Without knowing why, she snatched her woolen blanket from the floor and wrapped it tight around her shoulders. She secured it around her waist with the help of the belt attached to her new sheath.

After checking that her sword was in place inside the sheath, she moved toward the door. The spark in her gut stirred again.

Maybe it should have scared her, but it didn't. It didn't calm her either. The spark twisted and churned chaotically, forcing her to move forward. Her mind could have been playing tricks on her because of the late hour, but it felt like Faerie itself was trying to communicate with her.

How could she refuse?

With the green blanket around her shoulders and belted around her waist, she ducked into the hallway outside her room. Not a single sound filled in the hallway, not even the sound of fluttering vines.

Though she noticed the oddity, she didn't form any opinion on it. Instead, she moved forward without hesitation. She touched the stone wall at her side and trailed a finger across it with each step.

It wasn't until the stone disappeared from beneath her fingertips that she realized where her feet had been leading her. Once there, a part of her admitted she had known the entire time.

A stone wall stared back at her. The moss and vines and crumbles of rock matched the walls all around. But she knew it was a glamour.

Her hand swished around in the air in front of her. No stone or any other thing stopped it. Due to her first time finding this spot, she knew the empty space was the exact size of a doorway.

Something held her back the first time. Her curiosity had urged her to explore, but instinctively, she had known it wasn't time. That same instinct led her forward now.

Her stomach leapt as she walked straight into the wall that wasn't really a wall. Darkness enveloped her once she moved past the glamour. The magic must have worked on the sprites too because none of them flew in this hidden hallway.

Or perhaps they knew the hallway existed, but they avoided it anyway.

A shiver pulsed through her shoulders. She tugged the blanket tighter around herself while her eyes adjusted to the darkness. It felt denser than any darkness she had ever known. The sprites were just on the other side of the glamour, but their green light didn't come through it.

The only source of light came from ahead. Far ahead. And if she wasn't mistaken, it came from below as well.

Shuffling her feet forward slowly, she discovered a stone staircase leading down. Using the cool stone at her side to balance herself, she stepped down toward the tiny light. Her boots tapped each step quickly. The air cooled around her as she descended.

Soon, her hands no longer touched just cool stone. Every so often, a thorn would prick against her finger. After a few more steps, she couldn't even keep her hand on the stone wall. Too many thorns stretched over the stone surface. After even longer, her boots began crunching over thick vines, which also had thorns.

Darkness continued to pool around her, but the creaking made it clear that thorns were everywhere. They curled over the walls, the steps, the ceiling. The tiny light ahead grew, but everything still looked black. Maybe it was just because of the black briars filling so much of the space.

It probably should have scared her. A vague notion of fear danced around in her mind, but it didn't plague her. Curiosity won in that fight. Despite the darkness, despite the thorns, even despite the cold, she continued down the steps. Something inside pulled her forward, drew her to the bottom.

When she reached the bottom of the staircase, she didn't stop to think for even a moment. Her hand reached for the leather strap attached to the door in front of her. Somehow, even before she opened the door, she knew what she would see. She had a vague idea of the layout of the castle and where rooms inside met the castle walls outside. That helped her know what was beyond the door, but that wasn't the only thing.

Her heart could feel it. Perhaps it wasn't her heart but her gut. Whatever it was, she stepped into a large room, glancing straight up at the chandelier near the ceiling.

It gave off soft light just like it had when she saw it the first time. There were still no sprites. If she hadn't been so entranced by the room around her, it might have been disconcerting. But the spark inside her continued to pull her forward.

The chair made of leather and bundled sticks sat empty now. Neither Brannick nor his wolf were anywhere in sight. Briars and thorns dotted the room in haphazard growths.

After carefully closing the door behind her, she moved straight toward the chair. Flutters went through her stomach with each step. She couldn't explain why, but a smile played on her lips.

Drawing her sword, she sliced away every thorn that curled and twisted over the chair. There were other places to sit. The plush chair she had lounged in the other night still sat across from the stick and leather chair. It didn't even have any thorns wrapped around its arms or legs.

But she wanted to sit in the chair Brannick had been sitting in. The reason for it remained elusive. Or maybe she just didn't want to admit the reason. The point of her sword dipped and sliced until every thorn had been broken away.

As she lowered herself into the chair, a gasp escaped her lips. Something happened the moment she finally took a seat.

Something magical.

A daydream flashed in her mind, but it felt more like a memory. She saw Prince Brannick sitting in front of an ice tree growing out of a glittering, snowy landscape. He clutched his side while thick weariness dragged on his features.

She had certainly never seen him in a place with snow or frost, but she could still picture the daydream as clearly as if it had really happened. Then the prince repeated words she had once spoken to him.

A prince never accepts defeat.

She had chuckled then. Or… She shook her head, trying to reconcile this non-memory. This was only a daydream, so she hadn't chuckled *then*. She chuckled now at the thought of Brannick saying those words. It was so like him to say something so daring and egotistical all at the same time. And of course he would say it while injured and unable to stand.

Glancing over the room, she discovered one corner had an entire tree's height of briars twisting around each other. For the same reason she had entered the room in the first place—

which was really no reason at all—she found herself walking toward the corner.

Her sword lifted, very nearly of its own accord. The same urging inside herself pushed her feet until they had reached that corner. Once her sword started moving, she only had a vague understanding of what she wanted to do. She just let her hand move the way it wanted to move.

Expert swipes sent her sword through the vines of the briars. When finished, the twisting vines looked almost identical to how they had looked when she first arrived in the room. But there was an important difference.

Taking a deep breath, she leaned forward. Her eyes narrowed. Stretching one hand out, she plunged her fingers straight into the depths of the briars. Except she met no resistance. Not a single thorn brushed against her skin. The careful slices of her sword had carved a path for her.

With her hand deep in the briar, her fingertips brushed against a stone of some sort. The small rock was easy to pick up. Soon, she had it out of the briars and in the palm of her hand.

A crystal.

The light green rock had a raw cut with the rough lines of the crystal still intact. Its light green color reminded her of sage and pears. A thin striation of purple stretched through the crystal at one end.

It was cool to the touch, but it didn't feel like normal stone. When she held it between two fingers, her fingertips buzzed. And it was glowing. It didn't physically glow. It looked like a rock, a beautiful rock, but a rock nonetheless. But she could *feel* it glowing. It gave off energy, which she couldn't explain. And she couldn't ignore.

The same energy threaded into her arms until it bloomed in her chest. The buzzing of her fingertips crackled along her skin.

Brannick. Something about the crystal reminded her of Brannick.

That's when she noticed the thorns.

All around her, the thorns had multiplied and twisted. Several vines trailed up her boots, very nearly wrapping around her legs. With the tip of her sword, she sliced them away.

The crystal had to be protected. Even as the thought sounded in her mind, she couldn't explain it. But she wasn't about to argue with it either. Wrapping one hand tight around the small crystal, she raised her sword and moved toward the door once again.

It took a few slices and jabs to move past the thorns without incident, but she made it. With the crystal in one hand, she carefully closed the door behind her and began climbing the darkened staircase.

Her boots crunched over twice the amount of thorns that had been there before.

At the back of her mind, she couldn't help wonder if this moment was real. Was it a dream? It felt like a dream. In fact, the crystal in her hand was the only thing that *didn't* feel like a dream. But maybe that only proved it was.

She moved up the staircase and past the glamour that hid the hallway from view. She didn't stop to think or even listen. By the time she made it to her bedroom, she was panting from exertion. She ignored the discomfort that burned in her legs after climbing so many stairs.

As she tucked herself back into bed, she discreetly covered her face with the woolen blanket. Only once her face was covered—and out of sight of the sprites—did she take another glance at the crystal.

Its energy continued to glow and buzz inside her. It almost felt like a part of her now. And it still reminded her of Brannick. Maybe that meant something. Maybe it didn't.

Either way, she knew one thing with complete certainty. This crystal was hers. Even when Brannick forced her to return to the mortal realm, even if she never learned to fly properly, she'd still have this crystal.

It was the one thing from Faerie that she'd keep forever.

And maybe someday, she'd know why she had been drawn to it.

CHAPTER

9

After a bath with soaps of honeysuckle and lavender, Elora tucked the green crystal under her black leather corset. Faerie had many delights, but the stone seemed extra special. Perhaps it was because she had discovered it all on her own in a moment that felt like a dream. Upon waking, she had assumed it *was* a dream. But the existence of the crystal proved otherwise.

Once it was secured under her corset, she went for her sword and sheath. She had to pat the area under her mattress several times before her hand hit against the invisible sheath. Buckling the clasp without being able to see it always caused her to grunt a few times.

As she worked, she remembered when Brannick had given it to her. There was something tender in the way he did the glamour. Or maybe it was only concentration, not tenderness.

Considering he ended their training session by saying his feelings for her were an inconvenience, it was probably not tenderness at all.

That small memory was enough to set her blood to a low boil. Now the clasp of her belt became difficult but only because her fingers had too much tension to move right. With a loud huff, she finally managed to secure the belt around her waist.

The moment she finished, the sound of snapping twigs interrupted the usual forest sounds outside her window. Sucking in a breath, she crept toward it. Another kind of tension rocked through her fingers as she gripped her sword hilt.

Her feet shuffled as she edged herself toward the window. Though she had complained about the enchantment that went over her window at night, she found herself praising it now. The enchantment kept her from sneaking out, but it also kept anyone else from coming in.

Twigs continued to snap. By the sound of it, someone was just outside her window. Her fingers gripped tighter on her sword. Brannick insisted she was safe inside the castle, but where was her safety now? The enchantment would vanish soon, if it hadn't already.

When she finally reached the stone wall just next to the wide window, she leaned her head out a smidgeon. Just enough to peek outside but hopefully not reveal herself to whoever was out there.

She had to look down since her bedroom was on the second story, but she could still see the person clearly. Scoffing dramatically, she shouted down to the forest floor. "Why are you sneaking around outside my window, Brannick?"

The prince's head snapped upward, causing his hair to whip back. At his side, Blaz let out a delighted yip. Brannick had one toe digging into the ground. The moment her voice hit the air, his foot pulled back, and he clasped both hands behind his back.

With a carefree shrug, he glanced upward. "I have business here, never you mind."

Her hands curled into fists. She would have leaned out the window to get a better angle for glaring at him, except the shimmery gold enchantment held her inside.

Did he always have to act more important than her?

Rolling her eyes, she settled herself onto the ledge of the window, while staying inside the protective barrier. "Let me guess, you were so overcome by your feelings for me that you had to hide just outside my window."

The prince wrinkled his nose, clearly attempting to appear as disgusted as possible. "No. That is not correct."

Since fae couldn't lie, it must have been true. Her fists clenched, which didn't help her ignore the sinking in her gut. He considered her an *inconvenience*. She had no business being disappointed about him not wanting to be near her.

Pressing her back into the stone edge of the window, she turned her nose into the air. Another quippy remark would have left her lips. It *should* have left her lips. But Blaz caught her attention.

The wolf's ears bent as he nuzzled his nose into the prince's leg. The gesture caused Brannick's face to fall. His shoulders hunched while he took in a shallow breath.

Something etched across Brannick's face. Something Elora knew well.

Pain.

Just like that, her fists relaxed. She sat up straighter, searching for clues to explain the prince's demeanor. Nothing obvious revealed itself.

Did it feel colder now? Blaz rubbed his head against the prince's leg. Brannick patted his wolf's head. The gesture didn't have the same vigor as usual. It had to be his essence. Probably. Whatever it was, it was making him miserable.

Elora brushed a finger over one of the feathers in her hair, already regretting the words she hadn't even said yet. But they came out of her mouth anyway. "What's wrong?"

His face twitched as he narrowed his eyes at her. "Why do you believe something is wrong?"

"Really? You need me to explain?"

Now his eyes narrowed tighter.

It seemed like a good moment to shake her head. "You look as grumpy as Soren."

"I am not grumpy." The words would have been more believable if he hadn't spoken them through a grunt.

She raised both eyebrows. "Stop being difficult. Just tell me what's wrong?"

He responded with a razor-sharp chuckle. "Do not ask me such a question. I will not answer."

"Fine." She lifted her chin and turned away from him. "I won't offer my suggestion then."

He turned away from her. "I do not need your suggestion." With his hand on the wolf's head, he lifted one foot to walk away. But before he stepped, both he and the wolf glanced back at her. The prince opened his mouth but didn't speak. He didn't have to. She knew his question anyway. He wanted to know the suggestion.

Gesturing to the tree a few paces away from her window, she said, "Climb that tree. It will lift your spirits."

At the sound of those words, he glanced down at Blaz. Skepticism trailed across both their faces. Brannick flicked his hand, as if waving her off. "I have matters to attend to."

She leaned back into the stone again. "Fine. Ignore my advice if you want to keep getting worse."

One of the prince's feet hung in the air as he went to step away. His foot hovered as he glanced up at her. Light and swirls shimmered in his eyes, causing her stomach to flutter. But it wasn't his eyes that did her in this time. It was his action.

Letting out an annoyed sigh, he stomped over to the tree. He ran up its trunk much faster than she had ever done. Blaz sat at the bottom of the tree, looking far more relaxed than he had only moments ago.

With the strength and reflexes of a fae, Brannick reached the top branches of the tree in almost no time at all. Running one hand through his long hair, he glanced back at Elora. Showing off. "I did it. What is supposed to happen now that I am up here?"

Grinning, Elora tipped her eyebrows toward her forehead. "Now look around."

The prince stared at her with no expression for several moments before letting out a sigh. Yet again, he did what she asked, despite his outward attitude. Brannick had lived in Faerie his whole life, so it was probably easy for him to take advantage of his surroundings, to forget to notice them. But it turned out, the forest was magical enough to work even on a brooding prince.

The glare on his face softened once his eyes glanced out at the forest. Though he tried to be stubborn and find nothing of value, his eyes lit up at the sight. His shoulders rolled back while he leaned forward in the tree. When he looked at the castle, the beginnings of a grin tickled at the corners of his mouth. By the time his eyes met Elora's again, his entire demeanor had lifted.

He stared at her. Even without speaking a word, his gaze sent a knot through her insides. But the longer he went without looking away, the more the knot inside her untied.

She began running a finger over one of the feathers in her hair, trying to keep herself from flashing too wide a smile.

He glanced over the forest again, more color filling his cheeks. Maybe he wouldn't admit it, but his spirits had certainly been lifted. Settling down on the branch, he looked toward her window once again. "Is this why you like to climb trees?"

"Yes." She let out a sigh. "The world looks different when you force yourself to see it from a different perspective. It reminds me my troubles aren't as big as they seem."

The prince let out a chuckle as he pinched the bridge of his nose. "I see. And have your troubles ever been as big as a curse that affects your entire court? I fear that no amount of tree climbing will be enough."

Instead of answering, she swallowed. He sat in a tree several paces from her room, and she sat in the window. They were far enough away that they both had to speak louder than usual. And yet... She stroked a piece of her hair while feeling the weight of what the prince had just said.

He'd confided in her. Maybe he said the words in an offhand way, but that didn't change the truth. He shared a fear, one that clearly plagued him. Even more surprising, sharing it seemed to lift another weight off his shoulders. For a moment, the serious prince she knew melted away. He left behind someone she didn't know. But she wanted to.

Poking the open space of her window, her finger ran into the shimmery enchantment locking her inside.

Brannick waved his hand, and the enchantment disappeared. He raised one eyebrow. "The enchantment will still return this evening. I am only removing it temporarily."

She tried to act like it meant nothing to her that he removed the enchantment. Considering her cheeks bloomed with heat, her desire to act indifferent probably failed. But at least now she could sit on the ledge of the window and dangle her legs out of it.

Her gaze moved to the prince only to drop down to her skirt. While she rubbed away a spot of dirt, she glanced up at him again. "You know that room I found you in the other day? The room with the chandelier?"

Rather than answer, he merely narrowed his eyes.

She sat up straighter. "Why aren't there any sprites in that room?"

He turned his eyes downward. Blaz was already looking up at him. They shared a look that apparently had some kind of meaning behind it. It wasn't fair that Brannick knew how to communicate with a wolf. Even if it wasn't speaking exactly, they clearly shared some sort of thought process in that moment.

Blaz tilted his nose downward, almost like a nod. At the sight of it, Brannick settled himself back into the tree again. "That room is uncomfortable for sprites. The curse is strong in there because it is filled with trophies that mostly belonged to my mother."

"Trophies?" Elora continued to rub at the spot of dirt on her skirt, but she wasn't paying attention to it anymore. She remembered when Brannick had taken her to his room when they prepared for the first phase of testing. "You called that bear rug in your room a trophy."

Brannick scratched one eyebrow. "Yes, that rug is a trophy of mine. The chandelier is a trophy also, though technically it is not my mother's." His head tilted to the side. "Sometimes they are also called tokens."

At some point, Elora had leaned far enough forward that she had to grab the window to keep from falling out. Her eyes widened. "What are they?"

When the prince glanced at her, something new wriggled onto his face. It wasn't ease or joy, but he definitely had a hint of lightheartedness that hadn't existed before. Was this the real Brannick? One that didn't brood all the time?

He gestured toward the beaded necklace around his throat. "When the essence of an object has been greatly altered by a person or an experience, the object becomes a token."

Elora felt both her eyebrows raise up high. "Objects have an essence?"

"Everything has an essence." He let out a chuckle, though it wasn't cruel.

When she continued to stare at him with one eyebrow raised, he tapped his chin. "I will explain better. The chandelier in that room has a rich history. It was made in the mortal realm in a renowned glass-making shop. There was a master and an apprentice. The apprentice wanted to leave his master so he could open his own shop in another town. The master said the apprentice could leave but only after he created a masterpiece that was worth some specific amount of money. We do not have money in Faerie, so I do not remember the particulars."

Energy danced on the edges of Brannick's words. With every utterance, he seemed to grow both stronger and more relaxed.

"The apprentice made that chandelier?" Elora guessed. "That was his masterpiece?"

Brannick nodded. "He toiled over it, building his skill with each crystal. To him, it represented his freedom. He flooded every piece of the chandelier with his desire to be free and create whatever he wanted. When it was finished, everyone who saw it called it the most beautiful creation they had ever beheld." His lips turned down. "But the master was jealous. He told his apprentice that his skill was too valuable. The master insisted that he needed the apprentice and that he could not ever leave. The chandelier was not freedom, it was merely another shackle in disguise."

Elora screwed her mouth into a knot. "I'm guessing the master was even worse than he sounds."

"Good guess," Brannick said through a soft chuckle. "But the apprentice's bondage did not last long. My mother found out that the master had broken his deal, and she killed him for it. Then she offered to bring the apprentice to Faerie. She promised he could make any creation his heart desired for the rest of his life. He took the chandelier with him and lived in this castle until his death. In the end, the chandelier *had* given him freedom. The essence of it is still full of that."

Nodding, Elora thought back to Brannick's bear skin rug again. "You said you got the bear skin rug when you escaped Fairfrost." Her eyes jumped to his. "So, that experience was strong enough to change the essence of the bear skin rug?"

"Yes."

She reached for a piece of her hair, smiling toward the forest floor. "Looking at the rug made me feel adventurous. I must have felt its essence, if that's possible."

When he looked at her, the distance between them vanished. They still sat far from each other, but it felt as though he were at her side. Did he look at everyone that way? As if they were a mystery he was dying to solve? "Escaping Fairfrost *was* an adventure." He leaned forward. Even though he sat in a tree, she almost felt the need to move backward. Somehow, he still felt too close. His eyes narrowed, causing the colors in them to spin and burst. "The rug reminds me of you sometimes."

Heat burned all across her cheeks much too fast for her to stop. Flipping a section of hair behind her shoulder, she attempted to act unaffected. "That's nice to know you think of me even though I'm supposedly an inconvenience to you."

He scowled in response. Looking away, he folded his arms over his chest and leaned back into the tree branch behind him.

As the forest air stilled with silence, she glanced around. Glowing green sprites looped and hovered above, but no other creatures were near. Even still, she lowered her voice. "What is happening to your essence?"

Her voice came out more concerned than she wanted. But she probably couldn't have helped it even if she tried. She feared Brannick would scold her for being impertinent, but he didn't. He just let out a sigh that held the weight of pain. "I do not know. I used to be audacious and defiant." His hand rested against his forehead. "I used to have fun. Perhaps I am merely growing older and more experienced. But I must admit, I do not like the change."

The words dug deep into Elora while she stared back. The pain of her own past bubbled in her chest the way it often did when Brannick was around. It stung and twisted. Almost as soon as it resurfaced, she pushed it down.

Maybe it was a sign that she'd been pushing it down too much lately, but the pain curled in on itself until she almost couldn't feel it at all. Of course, it didn't disappear completely. Part of it still writhed deep inside. But at least now, she could ignore it.

Jumping back inside her room, she snatched one of the lavender-scented soaps from the table near her bath. When she returned to the window, she tipped an eyebrow upward. "Maybe it doesn't have to be so complicated to fix your essence. Maybe you just need to have more fun."

Hoping the cork stopper would stay in place, she chucked the tiny clay pot of soap right at the prince's face. Brannick blinked at the object as it flew toward him. He jerked backward in surprise, but he still managed to catch the pot without trouble.

Standing up on the branch, he shook his head deviously. "You should not start a game you cannot win."

As his arm reeled back to throw, Elora grinned. Yes, fae were stronger and had better reflexes, but she knew how to catch. Hopefully she wouldn't embarrass herself too badly.

But just as she lifted her hands, a gasp erupted from her lips. She placed one hand over her mouth. With the other, she pointed toward the looming object flying nearer by the second.

A dragon.

CHAPTER 10

Iridescent scales covered the dragon in the sky. Its wings flapped hard enough to send the leaves in Bitter Thorn forest fluttering. Elora took a step back from her window. Her heart hammered as she tried to ignore the pit in her stomach. The milky white dragon gave off a tint of bright green as it flew closer to the forest.

Clutching her heart, she jerked her head toward Brannick, who still sat in the tree outside her room. His eyes had lost all the brilliance they gained from his tree climbing. Now he cowered in the tree, swallowing even more often than she did.

From the forest floor, Blaz let out a low growl. Instead of sitting at the base of the tree like he had been doing only moments ago, the wolf stood alert. His nose pointed toward the sky while his growl deepened.

Shouts erupted as a crowd of white-clad soldiers charged toward Bitter Thorn Castle. Elora only managed a glimpse of them before her angle in the castle made them impossible to see.

The sight of the soldiers must have stirred Brannick to action. He descended from the tree with even more agility than he used to climb it. Blaz fell into step beside him as they both moved toward the front of the castle.

"Brannick." Elora bit her bottom lip as soon as the words left her lips. The prince who turned back to her was the broody fae she had met in the mortal realm. The Brannick who liked to have fun was nowhere to be seen. She chewed on her lip as she looked into his eyes. "Be careful."

His eyes went alight at the sound of those words. It only lasted a moment, but she could feel it inside her. He nodded. "Go find Soren. The outer castle guards will be ready to stop these soldiers, but it won't hurt to have reinforcements right away."

Before she could respond, he turned his gaze upward. The dragon drew closer. The rider on its back was still too far away to see, but Elora guessed it might be a fae who wore a white, beaded crown.

Both Elora and Brannick turned at the same moment. He moved toward the front of the castle, already waving one hand in the air. She rushed over to her bedroom door, quickly yanking it open.

Just as she reached the hallway, a pink sparkle among the glowing green lights ahead caught her attention.

"Tansy!" she yelled as she ran.

The sprite zoomed down from the ceiling until she landed on Elora's shoulder. Her limbs looked frailer than they had since the fight in Dustdune. The sprite's voice came out softer than usual. "Queen Alessandra has brought her dragon into Bitter Thorn. Most dragons are harmless, but the queen's is fierce. The soldiers attacking the castle are well trained, but I believe they are only a distraction. The queen herself only comes if she does not trust anyone else to do the job she needs done."

Nearly tripping over her feet, Elora sprinted down a new hallway. "Can you find Soren and give him that same message?"

Tansy barely had time to nod before she zoomed off again.

The halls of the castle blurred as Elora continued to run. She kept hoping she'd run into Lyren or even Vesper or Quintus, but none of them appeared. Still, several fae noticed her running at top speed toward the front castle doors. Surely, they would recognize that something was wrong.

Her running must have done the trick. By the time she reached the doors, a small crowd of fae were following behind her. The thick wooden doors creaked open, only to be met with a barrage of flying axes. Too bad for them, she had plenty of experience with avoiding blades.

Ducking into a roll, Elora dodged every axe easily. She reached for her sword, nearly pulling it from its sheath before she remembered using it would reveal the secret of her sword skill.

From behind her, fae let out war cries as they ran toward the Fairfrost guards. The fae reached into pockets only to pull out long spears and heavy bows and arrows that never would have fit inside pockets in the mortal realm.

Their screams filled the air while she turned toward the side of the castle Brannick should have been coming from. Just as she spotted him and Blaz around a turret, a shadow slithered over her.

Gulping, she turned to meet a large green creature with legs as thick as tree trunks. Even without someone explaining, she knew to call it a troll. The creature bared yellow teeth with black spots of decay. It wielded an axe with a rounded edge.

She had only just gained her footing before she had to duck and roll again. The blade of the troll's axe narrowly missed slicing through her leg.

Though she would not have liked getting cut, she feared even more that the axe would clash against her glamoured sheath. It wouldn't matter if the sheath was invisible then. If the metals clashed against each other, the sound would be loud enough to give its location away.

The desire to pull her sword from its sheath grew into a necessity. What had Brannick said? As long as the sword touched the sheath, it would remain invisible.

Hoping the troll couldn't climb trees, she scurried up the nearest trunk. While the troll swung its axe against every branch he could, she moved just fast enough to avoid his blade. Eventually, she climbed high enough that he couldn't reach her.

With the utmost care, she drew her sword. Even the scrape of metal against metal while unsheathing her sword might give away her secret, so she pulled it out as slow as she could. While she worked, more fae charged out from the castle. These fae wore brown and green coats with thick woolen belts of black around their waists. She recognized their weapons as the ones from the armory she and Brannick trained in.

They would help, but she was still concerned about getting to Brannick as quickly as possible. The other fae could handle the Fairfrost guards, but if Tansy was correct, something else was at play here.

Once everything but the very tip of the sword had been removed from the sheath, Elora slid the tip of the sword down the outside of the sheath, holding her breath all the while. As she hoped, the sword remained invisible. When it touched the very end of the sheath, she laid her sword against it. Now even the cross guard and hilt were touching the sheath.

The troll slammed his axe against the trunk, causing the leaves around her to shake. Steadying her feet, Elora now moved the tip of the sword away from the sheath. It stayed invisible because the cross guard still touched the sheath. She'd have to hold the sheath against the cross guard while she used her sword, which wasn't ideal, but it was better than not having a sword at all.

When the troll slammed his axe into the tree trunk a second time, she was ready. She threw herself off the tree, aiming straight for the troll's back. The faintest thought about her wings flitted through her mind, but she swiped it away almost as fast. The wings would just get in the way.

Her body jolted as she landed on the troll's back. The green-tinged skin had the texture of stone with the temperature of ice. She struck the sword across the troll's back while still keeping the cross guard against her sheath.

To her dismay, the sword bounced when it met the troll's skin. Apparently, the blade wasn't strong enough to penetrate the creature's thick skin. She grunted at the thought. When she hit the troll a second time, the blade still didn't puncture the thick skin. But just before her heart could sink completely, she noticed the sword *did* have an effect on the troll. Its green skin sizzled exactly the way Brannick's had when she accidentally cut him with her sword.

That moment of revelation gave the troll just enough time to throw her from its back. She landed with a thud on the forest floor. Damp earth covered her as she forced herself back up again.

The sword had become visible for the slightest moment when she fell. There was no time to worry about it, and probably no one but the troll had seen anyway. She gripped the hilt tight again, keeping it carefully touching the sheath once again.

Time to get serious about defeating this troll. The dragon's flapping wings beat against several trees as it finally landed on the forest floor.

Doing her best to ignore it, Elora focused on the troll. Maybe it was instinct, but something told her to aim for the soft skin under the troll's arm. A grunt escaped her as she charged.

Her aim was perfect, and the sword punctured the troll this time. Only the tip of the blade went in though. Before she could force it any deeper, the creature sent its fist into her stomach.

Air burst from her lips, escaping her body entirely as she fell. It wasn't until she landed that she realized she had lost her grip on the sword. Her heart stopped.

It wouldn't matter if she had any breath in her chest; she wouldn't have been able to breathe anyway.

The troll let out a screech that sounded like gravelly stones rolling around in a bucket. That sound was paired with a gargle as the troll pinched the sword between two fingers. It ripped it out from its skin and threw it toward the castle.

In full view.

Even as the troll lumbered toward her, she couldn't move. What if someone saw the sword? What would they think?

Of course, the first person to see it had to be the worst possible person of all.

Queen Alessandra dismounted her dragon with the beads of her white crown bouncing against her forehead. At the sight of the sword, the queen's teeth gritted together. After the shortest glance, she reached for the nearest guard to her.

Her fingers dug into the shoulder of the guard while she punched her other hand toward the sword. The sword had nearly reached the ground when a layer of icy blue fire engulfed it. By the time it fell onto the forest floor, the fire shot upward and outward in undulating bursts.

Curling her hand into a tight fist, Queen Alessandra pulled her hand back toward herself. All at once, the icy blue fire vanished.

And so did the sword.

The troll swung its axe toward Elora's heart. Her feet tumbled as she skipped backward to avoid it. Even as she moved, she glanced across the forest to the spot where her sword had fallen. Fire couldn't make a sword vanish. It couldn't.

Instead of fighting the troll, she only cared about getting closer to her sword. If the troll followed after her, it didn't matter. She could move faster than the large creature anyway.

Her eyes darted over the forest floor, desperate to find some hint of her sword. It didn't make any sense. Her father had forged weapons all her life. She knew how metal worked. Even if the queen's fire had been hot enough to destroy the sword, there would still be melted metal left behind.

Just as she had that thought, she caught a glint of something near a tree. Her heart skipped as she increased her speed. The sword was still there, she just had to get to it.

Only moments later, a large boulder fell from the sky. It landed right on the small glint she had noticed. At the same time, the troll swiped its axe at her legs. She tried to jump away, but the edge of the blade still hit against the bottom of her boots. Tucking her head, she turned her fall into a roll.

A growling snarl moved close to the troll. She barely caught sight of furry black ears before Blaz had clamped his teeth down on the troll's leg.

The troll let out a yowl, eager to now plunge its axe in the wolf's body instead of Elora's. But when its green arm raised, the branch of a nearby tree whipped across its chest. The force of the hit caused the troll to fall onto its back.

"This way." Brannick jerked his head toward the castle. Just as the troll began to stir, he waved his hand through the air. The movement caused another branch to slam the troll down once again.

Soon, she and the prince were both running back toward the castle. Relief flooded her so completely, she almost forgot the reason she had been so eager to find him. But soon it came back to her all at once. "The queen."

Brannick's shoulders jerked.

But Elora couldn't stop now. "Her guards are only a diversion. She's here for something else."

She spoke the words, but deep down, she already knew it was too late. From the front of the castle, Soren led another group of fae out toward the Fairfrost soldiers. Those in white uniforms had already started retreating.

Queen Alessandra had mounted her dragon once again. Her back was straight as she reached a hand toward the castle. When she clenched a fist, a corner of the black castle cracked.

Brannick's feet froze in place. He reached for his heart, as if the crack in the castle had physically pained him.

While the queen's dragon flew closer to the crack, she waved and twirled her hand until a small chunk of the castle broke away.

Brannick dropped to his knees, his breaths coming out in sharp bursts.

The chunk of castle fell, but with a graceful swoop, the dragon moved into the perfect position to allow Alessandra to snatch it out of the air. A truly wicked smile adorned her face as she pulled the chunk of castle toward herself.

Glancing over to the side, she threw a smirk toward Brannick. Her dragon beat its wings so fast, it rose above the trees in only a moment. Soon, the queen had flown out of sight. Her remaining guards were all fleeing.

Elora gulped as she turned toward the prince. Both he and Blaz glared at the retreating dragon with an identical growl in their throats. Whatever had just happened, it was bad.

Still, the need to find her sword stirred her feet to action. Just as she turned on her heel to find it, Brannick let out a hiss.

"Go back inside the castle immediately."

She forced her eyebrows together, hoping he would see the urgency in her eyes. "I have to find—"

He cut her off with a shake of the head. "Go." His jaw flexed. "Now."

He didn't just pair his words with urgency, he stabbed them with fear.

Without a word, she began running back toward the castle. Perhaps now wasn't the best time. And that boulder had fallen on top of the sword, so it wasn't likely to be found by anyone else anyway. She'd go back inside the castle now.

But she'd go back for her sword soon.

CHAPTER 11

After the soldiers and the queen left, nothing else of interest happened. Or maybe it did, but Elora didn't know because she spent the rest of the day in her room. She climbed her tree at least two dozen times, took an unnecessary bath, and paced the room enough to wear out the moss on one part of the stone floor. She even checked to see if her wardrobe had been restocked with dresses and jewelry after she had stolen the others. It had. New fabrics and gems stared back at her, but she simply slammed the wardrobe door on them.

The waiting wasn't too hard. She knew how to pass time when she wanted to. But it did have an unintended side effect. It allowed her way too much time to think on what had happened. Waiting didn't decrease any of her feelings. They festered inside of her until they felt like a physical entity deep in her gut.

Throughout the day, she teetered between believing her sword was unharmed and sitting in the forest to believing it was gone forever. The longer she paced, and climbed, and festered, the more she circled around to the same thought over and over.

Even if Brannick insisted on returning her to the mortal realm, she had one thing she absolutely had to do before she left. Get rid of Queen Alessandra. Or maybe anger her at the very least. No one could hurt her sword without a consequence.

Elora's fingers curled into tight fists, but at least the resolve gave her a sense of purpose. The queen had destroyed, or at least tried to destroy, her father's sword. She stole emotion from the renewal magic the fae of Swiftsea desperately needed. And she manipulated and betrayed Brannick in the worst way imaginable.

Elora shook that last thought away. It was mostly about the sword. If something had happened to the sword... She gulped. After her cottage burned to the ground and her parents died, that sword was the only item she had left from her father. If something happened to it, a part of her would never recover. Never.

Once night fell, she checked the clasp on her invisible sheath and went straight into the hallway. Marching over the stone fueled the determination inside her. Tension from the battle still hung in the castle air. To avoid getting caught, she ducked into the hallway hidden by a glamour.

Soon, she descended the darkened staircase and entered the room with the chandelier. Knowing its history, she took a long look at it before dashing across the room. It really was spectacular. A masterpiece like that should have been enough to buy anyone freedom.

After pushing open the door that led outside the castle, she glanced around. No fae lingered anywhere nearby. There were almost certainly guards standing near the entrance of the castle, but none of them could be seen from that part of the castle.

A gentle wind blew through the trees. The nearby streams trickled over rocks. The crispness of the usual Bitter Thorn air had been tainted by the smell of blood and metal. Despite that, no creature, fae or otherwise, could be seen.

Nodding to herself, she stepped out onto the damp forest floor. It seemed appropriate to hold her breath, though she didn't really know why. When nothing happened after that first step onto the soil, she took another. Brannick insisted she shouldn't leave the castle without an escort. Maybe it wasn't the safest place for her to be, but she couldn't just leave her sword in the middle of the forest, *if* it was still there. And either way, she had to know. If anyone appeared, she'd just run back to the castle as fast as she could.

On her third step, a swirling tunnel appeared at her side. She recognized Brannick's signature Faerie door at once. By the time he and Blaz walked through it to stand in front of her, she was already folding her arms over her chest.

"How did you know I was here?" It seemed like a good idea to interrogate him first.

He glanced down at his wolf while they shared a look she tried but failed to interpret. When Brannick turned back to her, he was shaking his head. "After I caught you sneaking out before, I set an enchantment on the forest to alert me if you step outside." His eyebrows drew together. "And you did it, even though I have repeatedly told you not to. It is not safe."

Concern laced his words enough that she dropped her hands to her sides. Maybe he was broody and grumpy, but he did care for her safety. No matter how he tried to hide it.

She started walking forward, hoping it might distract him enough to follow after her. Conversation would probably distract him even more. "Queen Alessandra stole a piece of the castle."

"Yes." His nose twitched, but he did follow her. Blaz padded after him.

Elora glanced up at the part of the castle which still had a crack through it. "Why would she do that?"

Brannick reached down, running his hand over his wolf's head. It was as if he needed strength before he could answer. Letting out a long breath, the answer finally came. "She is trying to remember how she knows me. She is hoping the castle will have some of my essence. She wants to use it like a token to restore the memories she has lost."

"*Does* the castle have some of your essence?"

Brannick's head dropped to his chest as he continued moving forward. "Yes, but Queen Alessandra's greatest magic is in emotion. She is not very good with essence." Those words caused his lips to twitch up in the lightest grin. The colors in his eyes swirled and tumbled in mesmerizing bursts.

Elora had to jerk her head away just to clear her head again. Now her eyebrows drew together. "Don't the other guards and fae in Fairfrost know who you are? Couldn't Queen Alessandra just ask them?"

An even bigger grin split across Brannick's face. "Most of the fae in Fairfrost never knew my name or position. They only knew me as one of the queen's guards. And the guards have a code with each other. They do not volunteer information. If she orders a guard to answer a question, nothing can stop them, but she would have to know the right questions to ask. She probably does not yet realize her guards know me."

But then, they had made it to the boulder that hid her sword. At least she hoped it hid her sword. "Can you move this?" She gestured toward the stone.

Without the prince there, she would have attempted to move it with a tree branch. Having him move it instead would save some time. With a simple wave of his hand, the boulder lifted off the ground and moved backward toward a nearby tree.

At once, she saw what had caused the glint. A small, smooth pendant sat in the grass. Its metal shined the same way her sword would have.

The pain bludgeoned into her, causing her breath to stop completely. She clutched her chest, but it did nothing.

The sword was gone.

Tears pooled in her eyes. She couldn't ignore them. Her feet kicked at the ground, hoping to uncover her sword. When nothing appeared, her throat burned. She tried to suck in a breath, but it was too shallow.

"What is it?" The prince leaned toward her, his eyebrows drawn tightly together.

"My sword." Now her breaths came in too fast. Too hard. "It's gone. Queen Alessandra burned it up, but that doesn't make any sense. It should be here. Some trace of it should still be here."

Each word came out faster than the last. Her chin quivered so hard, her words came out shaky. A well of tears had built up inside her. Her parents were dead, and her sisters still needed her. After the fire, she set the pain aside so she could care for her sisters. Then she'd been taken to Faerie which helped her forget just enough.

But the grief hadn't gone away. It was building and growing inside, getting stronger the more she ignored it.

And now the flood was coming. Too strong. Too fast.

She wrapped both arms around her stomach as the first tears streamed down her cheeks.

Blaz's ears twitched. Brannick stiffened. His lips pulled tight.

Her fingers squeezed into tight fists. "It can't just be gone."

Brannick took several steps toward her. When he got too close, she had to back away from him. But he leaned closer still. Soon, he had her pinned against a tree and yet he continued to move closer. His shoulder leaned against the tree trunk at her side while his opposite hand reached around her until it touched the tree trunk next to her head.

Pressing her head against the tree trunk behind her, she shot him a glare. "Be careful. You can't touch me, remember?"

His voice came out tight. "I know what I am doing. You must stop crying immediately."

The urgency in his voice stopped the pain at once. Fear did a remarkable job of masking the pain she so desperately wanted to smother.

She turned her gaze toward Brannick, ready to ask for an explanation.

Before she could ask, an answer came in the form of a familiar voice.

"Enjoying your pet, Prince Brannick?"

Ansel. The fae's voice sent a shiver down Elora's spine.

Donning a vaguely pleasant expression, Brannick dropped his hand to his side. His shoulder still leaned against the tree trunk, dangerously close to Elora's body. As he turned to face the fae behind him, he raised one eyebrow. "I do enjoy this mortal." He clenched his jaw. "And you are interrupting. Is there a reason you are here?"

While the prince spoke, heat surged into Elora's skin. It wasn't a blush this time. Rage burned inside her as she watched the fae who had once tried to keep her father as a pet.

Ansel twisted a red gem on the lapel of his coat. When he glanced up, his eyes flashed yellow. "Are you sure you will not reconsider my request? I have several pets I would trade in exchange for this one. You could take four or five of mine. And I will even throw in a bargain of your choosing—and perhaps even a debt."

Blaz bared his teeth as he let out a low growl. The wolf stepped in front of Elora, putting his body between her and Ansel.

While he moved, Brannick's jaw clenched tight enough to send pulsing through the veins in his neck. "No."

Ansel let out a sigh. "Fine, but please let me know as soon as you have grown tired of her."

At the sound of those words, Blaz tapped his pointed teeth together. He was too far away to bite Ansel or any part of his clothing, but the threat was still clear.

Taking a step back, Ansel narrowed his yellow eyes. "Prince Brannick, control your creature."

A devious smile danced across Brannick's lips. "I do not control Blaz. He controls himself. Besides, he did not injure you. He just made it clear how he feels about your suggestion." The prince's face softened for a moment as he patted the wolf's head. "Well done."

Pointing his nose in the air, Ansel glanced away. "High King Romany requests your presence in his throne room. He sent me here to retrieve you." With the wave of one hand, a rocky, gray tunnel appeared at his side. The sound of mountain springs and the smell of open air wafted through it. "The high king expects you right away." One corner of his mouth tipped up. "Your mortal can return to the castle on her own, can she not?"

Brannick leaned closer, his skin giving off heat that warmed Elora's. "She will accompany me. Go on. We will follow after you."

When Ansel began walking through the door, the rest of them followed. Brannick stood close on one side of her. Blaz stood on the other with his body nearly touching her leg.

CHAPTER

12

The scent of roses assaulted Elora's senses. After walking through the door, she expected to be inside a rose garden. Instead, she stepped onto a thick rug of red and cream with patterns of flowers and greenery woven through it. Cream and golden columns visually broke up the rich red walls of the large room in front of her.

At the head of the room, a dark red velvet curtain hung from ceiling to floor. Just in front of the curtain sat a carpeted dais. On top of that was a high-backed chair upholstered with rich, red velvet. The legs of the chair were cream with golden streaks peeking through.

Intricate gold and ruby chandeliers hung from the ceiling, giving off a soft yellow light amongst the green lights of glowing sprites. On every flat surface, metal and porcelain vases held bundles and bunches of roses.

The sweet smell hung thick and heavy in the air, quickly taking away the joy that might have come with a fewer number of roses. Despite the strong smell, magic showed itself in every corner of the room, in every fae standing near. Even far from her favorite court of Bitter Thorn, Faerie still carried wonderment.

Brannick and Blaz continued to stand on either side of her. When Ansel stepped through his door, he glanced toward the throne across from them. From atop it, High King Romany nodded once.

In response, Ansel offered his own nod. He then opened his door again and disappeared. The high king beckoned Elora and Brannick forward.

As they began walking, she opened her mouth to speak in a whisper. "I'm surprised Ansel opened a door straight into the throne room. I thought there would be an enchantment or something preventing that. It doesn't seem safe."

The prince moved forward with a step that made him stiff. "Fae do not create doors that go straight inside a home or room, or even a castle, unless they are specifically invited. It is a rule of Faerie, but it is not impossible to break like a bargain is. Still, I have never known a fae to break it." His mouth barely moved as he answered, somehow managing a quieter whisper than she had. At that moment, he spared her the smallest glance. "Remember, fae use bargains and vows and rules to ease our consciences. We do not break rules if we can help it."

Nodding would have to wait because now they had moved close enough to the throne that High King Romany would hear their conversation, even in whispers. Atop his light brown hair, the high king wore a red velvet and gold crown trimmed with white fur. A cream velvet cape had been fastened around his throat with a large golden clasp.

He raised his golden scepter, which made the ruby on top of it glint in the light of the room. "Welcome, Prince Brannick." His voice came out scratchy, like the fibrous end of a broken stick. So much red filled his eyes, the blue irises were difficult to make out.

By the time Brannick came to a stop, his wolf had padded over to stand next to him. The prince set his hand on top of the wolf's fur. "You requested my presence?"

Taking in a shallow breath, the high king set his scepter onto the ground once again. "I hear part of your castle has been damaged."

Setting his hand deeper into the wolf's fur, Brannick narrowed his eyes. "You have spies in my court?"

High King Romany tilted his chin high. "I have visitors in your court, as you know."

Before either of them could continue, a whirring noise sounded at the back of the room. Elora glanced over her shoulder long enough to see the rocky, gray tunnel of Ansel once again open at the back of the room.

Raising his scepter higher, High King Romany said, "Ah, just in time."

Queen Alessandra stepped out from the tunnel wearing a thick brocade dress with a sewn-in cape that matched. Among the white fabric, iridescent threads in the brocade gave off every color as the light caught it. Her white crown sat tall on her head with several rows of white beads falling down over her forehead.

She made an expression like she had just discovered animal droppings and now had to step over them. While moving to the front of the room, the expression didn't mellow.

High King Romany had lowered his scepter by the time she moved in front of him. He pressed one hand against his chest before taking a deep breath again. Even if Faerie kept him alive until the end of the testing, it couldn't have felt good to be dying. Sitting up straight, he turned a piercing gaze toward the queen. "You took a piece of Bitter Thorn Castle."

A light flashed in Queen Alessandra's icy blue eyes. Every fae looked young. Their immortality left them looking perpetually only a year or two older than Elora. But flashes like that gave a reminder of just how much these fae had experienced. Even without time in Faerie, these fae were older than they looked.

The queen stood tall and glanced away from the others. "I needed that piece of the castle. I will not explain why. The prince knows."

Pointing the ruby on the end of his scepter toward Brannick, High King Romany raised an eyebrow. "Did you give the piece freely?"

Each stroke through his wolf's fur seemed to calm the prince. Brannick kept his expression even as he answered. "No. It was taken forcefully."

The high king nodded. "Does its absence injure you still?"

An extra beat of silence filled the room before Brannick answered. "No."

Fae couldn't lie, which meant Brannick's answer had to be true. But the stiffness strangling the word made it harder to believe.

"Very well." Coughs erupted from the high king's throat, which only subsided after he leaned back in his throne. "Queen Alessandra, you know what you must do."

She continued to stare at one corner of the room. "I vow to have the crack in Bitter Thorn Castle repaired by the next phase of testing. I will also place a protective enchantment over the castle that will injure anyone who tries to damage it. The enchantment will last until a new High Ruler of Faerie has been chosen."

The high king continued to clutch his chest, but only let out a few small coughs. "Very well. I will not be lenient if I hear of any more sabotage during my testing." He waved at Queen Alessandra dismissively. "Go back to your court to prepare. The second phase of testing draws near."

After a stiff nod, the queen spun on her heel and marched to the back of the room. She opened a door of glittery white but stepped through it before any smell or sound from the door could be sensed.

Turning back to the prince, High King Romany raised his scepter again. "It is curious that you brought your mortal along with you."

Blood drained from Elora's fingertips at the sound of those words. She curled her fists to eradicate the sensation, but it did not temper the stammering of her heart.

With his face as even as ever, Brannick glanced toward her before turning to the high king again. "I do not like parting with her. I hope you do not mind."

Such simple words, but they sent her heart skipping. The fact that fae couldn't lie had never been so delicious. She was even happier to realize the only reason Brannick had brought her was because of Ansel. So, the prince did not like being parted with her, *and* he sought to protect her even when it was curious.

High King Romany let out a chuckle, which immediately turned into an abrasive cough. "I do not mind. I was most delighted by her harp playing in the first phase of testing."

Her jaw clenched at the words. She'd have to have a talk with the prince about how everyone liked to speak about her as if she wasn't there.

But just as the complaint filled her head, the high king looked her right in the eyes. "I am eager to see how your propensity for emotion affects the speech you will give during the second phase of testing."

If she hadn't been standing before the High King of Faerie, she probably would have gasped on the spot. Apparently, Brannick had been right. Romany planned to require speeches from more than just those in the testing. Heat curled into her toes, making her squeeze them against her boots. It probably wasn't best to show fear to the high king, so she did the only thing she knew how to do.

Raising her mouth in a smirk, she did her best to hide the fear and force fake confidence over it instead. "You will not be disappointed."

The high king responded with a smile before he waved her and the prince away. After walking to the back of the room, the prince opened a door that brought them back to Bitter Thorn Castle.

He leaned one shoulder against the stone wall of the hallway once the door disappeared behind them. "I will find a replacement sword for you, but it may take a few days."

This time, she *did* gasp. How could she have forgotten about the sword? It was her one last connection to her father, and now it was gone.

The moment her face began to twist in horror, Brannick turned from her to walk away. He waved a hand over his shoulder, which made a clump of purple wildflowers appear at her side. With his back turned away from her, he said, "For your brownie."

Whatever pain she was about to feel, she quickly pushed it down. "Wait."

He stopped, but only his wolf turned to face her again.

She swallowed over the burning in her throat, doing her best to ignore it. "I have no bargain with you now, which means I am only helping you because I choose to."

The prince's hands twitched at his sides, but he kept the rest of himself still.

A deep breath entered through her nose, giving her just enough strength to continue. "You should owe me a debt after the testing. If I help you win."

Now his head turned, so quickly that it almost seemed against his will. "A debt?" His eyes narrowed. "You are learning too many Faerie rules."

It seemed like the perfect time to offer a devious smirk. "I already know what debt I want you to pay." Her heart skipped as she prepared to speak. If fae were so particular with their rules, there *had* to be a way she could make them work in her favor. "I want you to let me stay in Faerie. Forever."

He stared for a long while after that. In the end, he never answered. He simply turned and walked away.

It didn't matter. He was definitely considering the idea. That's all she needed for now. As long as she played an integral part in helping him win the testing, he would surely abide by her request. How could he refuse when he had already admitted he didn't like being parted from her?

And how could she ever want to leave?

Was it because Faerie provided the perfect place to escape from the pain of her past? Her stomach filled with weight. If she stayed long enough, maybe she'd forget and never have to hurt again.

CHAPTER

13

When Elora woke the next morning, strain burned through her muscles. She must have been unintentionally tensing them in her sleep. Shaking out her arms and legs helped a little, but it would take time before she could relax again. A bath might help.

Her muscles continued to ache as she moved across the floor. The large stone basin that made her bath sat behind a thick wall of hanging vines. Steaming water filled it nearly to the top. On a little wicker table next to it, tiny clay pots had been filled with oils and soaps. Today they smelled of evergreen and citrus.

It only took a few minutes inside the steaming water to relieve most of the tension in her muscles. Nothing helped with the weight in her stomach though. The events from the day before were still fresh on her mind.

As she pulled on the purple woolen skirt her mother had given her, she tried to forget that the sword she usually wore with it was now gone. After donning her corset, she found herself reaching under her bed for the invisible sheath from Brannick. There was no point in wearing it now that the sword was gone, but a part of her still wanted to.

While the cool metal sat in her hands, the door to her room creaked open. Sucking in a breath, she threw the sheath under the mattress and stood up with a start.

Luckily, the tiny creature who had entered the room was too intent on sweeping the dust out of one corner to notice her standing there. His light brown feet had hair sticking up from every angle. When the creature turned, his bulbous chin and large eyes bulged at the sight of her. Using one long, spindly finger, he scratched his short nose.

"Hello, Fifer." Elora sat down on her bed, hoping it didn't look suspicious when she began smoothing her skirt.

With a chuckle, the brownie opened the door to her room and returned with a large tray of blue and red berries sitting next to a muffin that smelled like corn. A melting pat of butter sat atop the muffin. Both gave off wafts of steam when he handed them to her.

Setting the tray on her lap, Elora snatched up the muffin first. "This looks delicious."

Using his spindly fingers, Fifer took up his broom and began sweeping once again. "You are awake earlier than I expected."

The muffin practically melted in her mouth. Speaking over the large morsel, she said, "I am worried about the testing. It woke me sooner than I expected."

She decided not to mention the tension in her muscles.

After sweeping, the brownie tucked the broom into a tiny pocket of his coat that couldn't possibly fit a broom. And yet it did. He pulled out a rag next and began dusting. "Worry is a mortal emotion. If you try, it will be easier to ignore it while you are in Faerie."

With the half-eaten muffin in one hand, she leaned forward on the edge of her bed. "*How* do I ignore the worry?"

In truth, worry was only one of many emotions she wanted to ignore. It didn't feel right to pretend they didn't exist, but feeling them hurt too much. And she had to focus on the testing right now, didn't she? The emotions would only get in the way.

He chuckled and dusted every crook in her wooden wardrobe. "Just push the feeling away. It is not difficult. Not here."

Perhaps being mortal made it harder, but it hadn't been so easy to forget the pain of her past. She finished off the red and blue berries. Just then, a glowing green light zoomed into the room from her window. She smiled at the sight of it but quickly realized it didn't have Tansy's signature pink sparkle.

Soon, a sprite with long, velvety green hair and a toe-length green dress stood on Elora's palm. She didn't move as she waited for an offering. Elora quickly pulled a hair from her own head and handed it to the tiny creature.

With a nod, the sprite tucked the hair into her pocket. She held her hands behind her back as she spoke. "Elora of the mortal realm. Here is a message to you from Prince Brannick: Your presence is requested in the council room."

At the end of speaking, the sprite shot back toward the ceiling, glowing all the while.

Fifer took the tray from Elora before she could set it down. The brownie's squat nose wrinkled as he glanced at Elora's skirt. "Are you certain you do not want to wear anything else? I had Prince Brannick fill your wardrobe again after the other clothes went missing."

She reached for a lock of her light brown hair just so she wouldn't pinch her skirt. "No." But then again, if she wanted to ignore her emotions, maybe the clothes from her mother weren't helping. She swallowed and shook her head. "No, I want to wear these clothes." As she moved toward the door, she glanced back. "But maybe I'll wear something different tomorrow."

On the way to the council room, she thought of High King Romany's throne room. Did Bitter Thorn Castle have a throne room? Brannick's council room had a throne of course, but it didn't seem as grand as an *official* throne. Maybe she'd explore the castle sometime to look for the Bitter Thorn throne room.

Lyren's bright eyes met Elora the moment she stepped into the council room. The fae offered a wide smile before brushing a set of tight, black curls over her shoulder. "I have finished with the writing. Now we are all practicing our speeches for the second phase of testing."

Despite Lyren's obvious excitement, dread knocked its way into Elora's knees. She swallowed as she stepped into the room.

Brannick sat on his throne with twisting black thorns crawling up its stone sides. Blaz gave a happy pant at the sight of her, then he immediately nudged his nose against the prince's leg. A smile appeared on Brannick's lips for only a moment before he smothered it. He turned toward the table in front of him.

Quintus stood reciting words from a small piece of paper. His light brown skin almost shined as the words left his lips.

Vesper sat next to him. Once Elora moved closer, Vesper stared at her for no discernible reason. She remembered following him deep into the forest outside and then through his door to Dustdune. Vesper had been the reason she first met King Huron.

Did he distrust her still for conspiring against Brannick? Or did he perhaps admire it? The steadiness of his gaze didn't waver, but it also didn't answer any of those questions.

Lyren gestured toward a seat at the table and quickly sat in the chair next to it. When she handed a folded piece of paper to Elora, the fae's brown skin glowed with the same energy as her brown and silver eyes.

Quintus had finished reciting his speech. Elora didn't notice because she could only stare at the paper while a weight as heavy as iron dropped in her stomach. She swallowed.

Touching a hand to the white sea flower behind her ear, Lyren raised an eyebrow. "Prince Brannick told us High King Romany confirmed that he intends to ask you for a speech. I already prepared one for you, but now it is even more important."

Quivering shook through Elora's hand before she could stop it. "I don't have any skills for that sort of thing."

Lyren shrugged as she sat back in her chair. "We are hoping your mortal emotion will make it good enough. We fae usually use magic and exquisite speech patterns to improve the quality of our speeches."

The iron in Elora's stomach grew even heavier. "Magic?"

At the head of the table, Brannick gestured to Vesper. "Give yours, so she can see."

With a nod, Vesper stood at once. He took in a deep breath. As he did, the tiny noises of fluttering leaves and fae moving outside the room vanished. Once the silence became complete, Vesper stood taller. "The Court of Bitter Thorn has been cursed for the crimes of its first ruler, High Queen

Winola. When she created a portal to the mortal realm, it brought emotions here that have changed Faerie forever." Now Vesper breathed out, and the sounds in the room intensified to a volume even louder than when they started. After a few moments, the noises died down to what they had been at first. "Prince Brannick has paid for those crimes. He has endured his curse." An entirely different sound entered the room now. It sounded like glittery bursts in a dark room. It sounded like magic. "It is time for the prince to become High King. He will rule Faerie with the strength of one who has learned from punishment."

At the end, more sounds erupted that filled Elora with awe. Vesper breathed in again, and silence sucked away every bit of the noise. It stirred something within Elora, not emotions exactly, but something close.

Swallowing over a sticky ache in her throat, she tried to let out a chuckle. "I certainly can't do anything like that."

Lyren tapped the paper in Elora's hand. "Just do your best then. We all want to see how you can do."

By the time Elora stood, her hand was shaking again. She had to hold it against her stomach just to keep the paper from quivering. It forced her to tilt her head at a strange angle just to read the words. Her throat already felt tight before beginning, but the angle made it even more so. Somehow, she managed to begin reading anyway.

"Prince Brannick has the heart of a leader. Faerie needs strength. It will find it in him. Faerie needs wisdom. It will find it in him. The prince of Bitter Thorn will heal the mistakes of his fallen mother. Make him the high king, and Faerie will prosper like it never has before."

Even against her stomach, her hand shook by the end. At least the speech was short. Brannick's was probably longer, but maybe short speeches were common in Faerie. With her eyes still on the paper, she knew it was hopeless. Her words had come out clipped and unsteady. They obviously had no magic, but they had no feeling either. In a word, it was unimpressive.

Gulping, she managed to glance toward the head of the table.

Brannick had both arms folded over his chest. His eyebrows furrowed in disappointment, which hurt more than she wanted to admit.

She didn't want to, but she couldn't help looking toward the others as well. Lyren had sunk in her seat, wearing a frown that didn't suit her at all. Quintus was clearly unimpressed, but he didn't seem surprised either. Had he expected her to fail? Vesper was staring at her intensely again. Maybe he didn't have an opinion on her speech. Maybe he didn't have enough emotion to care.

"Quintus." Brannick's voice came out sure as he sat forward in his throne. "Can you craft her another harp? It does not need the designs you carved onto the one we gave High King Romany. In fact, a simpler pattern might be better. Something with trees and maybe wildflowers."

Now surprise took hold of Quintus's face. His eyes widened. "Another harp?" After a moment of silence, he gave a tiny nod. "Yes, my prince." He cocked an eyebrow upward. "But is there a reason for it?"

Ignoring the question, Brannick nodded. "Make it quickly and inform me when it is ready." He stood from his throne and waved a hand toward the table. "You are all dismissed."

"Wait." Elora jumped from her chair before the prince could disappear. "Will you…" Her voice quavered when he pierced her with a glare. Swallowing, she tried again. "Or will someone else come with me into the forest? I want to gather some purple berries for my brownie." She attempted a smile. "They're his favorite."

"I will take you." With the speed only the fae could boast, Vesper jumped from his seat and ran to Elora's side. His intense stare had lifted, replaced with his eagerness that had no observable origin.

She turned to look at the prince, but Brannick only stared at his friend, Vesper. He gave a heavy nod that probably meant something important. The two fae shared a look that only lasted a moment, but it made her gut lurch.

When Brannick turned away and left her with Vesper, she had no idea what to think. But whether she wanted to or not, she'd probably soon find out.

CHAPTER 14

At Elora's side, Vesper didn't speak as the two of them passed through the hallways of Bitter Thorn Castle. Her hands quavered with each step, waiting for something terrible or unexpected to happen. Even once they reached the forest, the fae's mouth remained closed.

She continued down a path she had walked several times, one she knew would lead to the purple berries Fifer loved. Even after several glances to her side, which Vesper had to have noticed, he still didn't speak a word.

It wasn't until she found a bush with the berries and bent to retrieve them that he finally opened his mouth. "I married a woman from the mortal realm."

With one hand hovering in place on its way to the bush, Elora glanced up. "What?"

Letting out a sigh, Vesper settled onto a large boulder that had moss growing up its side. "I always loved traveling. I loved my court, but I loved visiting the other five courts as well. It was not long before I ventured outside them and into the mortal world. I met a lovely young woman there and found I could not stop visiting her."

He let out a sigh. "She was going to have my baby. At that place in the mortal realm, they would have punished her severely for having a baby without a husband." He shrugged. "So, I married her."

Elora lowered herself to the ground. Her eyes continued to widen, but that didn't help her know what to say. "Did you love her?" It was the only question she could think of.

Vesper scratched a bit of moss off the boulder using his thumbnail. "Not at first." His voice came out heavy. Burdened. "Fae do not often love." His thumbnail stopped; the rest of him went completely still too. "But that changed over time."

Maybe the conversation would be easier to navigate if Elora kept her hands busy. Plucking a purple berry from the bush, she dropped it onto her skirt. "Where is the woman now?"

The scratching over the moss continued. Vesper stared at his hand while he spoke. "When mortals are brought to Faerie, they continue to age as mortals. They do not become immortal like we fae are."

Only a few berries sat in her skirt, but Elora already wanted to escape. This conversation didn't seem likely to turn in a good direction. Taking a deep breath, she plucked another berry from the bush. "She died?"

After several slow shakes of the head, Vesper set both his hands in his lap. "She is in the mortal realm. High King Romany is opposed to emotion more than any other ruler. He found out about my mortal family and banished me from my Court of Noble Rose." His face went slack. "He cursed me so that I cannot open a door to the mortal realm, nor can I step through one that leads to the mortal realm. I am forever separated from my court and from my beloved."

Squinting her eyes, Elora tilted her head to the side. "Couldn't another fae travel to the mortal realm and bring her to you?"

The little light in Vesper's eyes dimmed. "No. If they did, High King Romany would execute that fae for helping me. He would execute my beloved as well. She is safer where she is."

With no idea how to respond, Elora only nodded. She plucked almost a handful of berries before speaking again. "Why are you telling me this? It seems personal. I thought fae didn't trust easily."

Light sparked in his eyes when he glanced up. "You have blood of Noble Rose in your veins. It is many generations back, but it is there."

She pressed a hand to her collar. "How do you know that?" She sniffed the back of her hand, as if that might provide the answer. "Can all fae tell?"

Chuckling, he shook his head. "No. Very few can tell something so intimate."

Struck with the sudden urge to back away, she narrowed her eyes at the fae. "Then how do *you* know?"

"Prince Brannick told me."

"How does *he* know?" As soon as the question left her lips, a memory provided the answer. When the prince had given her the wings on her back, he mentioned that she had fae blood in her veins. It must have been his magic with essence that helped him sense it. "Why would he tell you that?"

Vesper scratched the bit of moss with his thumbnail. "Very few fae from Noble Rose have ever ventured into the mortal realm. I may be the only one. High King Romany has always been against it and punishes severely for it." The light in his eyes bloomed again. "When fae have mortal children, they always pass on one unique trait that is found in every generation to follow. I happen to know that my trait is the spirit of adventure."

Now the light in Vesper's eyes lit inside her own. Gathering the berries in her skirt, she raised herself to her knees. "I've always had the spirit of adventure. I got it from my father. He always encouraged my sister when she read about Faerie. And with me…" Her voice trailed off when Vesper's chin dropped to his chest.

"No. It is not from your father. Remember the fae your father bargained with? Ansel's greatest magic is in blood. He never would have given your father a chance to escape if he had a trace of fae blood in him."

Elora considered her other parent for only a moment before lowering herself down again. "It can't be from my mother. She never longed for adventure. I hate to say it, but she was boring when it came to that sort of thing."

With his eyebrows furrowing, Vesper glanced over the forest floor as if it might provide a different sort of answer. "But the trait does not always pass to every child in each generation. It only has to pass to at least one child. Does your mother not have a brother or sister?"

"No." Elora had to stare at her skirt to keep her disappointment at bay. How could it hurt when she had only found it might be a possibility only moments earlier? "My mother's mother died after giving birth. My mother's father died less than a year later when there was a siege on the castle.

My mother was raised by castle servants, brought up to be a great musician for the lord who lived there."

Vesper stood from the boulder, looking anywhere but at her. "I see. Another fae from Noble Rose must have snuck into the mortal realm then. Perhaps that fae passed musical ability on to future generations."

Even with the muted emotion of a fae, Vesper's words still came out tight. "Are you finished? Prince Brannick will want me to accompany you back to the castle."

She plucked one last berry from the bush and dropped it into her skirt before standing. "I am ready."

Nodding, Vesper continued to avoid eye contact as they returned to the path. "You are good to help with the testing. I am certain you will make your speech grand by the time the second phase arrives."

The words came out distant. He only spoke as if saying such things were expected of him, not as if he truly cared.

Still, they dug inside of her, touching on the very fears she had been trying to ignore. What would she do about the speech? If she couldn't use magic, then she'd have to rely on the only other thing she had at her disposal. Emotion.

But how could she survive in Faerie with so much pain in her heart?

CHAPTER

15

Scratches clawed at Elora's door. She woke with a start, hoping the noise had come from a dream. It didn't. With each scratch at the door, she could feel an identical one inside her chest. It made her heart pound. Hammer.

Sucking in a breath, she stood from her bed. The green wool blanket drifted to the ground while she reached under the mattress for her sword. It was only once she grabbed the invisible sheath that she remembered. *Again.*

Her sword was gone.

An ache tightened through her throat, but she grabbed the sheath anyway. The scratching at her door continued. Each new iteration sent tremors into her knees.

After checking that her corset and skirt were in place, she clasped the sheath around her waist. Maybe it was only a sheath instead of a weapon, but it could work in a pinch.

Another scratch at the door sent a shiver through her spine. She wasn't one to cower in fear, but facing an unknown enemy didn't seem like the best way to spend the middle of the night either. Was it Faerie itself leading her somewhere again? Or something worse?

She gulped while her feet led her to the door. At the last moment, she unclasped the leather belt holding the sheath. Gripping the cool metal of the sheath like she would a sword, she yanked on the handle of her door.

The skittering of her heart paused and then calmed once she saw what stood in the doorway.

Letting out a heavy sigh of relief, she dropped to her knees. "What are you doing here, Blaz?"

As she ran her fingers through the wolf's black fur, his ears twitched. He jerked his snout side to side as if shaking his head. Her eyes narrowed at the sight. Soon, he let out a whimper.

Using both hands, she tilted his head upward. "What's wrong?"

With another whimper, he bit onto the hem of her skirt and began backing away.

She buckled the sheath around her waist again. "You want me to follow you?"

He dipped his head like a nod and turned away from her to prance down the hallway. Hiking up her skirt, she ran after him. The wolf moved much faster than she could. Her breaths came out huffing after several hallways. Stone walls covered in various degrees of moss and vines met her at every corner.

Then came the briars.

At first, the black thorns only stretched over intermittent areas of the hallways. After a few turns, the thorns became more numerous than the moss and vines. In the next hallway, the thorns had overtaken the walls completely. Even the floor was littered with them.

Blaz let out a quiet yip as he leapt over a particularly large clump of briars. A large doorway stood next to the clump. Even running, Elora couldn't stop herself from staring.

Two heavy wooden doors ran from ceiling to floor. Instead of the leather straps that opened every other door in the castle, these had silver rings. Each had at least two vines of thorns wrapped around them. Geometric carvings featuring triangles and diamonds were engraved on the doors in breathtaking designs.

Her feet had slowed. She remembered High King Romany's throne room and how she had wondered if Bitter Thorn Castle had a throne room. If it did, this door seemed grand enough to lead to it.

Whimpering, Blaz bit the hem of her skirt. He backed up, urging her to follow him once again. She hadn't even noticed stopping.

It only took one more turn before the wolf pushed open a door. Elora recognized it at once. Four trees stood at the four corners of a large bed. A thick wall of vines hung from the ceiling, blocking off one corner of the room. The chairs at the front of the room had thorns creeping up their legs. On the other side of the room, a desk sat against the stone wall.

Brannick's room.

She only had a moment to recognize it before the prince stole her attention. He wore suede pants and no shirt. His black hair hung disheveled at his shoulders. He held a long spear with feathers and leather strings tied to it at different heights.

If he had noticed her presence, he gave no indication of it. His fingers tightened around the spear and then he charged toward the wall of his bedroom. The black tip of the spear pierced the wall of his bedroom, causing a chink in the wall. A stone wall normally would have stood up better against a spear tip, but perhaps this tip had been magicked to be more resilient.

The moment the chink came away from the wall, a pulse resounded in the room. Shimmery, white light erupted from the chink, slamming into Brannick's chest. His face contorted. He clutched his chest and forced out a cough. While coughing, his limbs drooped, as if in pain.

Everything happened so quickly, forming thoughts was almost a burden. But what was happening?

The vow.

Sucking in a breath, Elora suddenly knew exactly what was going on. Queen Alessandra had damaged Bitter Thorn Castle and High King Romany forced her to offer a vow to make up for it. The words held little consequence at the time, but now they pounded inside Elora's head, as strong as a pommel to the gut.

I will also place a protective enchantment over the castle that will injure anyone who tries to damage it.

Brannick gripped his spear tight again, eyeing the spot in his wall that he had pierced only a moment ago. When he raised his spear, Elora shouted.

"Stop!"

His shoulders slumped at the word. He glanced at her and then at Blaz. The bursts and colors in his magnificent eyes dimmed. His eyes met hers once more before he gazed at his spear. "I cannot."

Without warning, he charged toward the castle wall again. Another chink broke off from the wall, which caused the white light to slam into his chest again. This time, he had to take a step backward to regain his balance.

Hot air burst from her nose. She stomped across the floor, standing between Brannick and the wall. Her fist clenched around the invisible sheath in her hand. "Don't you remember Queen Alessandra's vow to you? Anyone who damages the castle will be injured."

Kneading his knuckles into his chest, he nodded. "I remember."

And then he raised his spear again.

When he charged forward, she slammed her sheath against his weapon before it could make contact with the castle wall. He had to take several steps back to regain his balance this time.

She eyed him while tension stretched through her jaw. "Then *what* are you doing?"

Seeing his shoulders slump and his limbs droop wasn't pleasant, but she could handle it. But when his eyes lost every bit of magic, her heart dropped.

He didn't even speak when he charged forward again. He focused in on the wall, as if unable to stop himself.

Her sheath hit his spear, pushing him back immediately. But while he regained his balance, more pieces of this puzzle fell into place.

It took a hard swallow before she could speak. "Because of your bargain, you have to follow every order Queen Alessandra gives you." She swallowed again. "Even if she gives it all the way over in the Court of Fairfrost."

When he met her eyes, his head dipped in the slightest nod.

Elora's jaw clenched tighter. "She remembered you."

The prince didn't look at her anymore. His focus turned to the wall as he gripped his spear. "She may not remember everything yet, but she has certainly given me an order. This may simply be a test to see if I follow it."

His hair blew out of his face as he sprinted forward.

New anger filled Elora's muscles as she shoved her sheath against the prince's weapon. He stumbled backward, nearly losing his balance. Squeezing her sheath tighter, she turned to the side of the room. "Blaz, get some pillows and blankets from the bed and lay them on the ground behind Brannick in case he falls backward. Can you do that?"

The wolf let out a yip. He bounded toward the bed and used his teeth to pull a soft brown blanket from off the prince's bed. While he worked, she blocked another blow to prevent Brannick from piercing the castle wall with his spear.

"How long will this last?" She shook out her arms. "Will the order last until you die?"

"No." A little light had entered his eyes again. "While I was in Fairfrost, her orders only lasted until a new day dawned. Now that I am home in Bitter Thorn, I may have more power over the bargain than I used to."

The wood from his spear clashed against her sheath, straining the muscles in her arms. A grunt escaped her lips before she could stop it. "So, we only have to keep this up until morning? How long until morning?"

He gripped his knee for a moment to catch his breath. When he glanced up, it was with one eyebrow raised. "Oh, mortal." He raised his spear. "There is no time in Faerie."

His spear hit harder that time, but she still managed to fight him off before the tip of it touched the bedroom wall. "Right." Now she raised her own eyebrow. "I have a name, you know. All the other fae call me Elora, which they do at your request. Are you ever going to use my name?"

Rather than answer, he clutched a hand over his stomach. It seemed like an excuse until his shoulders jerked with a shiver. His jaw clenched as he winced.

"What happened?"

His eyes darkened at her question. When he gripped his spear again, the veins in his hands stood out. "The bargain can tell I am not really trying to destroy the castle wall."

"What does that mean?" She didn't intend for her voice to shake so much.

Darkness overcame his eyes. It wasn't the same as when they looked colorless. It wasn't even a black darkness. It was simply an absence of life. He charged forward with a new level of intensity.

When she slammed his spear out of the way, he jabbed his elbow into her side. The motion caused her stumble sideways. Her feet danced until she ran into the nearby desk. It wouldn't cause a bruise, but it had certainly taken her by surprise. Her arms flailed as she tried to balance herself.

The motion caused her to knock a tiny clay pot off the desk. It tumbled downward until it hit her skirt. Dark ink spilled from the pot, soaking into the skirt from her mother.

Before soreness could line her throat, Brannick's spear slammed into the castle wall. A crack spliced through the stone. When the white light blasted into him, he fell to his hands and knees. Heavy breaths burst from his nose. His face contorted in pain. "I did not," he let out a pant, "mean to injure you." His chest heaved. "The bargain is taking over."

Taking a deep breath, she stomped back to her position between Brannick and the castle wall. "Blaz, get a few more blankets on the ground. As many as you can manage."

Brannick gripped his knees as he forced himself to a standing position.

Her eyes flicked to the wolf who was pulling more blankets from off the bed. "And then I need you to help me hold the prince off."

When Brannick charged toward her again, she set her feet in the strongest stance she could manage. She shoved her sheath against his weapon, but he pushed forward even harder. Blaz leapt forward, pushing against the prince's chest with his paws.

With the force of the wolf and her sheath, Brannick teetered backward. He fell onto the pile of pillows and blankets his wolf had arranged.

The plan had worked. She let out a slow breath as she gripped her sheath. But it would take a lot of energy to make it until morning.

CHAPTER 16

Tremors attempted to peel Elora's fingers away from her sheath. Her arms shook so badly, even raising them took effort. At her side, Blaz panted like he'd just run the entire length of Faerie at least twice.

Neither of them suffered the way Brannick did.

The prince collapsed backward onto the pile of blankets. His arms and legs shook but so did his jaw, his neck, even his knees. The bargain only allowed him two deep breaths before he scrambled to his feet again.

Before he could retrieve his weapon from the ground, she took a moment to glance at the wall behind her. Several cracks stretched across the stone, one reaching all the way to the ceiling. A chunk as big as a fist had broken away from the wall. It served as a reminder of how many times her defenses failed and Brannick damaged the castle.

Pulling his spear in tight, the prince charged forward with piercing eyes. Her arms continued to shake as she slammed her sheath against his weapon. Blaz slammed into the prince's chest with the full force of a running jump.

The force of their blows caused Brannick to stumble backward, but the bargain wouldn't let him give up there. Flecks of spit burst from his lips as he snarled. He repositioned his feet and pushed against both of them even harder than before.

Moving one foot up against the wall behind her, she kicked off the wall to give herself more force against him. Even then, it took several pushes to finally knock him off his feet. While he fell, his spear lashed wildly through the air, still fighting the defeat.

During one wild lash, the tip of the spear sliced across the inside of Elora's arm. Warm blood trickled down her skin while she caught her breath. A sharp stinging sensation accompanied the slice.

It was not her first injury of the evening, but it was her worst. She winced at the pain—and tried to ignore it anyway. When Blaz caught sight of the blood, he let out a low howl.

Brannick shivered and curled himself into a ball. Before he could even breathe, he was pulling himself up to his feet again. At the sight of the blood, his eyes widened with horror. Of course, that didn't stop him from lifting his spear from the ground.

He glared at the spear while aiming toward the wall once again. When he glanced at Elora, he immediately slammed his eyes shut and turned away.

But just as he lifted a foot to charge, his body froze in place. He peeled one eye open, glancing at Elora and then at his feet. After releasing a heavy breath, he dropped to the blankets again. With his eyes closed, he threw the spear across the room, far out of his reach.

Holding her breath, she glanced out the large window near his bed. Soft light streamed through the branches just outside.

A new day had dawned.

She let out a single breath before her own body collapsed onto the ground. The stinging in her arm intensified. Reaching for it, she glanced toward the wolf. "Blaz, go get Kaia."

"No." Brannick sat up with a start and then immediately fell back onto the blankets. His voice came out breathless. "Queen Alessandra must have spies in my castle. She would not have given me an order without a way to test it. If I give any hint that I have been injured, she will know the truth. She will give me even more orders."

Elora stared at the ceiling as she nodded. The scrapes and bruises on her own body would give away that she had spent the night being injured, but no spy would be looking at her. The prince had his own bruises, but they were mostly on his chest. Those would be easy to hide.

Taking a deep breath, she forced herself to sit up. Her knees dragged across the blankets as she moved to Brannick's side. Did he have any other indications of injury? Anything that would alert a spy?

The answer came when he glanced toward her.

She let out a sigh. "Your eyes will give it away. They don't look the way they usually do. Even if you don't look injured, your eyes look different enough that anyone will be able to see something terrible happened."

With each new word that left her lips, he stared a little harder. Did he think gazing at her would make his eyes appear normal again?

He sat up, but the staring didn't stop. From his new position, she had to crane her neck upward just to see his face. When he leaned in closer, her heart jolted inside her chest.

She sucked in a breath and jerked her head away. "I have an idea."

The flutters in her stomach were easier to control once she stood and moved away from the prince. Now she snatched the bear skin rug from off the stone floor. By the time she turned to face the prince again, he was also standing.

She gestured toward the bear skin rug. "You took this trophy—or token—when you escaped Fairfrost, didn't you?"

"Yes." His gaze on her never wavered. He didn't even blink.

With a nod, she draped the arms of the bear skin rug over his shoulders, careful to avoid touching him. He had to bend his knees for her to reach, and even then, she still had to stand on her tiptoes. To avoid his eyes, she took her time arranging it. "Maybe wearing the rug will remind you that you can beat her. If you've done it before, surely you can do it again."

He bent his head in a motion that wasn't quite like a nod, but it was close enough.

The moment she looked back into his eyes, she knew it was a mistake. Her stomach flipped in on itself while she tried to swallow. But seeing the bear skin rug around his shoulders lit another desire inside her. It was so *wild* that it almost made her chuckle.

"I suddenly feel like dancing." This time, she did chuckle. "Isn't that odd?"

Brannick finally broke his gaze when he brushed a hand over the fur of the bearskin. "You can sense the essence of the rug then. I used it to disguise myself as a bear and then danced in front of Queen Alessandra during my escape."

"You had to disguise yourself as a dancing bear in order to escape?" The chuckle that left her lips was as soft and as warm as the bear fur.

Staring at the rug, the prince nodded. "Yes, but I do not remember why."

Her stomach started flipping again. Keeping busy would help her ignore that. She took a step back and waved her hand. "Show me. You said you wanted to have more fun anyway, right? This is the perfect chance to do it."

A grin graced his lips for only a moment before the prince vanished and a large bear stood before her. The bear moved with the agility of a fae but with the weight of a bear. As it swayed and circled across the floor, Brannick's voice came from it. "I was dancing with someone, a servant from the palace, I think. I would demonstrate, but since I cannot touch you, this will have to do." He took that moment to twirl in a circle the way a female usually did after being spun.

Snickering, Elora shook her head. "I'm sure it was a very magical dance."

"It was." He dropped the glamour and the bear vanished. Once again, he stood as a prince with a bear skin rug around his shoulders. "How do my eyes look now?"

"Better." They looked *much* better, but if she admitted that, her cheeks probably would have turned bright red. Now he pinned her with that enchanting gaze of his. The swirling magic in his eyes caught hold of her, refusing to let go. Her gaze turned downward to avoid the pull.

And then she caught sight of her skirt. The skirt her mother had given her. The one thing she had left from the woman who had given her life.

Spilled ink soaked deep in the fibers, staining a large portion of the skirt front. Several small rips and tatters lined the hem. A worn spot hovered over one knee where she had been forced to drag her leg across the stone while trying to keep Brannick from damaging the castle wall. A long slit tore up the side of the skirt, almost as high as her knee.

Swallowing would be impossible with the ache in her throat, but she tried anyway. "I should go. I need to change out of these clothes."

He stepped closer to her, holding one hand out until it hovered near her elbow. "Stay."

She shook her head. "I can't walk through the castle hallways wearing a ripped and stained skirt."

His head tilted downward. "I will make you something to wear. I cannot make clothes as fine as some other fae, but I can conjure something." With a wave of his hand, a simple suede dress appeared in the air from the bottom up. The soft fabric rippled while his magic created it.

She had to clench her fists to remind herself how much she did not want to fall into his arms. Maybe he had been entranced, but she wasn't about to fall for someone who called her an inconvenience.

Turning on her heel, she marched toward the door. "I also need to clean up this wound on my arm and maybe get some sleep." Her eyebrows jumped up as another idea struck her. "If I return to my room quickly, I might be able to ask Fifer if he can repair my skirt."

She could feel the prince's gaze on her, but she refused to meet it. Instead, she stared at the leather strap on his door. Nodding to herself, she turned around again. She looked at Blaz while she spoke instead of the prince. "Can you open a door to my room? That will be faster than going through the halls, and I don't want to miss Fifer."

Blaz padded across the floor and nuzzled his nose against her leg. Attempting a smirk, she finally glanced up at the prince. "I find it very telling that you sent Blaz to get me when you were in need."

The magic of Brannick's eyes continued to grow. He raised one eyebrow. "I did not tell Blaz to get you. I asked him to get help. He chose to go to you."

Blaz let out a yip while something very close to a grin stretched over his sharp teeth. He padded across the floor to stand at the prince's side. They shared a look before Brannick raised his hand. A quick wave later, a swirling Faerie door appeared before them.

Moving her gaze far away from her skirt, she marched toward the door. The sooner she got out of those clothes the sooner she could forget how much their destruction churned her insides.

CHAPTER 17

The moment the door closed behind Elora, she tore the skirt and corset off her body. Leaving them and the invisible sheath in the middle of the floor, she flung open the wardrobe behind her room's wall of vines. She picked out the first dress her hand came in contact with. She hardly noticed anything except the delicate shoulder straps and the sage green color. It slipped over her head with the ease of trickling water.

While crossing the room to her bath, her toe bumped against something hard that had been hidden underneath her corset. Her face screwed up, trying to remember if she had hidden anything in her corset that she had forgotten about.

Her fingers buzzed with energy as she reached under the black leather. Half a moment before she touched it, she remembered what it was.

The crystal.

That strange night when she had been woken from sleep and drawn to the room with the chandelier seemed like a distant memory. Was it a distant memory? It seemed to have happened just yesterday, but it also seemed like a dream, never really occurring at all. And all that time, the crystal had been hidden under her corset where she had forgotten about it completely.

Shaking her head, she stuffed the crystal deep into a pocket of the dress she wore. When the damaged skirt stared back at her, she huffed. Guilt prickled through her skin. Maybe if she shoved the damaged clothes deep into her wardrobe, it would be easier to bury the feeling. Fifer had said ignoring her feelings would be easier in Faerie. It would surely be much easier once she didn't have any visual reminders.

After slamming the wardrobe doors shut, she marched back over to the bath. The slippery green dress moved with her as she dipped her bare arms into the steaming water. Using a soap that smelled of crisp rain and wild berries, she scrubbed the blood away from her scratches. The gash on the inside of her arm continued to bleed.

Once everything else had been cleaned, she untied the sash around her waist and wrapped it over the bleeding gash.

None of it stole her attention away from the damaged skirt. She could still see it torn and stained in a sad heap at the back of the wardrobe. The corset sat next to it even though it hadn't been damaged.

Tears threatened to show themselves, but a sharp head shake whisked them away.

A distraction.

That's all she needed.

The sash had been secured over her arm, which left both hands free. It only took a moment of glancing over her room to decide what to do next. She climbed the tree in the middle of her room. After working so hard during the night, her muscles strained with even the smallest movements. Puffs burst from her lips by the time she reached the top of the tree.

But those tears attempted another appearance. Only something big could stop them.

Closing her eyes, her wings burst from their place on her back. Their glittery translucence caught the light.

Much better.

The distraction worked exactly as she hoped. It worked even better when she hurled herself off the branches of the tree, plummeting toward her bedroom floor.

Her shoulder slammed against the mossy stone only a moment later. It would cause a bruise, but she already had so many. What was one more?

On her second climb up the tree, she now had two things to ignore: guilt and disappointment. She pushed herself off the branches, but her flapping wings only fluttered enough to bring her a little farther away from the tree. She still fell hard against the floor.

The third try brought another bruise and another failure.

With a huff, she kicked the tree trunk as hard as she could. Her stomach churned and tumbled, but things only got worse when a little glowing light with a sparkle of pink flew down toward her.

She jerked her head away from it, not wanting to see Tansy at the moment. "Come to laugh at me again?" The words felt bitter as they left Elora's lips.

Apparently, the sprite had no concept of privacy. Or perhaps she simply didn't care. Tansy's pink dress sparkled as she landed on Elora's shoulder. "No." The sprite twirled her dress around. "I have been asked to help you."

"Help me fly?" Elora snorted. "No need. I am never going to fly again. It's too hard. Truthfully, I don't even care about flying. Not even a little bit. Brannick is just going to banish me to the mortal realm anyway. Why would I need wings while living there?"

Flying forward to face Elora, Tansy raised her mouth in a smirk. "You say *banish* as if Faerie is your home."

Heat trailed up Elora's neck. "I…" Why did no excuse come when she needed it? Letting out a sigh, her head dropped. "I do not want to go home. My sisters have money and gems now, more than we ever had before. Why do they need me?"

"Why did you do it?" The sprite's voice came out with a glittery quality.

Standing up straighter, Elora tilted her head. "Do what? Practice flying?"

Tansy's velvety hair quivered as she shook her head. "When you saw Prince Brannick's predicament, you did not hesitate to help him. When your skirt got stained with ink, you continued without question. When your arms and body grew weak, you only fought harder."

A heavy sigh left Elora's lips, coming very close to a scoff. The sprite's code of never speaking to other fae made a lot more sense, considering they saw everything and clearly talked to each other about it constantly. "What was I supposed to do? Just let the prince get injured over and over again?"

Tansy shrugged. "You had no obligation." Her eyebrow raised. "Besides, your actions were fueled by passion."

Elora forced out a laugh. "Passion?" She raised both hands in front of herself while shaking her head. "I understand what you're implying, but no." Her hand reached into the pocket of her dress. "Perhaps Brannick has fallen for me, but I do not feel the same for him." She rubbed a thumb across the raw cut of the green stone in her pocket. "I only fought so hard because I want to stay in Faerie. Because…"

The rest of the sentence vanished from her lips when she finally noticed what her hand was doing. Why had she saved the crystal but not her corset? Neither had been destroyed, only the skirt. Yet, she had shoved the black leather as deep into the wardrobe as it could go. But the crystal she had kept close.

Even that she could have ignored if the crystal weren't so peculiar. And by peculiar, she meant that it reminded her of Brannick.

"Oh no." Flutters moved in Elora's heart and stomach as she reached a hand to her head. "Oh. No. How did this happen?"

The truth dawned clear in her mind, too bright to ignore. It annoyed her. Frustrated her. But it also filled her with the kind of flutters every love poem liked to mention.

She pinched the bridge of her nose while shooting a glare toward the sprite. "Did you come here just to ruin my day?"

"No, I came to help you fly, remember? And to ask you something." Tansy snickered and placed a hand over her mouth. "But the face you are making *is* highly amusing."

Groaning, Elora kicked the tree again.

One last snicker left the sprite's mouth before she straightened her spine mid-flight. "We have a request."

"We?" Elora raised an eyebrow. "Who is we? The sprites? All of you?"

Tansy nodded. "That is generally the way we do things." Before she could continue, a knock sounded at the door. She glanced over her shoulder at it and then looked toward the ceiling where the other sprites floated around. "I will explain more later."

With stiffened shoulders, Elora moved toward the door. Fifer still hadn't come to her room yet, but perhaps that was only because it was early. Or maybe he had come already but saw that her bed was empty and left no food. She grabbed the leather strap and pulled her door open.

Prince Brannick stood before her wearing a tan coat and dark pants. The coat was tied loosely closed with a leather belt, which left some of his chest exposed. And his stupid, perfect hair was just as perfect as ever.

She swallowed at the sight of him.

"May I enter?" An air of solemnity floated around him. Even Blaz seemed more serious than usual.

Nodding, she opened the door wide for both of them. Once she closed the door again, she leaned against it with one shoulder.

Brannick held his arms stiff at his sides, one hand clenched in a fist as if carrying something, but nothing was there. He glanced over her. "You changed your clothes."

"Yes." Could he hear how guilt strangled her just for saying that one word?

Taking a deep breath, he stood taller. "The protective enchantment and my bargain would have gravely injured me without your help." He dipped his head, gazing at her with too much intensity. "Thank you."

Her back arched as she brought a hand to her chest. "I thought if fae said *thank you*, they had to offer a gift…"

While she spoke, the prince turned his hand that was clenched in the strange fist. He brought his other hand out in front of him. Her voice trailed off when a magnificent sword appeared in his hands. He had been glamouring it to be invisible, but she could see it now. The metal shimmered with colorful glints. Even without touching it, she could feel power and energy brimming from inside it.

He pushed it toward her. "It is made with a Faerie alloy. The blade is not as strong as the one your father made, but I enchanted it with extra strength. It will go invisible whenever it touches your sheath, just like the other."

Her mouth hung open, hardly able to look at the sword without drooling. She very nearly thanked him before remembering the Faerie rule that required a gift after speaking those words. Instead, she just took the sword. Her sheath was still on her floor somewhere from when she had taken off her clothes. She would have to find it after the prince left.

Keeping his eyes on her, he reached into his pocket. His hand went much deeper than it should have been able to, but Faerie pockets clearly had magic she didn't understand. When his hand emerged again, he held a necklace with beads of green and bone. White feathers were tied to the thick leather string. "This ward necklace will protect you from fae enchantments."

Touching a toe to her ankle, she frowned. "I already have a ward." At least she still had the red ribbon from Chloe. It was the only thing she still had from the mortal realm.

Brannick raised an eyebrow. "This one is far more powerful. Once it goes around your neck, it will be invisible to all except you and me. And it will help you feel whenever someone tries to place an enchantment on you."

She took the necklace when he offered it, but she had no intention of wearing it. Chloe's ward had worked well enough for now. She couldn't leave everything from the mortal realm behind.

Now she stared at the items in her hands. "Two gifts for one *thank you* seems unbalanced."

"These are still not enough to display the depth of my gratitude. I have one last gift to bestow." He pulled a small clay pot from his pocket. It was stoppered with a cork and had a small, white rag wrapped around it. "Kaia made the ointment inside of this. It holds great magic and will heal the gash on your arm."

He pinched the top of the clay pot, carefully positioning his fingers so he would not touch her as he dropped it into her hand.

Words failed Elora as she stared at the items once again. She was closer than ever to convincing the prince to let her stay in Faerie. If she asked him now, he might even agree. But could she? Could she really leave her sisters in the mortal realm?

Now that she knew the true dangers Faerie posed, she couldn't help admit to herself that her sisters were probably safer in the mortal realm. She couldn't possibly bring her sisters to such a dangerous place. Not now. Now when all trace of their former life would likely be destroyed as Elora's had.

But could she really leave them behind? Forever?

Running a hand through his hair, the prince tilted his head toward her. "Lyren has requested your presence in the council room."

Without even thinking, Elora nodded.

The moment she did so, a glowing light zoomed down from the ceiling. Tansy hovered behind Brannick's head, just out of his sight. Her velvety hair bounced as she shook her head.

After a few blinks, Elora glanced back at the prince. "I will be there soon. I just need to put these things away first."

He nodded and left the room with his wolf.

The moment the door shut, Tansy flew closer, ready to explain her mysterious request.

CHAPTER

18

Watching her sprite friend fly toward her, Elora stood still. She allowed herself one swift glance toward the closed wardrobe in her room. Images of the crumpled purple skirt and corset twisted in her mind. The same twisting writhed in her gut as well. So much guilt.

Tansy's soft green shoes landed with a thud on Elora's palm. The sprite's recent looks of amusement and fun had been wiped away. Everything about her spoke of seriousness now. "Lyren is going to ask for your help with removing a talisman from a certain spot in Swiftsea." Her tiny eyebrows lowered over her pink and green eyes. "You need to do it."

Elora blinked at the sprite. A huff left her as she shook her head. "Do sprites respect *anyone's* privacy? Or do you just fly around seeing and hearing everything and no one ever complains?"

Dropping her jaw dramatically, Tansy shoved her hands onto her hips. "We have a very strict code for respecting privacy. We do not watch or listen to anything intimate, which includes a whole range of activities and emotions. Even if someone is crying and wants to be alone, we do not look or listen."

Shaking her head again, Elora turned to retrieve her sheath and belt from the ground. Given that they were both invisible, it took some time to find them. "Why do you care about the talisman?"

Once she found the sheath, she dropped the sword from Brannick inside of it. The metals let out a glorious zing as the sword fell into place. It almost made her forget how the sword from her father had been destroyed.

Tansy's dress sparkled as she floated near. "Queen Alessandra placed the talisman where it is in Swiftsea. It draws on the magic there. She plans to use that magic to capture more sprites."

"More sprites than she already has captured in Fairfrost?"

Nodding gravely, Tansy glanced away. "She wants information on Prince Brannick, and she knows the sprites in Bitter Thorn will have it."

For one brief moment, the guilt lining Elora's stomach shimmered away. Now, she could only focus on the consequences if Queen Alessandra found out more about her bargain with the prince. The testing would end immediately. She'd simply order Brannick to give a terrible speech. And then the queen who imprisoned sprites and stole magic from another court would be High Queen of Faerie.

Suppressing a shudder, Elora's hand went straight for the crystal in her pocket. She glanced toward the wardrobe, but it was easier to forget the skirt and corset, and even her father's sword, when such a terrible consequence lay in the future.

Her fingers tightened as she gripped the crystal between two fingers. "I'll do it." The words came out softer than she intended, but they were fiercer too.

Tansy flitted behind as they entered the hallway. "Do not tell anyone else what I told you. I technically should not have even told you."

For someone with such a glittery voice, it was surprising that the sprite could lend so much weight to her words.

Elora merely nodded in response. By the time she made it to the council room, her sprite friend had disappeared among the sea of glowing lights up above.

As grave as the conversation had been, nothing could have prepared Elora for the way Lyren's eyes sharpened. The fae wore no smile. Even the sea flower that was usually tucked behind one ear was nowhere to be seen.

A blue-painted nail shimmered in the light as Lyren pressed a finger to Elora's forehead. Her voice came out clear but with a much sharper edge than normal. "I enchant you to agree to my every request until dusk falls this evening.

Sucking in a breath, Elora stepped back. The ribbon around her ankle burned with crackling energy. Her eyes shot forward at the fae in front of her. "You just tried to enchant me."

"It did not work?" The dark skin of Lyren's face wrinkled. "Did Prince Brannick give you a ward? He must have."

Elora's heart squeezed in her chest. "I thought you were my friend. If you need something from me, why didn't you just ask for my help?"

The brown and silver in Lyren's eyes sharpened even more. Rather than blend and burst like they usually did, the two colors pierced, as if trying to carve the other out. Her jaw tightened. "This is Faerie. I do not have to help a friend if hurting that friend serves me."

Even as she spoke the selfish words, the tension in her neck and shoulders loosened like a sigh. "You must help me. *Please.* I will owe you another debt, an even bigger one. And do you remember that shell I gave you that can clean water and make it taste as sweet as honey? It can also purify an enchantment out of any liquid. I will give you a matching bag of Swiftsea salt that does the same for Faerie food. You will be able to eat anything in Faerie without fear of enchantment or poison."

The desperation inside Lyren's eyes might not have been convincing enough on its own. But since it was paired with Elora's previous decision to help, Elora was able to brush off the betrayal more easily. "Tell me what you want from me."

Lyren winced as she opened her mouth. "Queen Alessandra placed a talisman on one of the islands in Swiftsea. It is drawing magic away from my court. Even more magic than she has ever stolen."

It took everything inside Elora to keep herself from grabbing her sword. "Is it related to the decay?"

"No." Lyren wrung her hands in front of her, glancing toward the ground. "It is the same as she has always done. It does not cause the decay, but it does take advantage of the magic we use to combat it. Except this time, it is different. It is stronger, and we cannot move the talisman."

Elora raised an eyebrow. "You cannot move it?"

"The talisman is made of iron," Lyren said, as if that answered the question.

After blinking twice, Elora tried again. "And that means…"

It took a long moment before the fae recognized Elora's lack of understanding. Lyren sighed. "Iron is a fae weakness. We cannot touch it without great consequences. Sometimes, it is even difficult to get close to iron, but that depends on how it is made."

Elora nodded like the words made any sense at all, though of course they didn't. But then a memory flashed in her mind. Before she had lost her father's sword, she had cut Brannick during one of their training sessions. Rather than simply scratch his skin, her sword had caused the prince's skin to sizzle with steam.

After growing up with a sword-making father, she knew well that her sword had iron in it. Her thoughts turned to the new sword now hanging invisible at her hip. And Brannick mentioned the new sword had been made with a Faerie alloy. Perhaps that meant it had no iron.

Lyren must have interpreted the silence as acceptance. She waved her hand in a circle, opening her Faerie door of foamy whites, shimmery blues, and salty breezes. "Are you coming?"

Since Elora had made the decision even before entering the council room, it didn't take much thought to nod and begin walking through the door. As long as she kept her thoughts far from the moment when Lyren tried to enchant her.

But Elora was getting good at pushing emotions down these days. A little too good maybe.

The door took them to a small island with soft ocean waves lapping at the backs of their shoes. Palm trees with thick trunks and lush palm leaves grew in a circle around the outside of the island. Without even looking back, Lyren began marching down a nearby path.

After traveling down the path long enough to wear out her feet, Elora stopped at the edge of a sparkling lake. The water rippled and waved, as if it had a life of its own. At the very center of the lake, a large white boulder peeked above the surface of the water. It was just large enough for three people to stand on.

With a pounding heart, she raised herself to her tiptoes to get a glance at the top of the boulder. Just as she feared, light glinted off a piece of metal sitting there.

She turned, setting one hand on her hip as she did so. "You failed to mention the talisman would be at the center of a lake. I don't know how to swim."

A sly smile broke across Lyren's face, which was not reassuring. "Well…"

The moment her voice hit the air, the ripples and waves in the lake water churned and bubbled. Soon, blue-green scales curved out and back into the water. After a few curves and dives, the creature's body was easier to make out. It had a head like a dragon but a body like a snake. Its blue-green scales almost perfectly matched the color of the water. Sharp teeth snapped in the water, tearing apart a large fish while blood trickled down the sides of its mouth. The jaw looked strong enough to snap her in half instantly.

With eyes opening wide, Elora took several steps back. "There's a sea monster living in the lake?"

The shrug Lyren offered in response looked just as sly as the smile she had given earlier. "Actually, there are five."

"Are they secretly kind and benevolent?"

Lyren snorted. "No. They tear anyone or anything apart the moment it touches their lake."

Gulping seemed like an appropriate response. It didn't help. Elora continued to gawk at the lake, wishing desperately that she could grip her sword without causing suspicion. This was a terrible idea. Why did she always throw herself into danger like this? Couldn't her need for adventure be just a little less potent?

Shaking her head, she glared at the fae. "How am I supposed to get the talisman then?"

Lyren bit into her bottom lip before answering. "Remember when you first arrived in Faerie? You showed me the wings Prince Brannick gave you."

A light dawned in Elora's mind, but it still took a moment to respond. "You want me to *fly* to the talisman? You didn't just need a mortal who could touch iron. You needed a mortal who could fly?"

Glancing away, Lyren nodded. "The Court of Fairfrost has dragons and Dustdune has firebirds, but we have no flying creatures here in Swiftsea." Perhaps she was trying to prevent any more questions, but the fae suddenly stuffed a hand into her pocket. She produced a large box made of a strange material that seemed to be a mix of both wood and metal. It glinted in the light, but it also had the striations and texture of bark.

"Put the talisman inside this box once you reach the boulder. As long as it is inside of here, the iron cannot harm any fae." Lyren shoved the box into Elora's hands.

But it didn't matter if the fae moved too quickly to allow any response. It didn't even matter that Elora had promised her sprite friend that she would help. If wings were needed, the task was already a failure.

Another wave of guilt twisted in Elora's gut. It curled up and around the guilt she had for casting off the skirt from her mother. Both of those danced around her guilt for losing her father's sword. If she had any more guilt, it would probably eat her up from the inside out.

Why hadn't she practiced flying when she had the chance? Why had she abandoned it just because it was too hard? Because now she had a way to help Lyren and Swiftsea and even the sprites.

And she couldn't.

She couldn't because she had given up.

Turmoil churned inside of her—so great that she almost didn't notice the fluttery wisp of wind around one finger. Not expecting to see anything, she glanced down.

Tansy used both arms to grab onto Elora's finger. The sprite jerked her head toward the boulder and pulled—or attempted to pull—Elora toward it.

Of course.

The tiniest smile spread across Elora's lips. The sprite had said she came to help Elora with flying. Even if she couldn't fly herself across, Tansy could get them both there.

Jumping upward, her wings popped out of her back and began beating in a single motion. They flapped hard and strong without any hesitation. The fear of failure or even injury had kept her wings from moving feely before. But now they whipped in the wind, eager to do what they were made for.

The guilt inside got buried because Elora had something new to distract her. She would not give up on flying. If Tansy said she needed to know how it felt to fly, then Elora would pay careful attention to how it felt as she flew over the lake. When she returned to Bitter Thorn, she'd beg Tansy to help her fly even more. She'd do it over and over again until she knew the feeling of flying as well as she knew the guilt.

Once the feeling became familiar, she'd figure out the rest.

Just as that thought entered her head, she drifted down toward the boulder. The sea monsters snapped their sharp teeth and dove their snake-like bodies until the lake bubbled. But nothing could frighten her when she was so determined.

Keeping her feet in the air where the sea monsters couldn't reach, she opened the box in her hands. The talisman was shaped like a flower with a sharp spear cutting through it, or perhaps it was an icicle. It made a loud plunk as it hit the bottom of the box. Once she closed and buckled the lid, Tansy let out a long sigh.

On the way back across the lake, Lyren's eyes switched from sharp to soft several times. Elora had done what Lyren asked, but it didn't change how the fae had attempted to enchant her first. Brannick insisted his ward necklace was more powerful than the red ribbon from Chloe. Even Tansy said the prince's necklace was better.

Elora took in a deep breath. She had already lost her father's sword and the clothes from her mother. How much worse would it be if she traded her sister's ribbon for the more powerful ward necklace?

Besides, surviving in Faerie took constant attention. It would be easier if she wasn't continually burdened by the distractions of home.

The moment Elora landed on the shore of the lake, Lyren grabbed the box and let out a sigh of relief. "I will bring you the bag of Swiftsea salt for Faerie food that I promised, and I still owe you a large debt. You do not know what this means for my court."

Elora glanced at the sky as a glowing green light with a sparkle of pink flew far away. She couldn't help but smile about what she had just done.

That sense of accomplishment lifted her spirits even more than listening to poems or playing the harp ever did. Maybe even more than sword training with her father ever did. Because now she was doing something useful.

The feeling stirred in her heart, aching. It made her want to stay. Stay in Faerie forever. Why did she need the red ribbon from Chloe anyway? It only burdened her. Deepened her grief and guilt. Maybe once she wore the ward necklace from Brannick, she could finally move on.

CHAPTER 19

Elora slept for two days straight. It felt like two days straight anyway. Since time didn't exist in Faerie, she had no way of knowing for sure. She just knew that after helping Brannick for an entire evening and then flying over a lake immediately after, her body needed rest.

If anyone disturbed her during her rest, she was blissfully unaware of it. When she finally woke, she devoured a delicious meal of herbed potatoes and cornmeal. She whipped open the wardrobe just long enough to pull a new dress from it.

The midnight blue fabric was softer than any she'd ever touched, and it had a shimmery silver fringe at the bottom. Brannick's ward necklace looked stunning on top of it, but no one else would see it except her.

When she finished getting ready, a sprite floated down to announce that Quintus had finished crafting her new harp and that it waited in the council room for her to play.

She ripped the last strand of red thread off her ankle as an offering to the sprite for delivering the message. They required something meaningful, and the thread did hold plenty of meaning for Elora. Even if she had cut the rest of the ribbon off with her sword and stuffed it into the wardrobe with the rest of her things.

The council room stood empty when she got to it. Wind blew through the leaves of the trees and vines. Her heart skittered at the sight of the harp. She hadn't thought twice about the instrument since playing for High King Romany. But staring at it now, a flood of memories knocked at the back of her mind.

She had terrorized her mother through so many lessons, always complaining as loudly and obnoxiously as she could.

But now the memories brought a single tear to her eye, which she quickly wiped away. She had no time to think on such distractions. Instead, focusing on the harp would be much better.

Her fingers traced over the simple tree and wildflower designs along the pillar of the harp. One of them looked suspiciously like the tree inside her room. The others were similar except one near the bottom that had a gnarly, knotted trunk.

Jerking her head toward the little stool, she now placed a hand on the suede cushion that had been attached to the top of it. While the harp they gave to High King Romany had been grand and eye catching, this one was simpler. Like Bitter Thorn.

After another moment of admiration, she lowered herself into the seat and pulled the pillar of the harp against her shoulder. But when she plucked the strings, they did not resound through the room like they usually did.

Narrowing her eyes, she leaned into the harp and plucked harder. Harsh notes accosted the air, far from the delicate ones she was supposed to create.

Would rolling her eyes help? It didn't. Closing her eyes, she used a lighter touch than before. The notes did come out softer, but they didn't ring. They hung in the air as single entities, refusing to wind together into a melody.

Something was not right.

Before making any decision, she felt a pair of eyes boring into her from behind. Soon, light footsteps moved toward her. Even playing the harp, her fingers longed to touch the crystal in her pocket that reminded her of Brannick.

She managed to keep her fingers playing the unimpressive harp, but her heart came alive each time the footsteps moved closer.

But it wasn't the prince who had come. It was only Vesper.

Just as her heart sank, she forced herself to melt the feeling away. It was dangerous to desire the prince's presence. And hadn't Lyren just reminded her that fae would always be selfish, even with someone they cared about?

She did not need her feelings for Brannick growing any wilder.

Vesper's brown curls tumbled across his forehead as he pulled a chair from the council table and moved it to her side. He settled into it without saying a word.

Her fingers continued to pluck across the strange strings that couldn't produce the right kind of sounds. She glanced toward him. "Do you have something to say to me, or did you just want to listen?"

He eyed her moving fingers for a moment before turning his gaze onto her. It held the same intensity as it had in the forest the other night. "Are you certain your mother did not have the spirit of adventure?"

The question sank Elora's heart even deeper. Her spine straightened, as if that might have the ability to counteract it. All the while, she continued to pluck the strings. "I don't think so."

But Vesper only sat forward. "Did she never desire to escape the life she was born into? She never longed for a new place to live?"

In a single moment, Elora's fingers froze on the strings. Her entire body hummed with energy while the weight of Vesper's questions dug deep inside her.

"What is it?" Vesper had moved so far forward on his chair, it was a wonder he hadn't fallen off it.

Elora touched her collar, brushing a finger against the white feather on her hidden ward necklace. "My mother and father both worked in a castle when they met. I've always thought of castle life as exciting and adventurous, but I suppose it was normal and boring to my mother."

His blue and gray eyes turned bright as Vesper nodded.

Elora took a deep breath before she could continue. "After my parents married, they moved to the country to raise a family. My mother is the one who wanted to escape castle life."

Vesper's mouth hung open for a few moments until he mouthed the word *escape*. And then he let out a laugh that lit up his eyes even more. "This proves it. You *are* my family."

His laugh warmed inside her until it traveled up to her lips in a smile. "If my fae blood is several generations back, then you must be my great-great-great grandfather. Or perhaps there are even more *greats*."

He chuckled in return. "No, relations in Faerie are much simpler than in the mortal realm. We have mothers and fathers and sons and daughters. Every other relation is simply called a brother or sister."

"So, you are my brother?"

"Yes." He confirmed it with an eager nod.

That brought a snicker to her lips. "I never wanted a brother."

The light in his eyes flickered for a moment.

She offered a smile to soften her confession. "But I am oddly glad to have one." Her fingers moved back to the harp strings once again.

Vesper leaned back, but he didn't seem capable of sitting anymore. His entire demeanor lifted him far above the chair. "I am glad too. I have been alone for…" He cleared his throat. "Too long."

Her head bent in a nod, but she had no idea what else to say. At some point, her playing got louder. And faster. She needed to say something quick or else he would notice her discomfort. "Does this mean I have fae magic? Can I get faster reflexes or better smell the longer I stay in Faerie? If I were half fae, would I have more abilities?"

"No, that is not how it works. No one is half, you are either fully fae or fully mortal."

She had to bite her lip so he wouldn't see the frown. "So even being in Faerie will not help my fae blood come out or anything?"

His eyebrows squished together as he shook his head. "No, it will not. The only way for a mortal to become fae is by using a pink balance shard. But don't get any ideas in your head about that. You saw what happened to King Huron. You would die if you attempted to use a shard."

A chuckle left her lips, and she didn't even have to fake it. "I have no intention of using a shard. I know they force you to relive all your worst memories. That alone is enough to keep me from using it, but I especially want to avoid the whole dying thing."

Now it was Vesper's turn to chuckle. "Good."

When her fingers stumbled over a simple run, she moved them with a little less vigor over the strings. "If a fae and a mortal have a child, is that child always fully mortal?"

"No. Prince Brannick's father is mortal, but Prince Brannick is fully fae. There are exceptions, but usually a child born in the mortal realm is mortal and a child born in Faerie is a fae."

Elora's hands had dropped to her lap. "Prince Brannick's father is a mortal?"

Vesper dismissed the question with a wave of his hand. "I should have said *was*. His father died long ago."

He spoke the words with the same dismissive attitude as he waved his hand. He spoke like this was a completely normal piece of information and not realm-shattering news.

But then again, Brannick always had seemed a little less selfish and unfeeling than the other fae. The story of the apprentice who crafted the chandelier came to her mind. Was *he* Brannick's father?

She raised an eyebrow. "Is—"

"Your harp playing does not sound the way it used to." Vesper stood from his chair as he spoke.

Glaring at the instrument, she plucked one of the strings with her thumb. "I know. There is something wrong with the harp. I'll have to find Quintus and see if he can fix it."

Instead of responding, Vesper simply stared at her. For too long. After taking in a slow breath, he threw her one of his intense gazes. "It is not the harp. It is because of you."

"What?" She touched a hand to her necklace, barely stopping herself from glaring.

The intensity of his gaze only deepened. "You cannot pick and choose which emotions to feel. If you block out grief, you block out everything."

If the words had trickled in, she probably could have handled it. But they didn't. They stabbed her and gutted her like a sword and dagger working in tandem. Even without moving or speaking, she had lost her breath. "Then how am I supposed to do my speech?"

Vesper used his eyebrow to point. "That is why Prince Brannick had the harp made for you." He leaned toward her. "I have seen this in other mortals too, so I know all is not lost yet. Dig deep. You will find your emotions again as long as you allow them into your heart."

CHAPTER

20

The crisp scent of rain and bark filled the castle hallway. Elora's feet dragged across the surface of the stone, wishing each step would bring her closer to her room instead of closer to the council room.

The second phase of testing had arrived.

Everyone was supposed to meet in the council room, where they would then travel together to Noble Rose.

Her hands clasped behind her back, yearning so deeply to be moving in the other direction that they sometimes pulled away from her back. But they couldn't have their wish. Neither could her feet.

With each step closer, one thought filled her head in pounding gongs.

I'm not ready.

I'm not ready.

I'm not ready, I'm not ready, I'm not ready.

She reached for the green crystal in her pocket, hoping it might bolster her somehow.

It didn't matter if Vesper had helped her recognize why her speech would fail. Deep down, she had already known. She pushed and shoved every painful emotion away until she had nothing left. She has spent so much time bottling everything up, but now it was closed away. Hidden.

She'd been avoiding the pain of her past for so long, she hardly remembered how to feel anymore. And her fae brother had been wrong about how to solve the problem. She dug and pierced, but she couldn't find the emotions.

Not anymore.

Her thumb stroked the crystal, but it didn't feel as magical as it had when she first found it. Had the crystal changed? Or had she?

By the time she reached the council room, the toes of her boots had deep scrapes in the top from dragging them over the stone. No one else had arrived yet.

The fact moved into her head with no reaction. No stirring. Not even the second phase of testing moved her. It should have scared her how unprepared she was. It should have made her feel guilty that she would fail the prince.

If Brannick lost this phase of testing, then Queen Alessandra would choose the weapons for the last phase of testing. The prince wouldn't even get to use swords and trick everyone like he planned.

He had to win the speech, or he would never become High King of Faerie.

Elora understood that, but she didn't internalize it. Her fingers ran across the wood of the council room table. Even the senses in her fingers felt weaker than usual.

Was this how her life would always be from now on? Would nothing make her feel ever again?

She vaguely sensed padding feet behind her, but she didn't register them until Blaz nuzzled his head against her leg.

Maybe it wasn't as strong as it could have been, but she felt that. It was nice. The smile on her face was fake, but it almost tricked her insides into feeling something. When she ruffled her hand through the wolf's fur, she forced her smile to grow.

But then it fell. Apparently, forcing it wasn't enough.

When another pair of footsteps entered the room, her heart skipped. If Blaz was here, then that meant...

Brannick's lips twitched, apparently doing the opposite of her as he tried to smother a grin. His eyes shimmered and burst with colors. When he lifted a hand in greeting, his muscles flexed.

Her stomach flipped at the sight of it. She felt *that*.

His gaze might have sent her heart pounding, except he didn't meet her eyes. Once she realized he was staring at her neck, the beating started all the same.

"You are wearing my necklace." He ran a hand through the glossy black strands of his hair as he said it.

She attempted to touch the necklace before remembering she still held the crystal between two fingers. "Yes, I..."

But he wasn't looking at the necklace anymore. His head tilted downward as the hand holding the crystal dropped to her side. He continued to stare at it as he moved toward her.

"Where did you get that?" He moved so close that only the width of a finger separated their shoulders.

When she lifted the crystal up, he leaned toward it. He traced a finger over the purple striation near the top of the crystal, just missing her own fingers which held it. Even though they never touched, she could still feel the movement as if they had.

She glanced toward him. He immediately pinned her with his stare.

Pinching the crystal tighter, she managed a little shrug. "I woke up one night, and… I don't know how to explain it. I was drawn to this crystal. I didn't know where I was going. I just moved, and suddenly I ended up in the room where I found you that one night. The room with the chandelier."

The faintest smile played on her lips. It was so small, maybe it didn't even look like a smile. But it didn't matter. Because she could *feel* it. Her thumb ran across the crystal. "It reminded me of you."

Brannick gestured toward it. "This holds my essence."

Her eyebrows yanked upward. Swallowing, she held the crystal toward him. "Do you want it back?"

"No." He shook his head but touched the crystal once again. "If Faerie itself drew you to it, then it belongs to you now." His eyes flicked up for a beat before they fell back onto the crystal. "You do not know what this means."

She pulled the green stone into her fist, forcing the prince to meet her gaze. "What does it mean?"

He pointed now. At first, she assumed he was pointing to the ward necklace, but she realized her mistake as soon as he spoke. "Your heart," now his finger turned toward himself until he touched his chest, "is tied to mine."

Blinking was all she could do.

One corner of his mouth turned up as he leaned close enough that their foreheads almost touched. "It means you love me."

If he kept standing so close, she'd forget how to breathe. Something wriggled inside her chest. It turned and twisted so subtly she almost couldn't feel it. But it was there.

Tilting her head upward, she reached for the wriggling. Embraced it. "I think I do love you." She swallowed, not even trying to ignore the lump in her throat. "And that terrifies me."

The colors in his eyes shifted, swirling even more magnificently than before. He lifted one hand. It hovered next to her arm for several moments, energy sizzling off it. How could she feel him even when they weren't touching?

Finally, his hand curled into a fist. He dropped it to his side. "It terrifies me too." He spoke the words under his breath.

He abruptly stepped away from her then, patting Blaz's head as he moved toward the table. In the next breath, Quintus entered the council room.

Elora carefully tucked the crystal into her pocket. Would the others notice the heat in her cheeks? At least she had managed to feel something again.

When Lyren entered the room, she pushed a small leather bag into Elora's hands. "This is the salt from Swiftsea. Sprinkle it over any Faerie food and you will be safe from enchantment and poison. Do you still have the shell from me as well?"

Reaching into the pocket opposite the crystal, Elora touched a hand to the shell. She had just found it the other day and promptly decided to start carrying it around with her everywhere. After a quick nod, she put the bag of salt into the pocket as well.

Brannick opened a door for them. Apparently, Vesper would not join them. Was it because he had been banished from his Court of Noble Rose? Probably.

Noble Rose's throne room met them on the other side of the door. The red-painted walls and cream-colored columns were the same as Elora's first visit, but this time, vines and bushes with red and white roses graced every corner and stretch of the room. On the dais, High King Romany lowered himself onto his throne while he coughed into a golden handkerchief.

A handful of guards and courtiers peppered the room, but there were no more than twenty.

Lyren snickered as their group moved forward. "After the chaos at the last phase, High King Romany must be eager for something simpler."

With a smirk, Quintus nodded. "I believe you are correct."

From behind them, the sound of icicles falling into a bank of snow filled the room. Brannick's shoulders tensed, but he still looked back. So did Elora.

Queen Alessandra emerged from her glittery white door, holding her head high. Two guards in white followed after her. She marched without hesitation, quickly overtaking Brannick and the others. Once at the front of the room, she turned her gaze toward the ceiling.

It only took a few more steps to reach the dais, but Elora's feet dragged the whole way. Once she reached the front, she noticed the king of Mistmount, King Jackory, standing alone on the right side of the coughing high king.

The golden handkerchief pressed tight against High King Romany's lips for two more coughs before he dropped it into his lap. "Welcome." The moment the word left his lips, more coughs erupted. His red eyes watered as his body shook.

At last, the coughing stopped. He waved his hand toward the other king, and this time, spoke in a whisper. "King Jackory of Mistmount, your speech will be first."

Elora remembered the last phase of testing when Brannick explained that the order demonstrated who the high king considered most powerful. If King Jackory was going first, that meant he was an even bigger threat than Queen Alessandra. A threat they hadn't prepared for.

King Jackory nodded toward the high king before standing tall. "I officially withdraw myself from the testing. May High King Romany be remembered forever."

A wince pulsed between the high king's eyebrows. He frowned at the other king. But though King Jackory's words were clearly a disappointment, they didn't seem unexpected to the high king. And now more of the first phase played over in Elora's mind. Brannick had said King Jackory did not want to become high king. Luckily, the prince had been right about that.

High King Romany's hand trembled as he gestured toward the other side of the room. "Queen Alessandra, your speech now."

Even before he finished speaking, the queen conjured snow and ice in a flurry around herself. Each piece caught the light, showering the walls in rainbows and iridescence. She probably used pretty words too, but Elora was too caught up in the beauty of the snow and ice to internalize them. Music danced along the edges of the speech, but maybe it was just magic. Elora couldn't tell if the music came from the room or from inside her head.

Sparkling snowflakes soon fell from the ceiling. Each one twirled until it burst into a shower of sparkles once it hit the ground.

The end of the speech came too soon. Apparently, her earlier guess that speeches in Faerie tended to be short was right. With the end of the speech came the end of the snow and ice show. Elora found herself frowning at the thought.

She shook her head. Queen Alessandra was supposed to be her enemy. The end of her speech should have been a good thing.

Needles pierced Elora's insides. If she liked the speech of her enemy enough to mourn its ending, what would High King Romany think?

His eyes were comically wide, and his jaw had dropped low.

That couldn't be good.

The high king didn't even ask to hear speeches from the other members of the queen's council. His eyes were still wide with awe when he gestured ahead. "Prince Brannick, you are next."

While he stood tall, Lyren tucked a piece of paper into Elora's hand. The fae adjusted the white sea flower in her hair before offering an encouraging nod. "If you are asked for a speech, you will do great."

Brannick used the roses in the room during his speech. He called on the wind. His voice came out strong and clear and impressive. Still, it was nothing to Queen Alessandra's speech.

Everyone knew it.

The other eyes in the room wandered, ignoring Brannick's speech in favor of the carpet or the walls or even the print on their gowns or coats. The speech had certainly been grand.

But it wasn't enough.

High King Romany gave a hearty nod at the end. He didn't seem one to fake agreement, so at least he had found the speech acceptable. Sitting up straighter, his blue eyes flashed against the red inside them. "Only one more speech."

He coughed into his golden handkerchief. When he emerged from it, his eyes turned straight to Elora. "Mortal, your speech is last."

Her fingers pinched the paper in her hand, attempting to hide the trembling that moved through them. It probably didn't work, but she couldn't tell because the rest of her was trembling too. Maybe the crystal would help.

She reached for the crystal in her pocket, turning it over inside her fist while her short moment in the council room with Brannick filled her mind. Without really meaning to, she closed her eyes. She let the memory of his piercing gaze run through her. When her eyes opened again, a smile worked across her lips.

"Prince Brannick has the heart of a leader." As she spoke, she remembered how the prince had writhed in pain inside Dustdune Palace because he destroyed the shards that would have destroyed fae. No one else would have cared for other fae the way Brannick did.

Taking a deep breath, Elora's spine straightened. "Faerie needs strength. It will find it in him." Now she thought of how the prince fought against his bargain with Queen Alessandra, so he wouldn't destroy his castle and be injured himself. Even when that failed, he continued to fight valiantly.

"Faerie needs wisdom. It will find it in him." Could anyone *else* in Faerie be clever enough to learn a new weapon just to outwit his opponent in a tournament?

The rest of the speech filled the paper in her hand, but the words wouldn't move toward her lips. Instead, the crystal in her hand buzzed with energy. New words came out of her mouth completely against her will. But that didn't make them any less true.

"Prince Brannick will never give up. He meets every obstacle, no matter how big or small." Her heart surged in her chest as she glanced toward the prince. "Even if it terrifies him." By the time she turned back to High King Romany, the speech from Lyren had been crumpled in her fist. "Make Prince Brannick the high king, and Faerie will prosper like it never has before."

High King Romany touched a finger to the corner of one eye. At the first phase of testing, he had done the same thing, but the gesture had merely been a show. This time was different.

One tear pooled onto the high king's finger when it met his eye. He pulled his finger forward, staring at the tear in complete silence. After a moment, he rubbed his thumb over the tear, letting the water spread across his finger. But now his finger moved to the other eye. That one produced two tears.

He stared at them again, as if they might disappear. But they didn't.

Finally, he dropped his hands to his lap. He whispered a single word, which didn't seem directed at anyone in particular. "Extraordinary."

He wasn't the only one in the room moved by her words. Several others wiped away tears and tried to cover sniffles. But the most dangerous tears were her own.

They teetered inside her eyelids, threatening to spill out at the smallest movement. Her stomach churned inside her, filling too fast. All morning she had tried to feel an inkling of emotion. That moment with Brannick allowed her to feel a little.

It wasn't just a little anymore. Everything burned inside her with no regard for the horrible timing of it all. Her insides shook. Quivered. She was only a moment away from curling into a ball right there in the middle of the throne room in front of everyone.

High King Romany stood from his throne. "Prince Brannick wins the speech. He will choose the weapons for the final tournament stage of the testing when it arrives."

Her heart should have soared at the words, but she was too busy trying to keep herself from crumbling into a wreck of tears.

Maybe she could be happy later, but now the pain she had been avoiding was hitting her fast. If she didn't move soon, the pain would erupt in front of everyone.

CHAPTER

21

Tears of grief didn't feel the same as tears of pain. Though grief held pain, it was nothing like being sliced with a sword. Of the two, grief hurt worse. It came in a shadow wrapped in ice. It nibbled at defenses until there was nothing left to do except welcome it with open arms.

And then it would crush those arms. Destroy them. It would crumble everything that kept it away from the heart and then it would crush that too.

By the time the second phase of testing ended, Elora already had single tears streaming down her cheeks. Brannick opened a door that led back to Bitter Thorn Castle immediately. When her boots hit the stone hallways, her single tears had turned to waterfalls.

She sprinted to her room, trying desperately to keep herself from collapsing.

Her room offered no relief.

She curled into a tight ball, letting out a wail that could wilt flowers.

The wail offered no relief.

Her arms wrapped over her legs, pulling her knees tight to her chest. Rocking her body back and forth, she tried to release the pain through her tears.

No relief came.

The more she cried the more it hurt. Grief didn't care that it tore her insides apart. It didn't care that she wasn't strong enough to deal with such things. It just charged ahead, splitting down every defense she had built.

She had never asked her father why he was so fascinated with Chloe's poems about Faerie. She had never asked her mother why she wanted to move to the country.

And those were only things she knew she had failed to ask about. What about her name? Why had they chosen to name her Elora? Maybe there had been no special reason for it, but what if there had been? Now she would never know.

Tears continued to fall, no matter how she tried to stop them. It seemed her ability to block emotions had vanished when she chose to let them in. But if she had known it would hurt so much, maybe she wouldn't have tried so hard.

Because now her chest ached. Stabbing pain shot through her head. Her arms strained under the pressure she tensed them with.

But she couldn't stop. She couldn't even breathe.

It wasn't just sobs that escaped her. Whimpers and wails came out too.

It was too much.

Her mind raced to quiet evenings in her cottage with the blue shutters. Her mother taught harp to the youngest sister,

Grace, while Chloe recited long poems in her bedroom. Elora and her father sat in the kitchen while he taught her to properly sharpen a sword.

And that was only one evening. Their lives had been good. Happy. And now her parents were gone. Her sisters were grief-stricken, and they relied on Elora to take care of them. She had left them money and clothes, but what about their pain?

If she couldn't even manage her own pain, how could she take care of theirs? How could any of them move on after something so tragic?

She wanted to hide the grief away. She wanted to drop it into a box like the one Lyren had given her for Queen Alessandra's iron talisman.

But deep down, Elora knew shutting the grief out wouldn't help. Even when she'd done so, it only masked the pain. It still always churned and writhed inside her, cutting away her insides even when she pretended not to notice.

Maybe giving in to the pain was all she could do.

Sheets of tears slipped down her cheeks as she peeled herself off the stone floor. Her arms hung heavy at her sides. Somehow, she lifted one to open the wardrobe.

Gorgeous dresses and sparkling jewels stared back at her. As always, she ignored them. Her eyes turned straight to the back of the wardrobe. On the bottom, a bright red ribbon cut with a sword sat on top of a crumpled corset.

Elora's lip quivered as she reached for the ribbon. Maybe it hurt, but maybe she was finally ready to face it.

The moment her finger touched the ribbon, it burned. Heat exploded in her fingertips, forcing her to let out a scream. Dropping it, she jumped backward and slammed the wardrobe shut.

Curling a fist over her finger, she took deep, heaving breaths. At least the physical pain had provided a brief distraction from the emotional one.

When she carefully opened her fist, the burned finger looked no different than all the rest. She poked it just to see if that changed anything.

It didn't.

Had she imagined the pain?

Her head shook side to side as she dashed toward her bed. She wrapped the green blanket tight around her shoulders and buried her face in her pillow. Grief would always be a part of her now. She knew that instinctively even though she *still* tried to ignore it.

It would always hurt. Always burn.

No matter how she desired to, she knew that blocking it would only make things worse.

She glanced toward the wardrobe.

But maybe she didn't have to let it all in at once either. Maybe she could open up gradually, heal a little at a time.

A knock sounded at her door. For a moment, she merely stared at it. When the knock came a second time, she pulled herself out of bed and went to answer it. She sniffled while pulling the door open.

"Oh, you are still crying?" Lyren stared back at her with a mixture of disgust and sympathy. But mostly disgust. She turned to the fae at her side.

A part of Elora had been hoping for Brannick, but it was Vesper who stood there. His eyebrows lowered. "Are you all right? Do you need…" His eyebrows dove even deeper while he looked to the side. In a flash, his eyebrows shot up. "Tea? That helps when mortals are upset, does it not?"

The question came with such genuine desire to help that it calmed some of the burning inside. Elora even managed a short chuckle, though it came without a smile. "I don't need tea. Why are you two here?"

Lyren beckoned before turning to walk down the hallway. "It is about Prince Brannick. He will not speak to us about the final phase of the testing."

After taking a moment to drop her blanket back in her room, Elora shut the door and followed after the two fae into the hallway. "The tournament?"

Slowing his steps, Vesper nodded. "The prince's magic is very powerful, but so is Queen Alessandra's. It will not be difficult for her to learn about his magic. She could ask any number of fae. They would give the answer willingly as long as she offered a great enough reward or bargain in return. Soon, she will know exactly how to combat Prince Brannick's magic."

Lyren nodded gravely. "He will have no advantage."

Grief still roared in Elora's chest, but the conversation brought it to a manageable level. "I'm sure he has thought about this."

"Then why has he not spoken to us about it?" Vesper raised an eyebrow as he asked.

Elora shrugged. "Has he spoken to you about the other two phases of testing?"

"Yes," Lyren answered immediately.

Vesper gave an eager nod. "Extensively."

"Oh." Elora tried to keep her face neutral. Of course, she knew Brannick had a very good plan for the testing. He would choose swords as the weapons, which Queen Alessandra would never expect because no one in Bitter Thorn trained with swords. It would take the queen off guard, but it would also put her at a strong disadvantage because no one in Fairfrost trained with swords either, including the queen.

Lyren hooked an arm around Elora's. "Will you speak to the prince? If he becomes high king, it could save my court. I need him to win."

Vesper gave Elora a pointed look. "He does listen to you, even if he often acts like he does not."

Elora stayed silent for a beat too long, trying to think of how to navigate this conversation without giving anything away. Going along with their plan would probably be the easiest. "Of course I'll speak to him."

"Wonderful." Lyren clapped her hands together.

With a crooked smile, Vesper gestured down a long hallway. "Soren said Prince Brannick is in the kitchen wing, speaking to one of the brownies."

Elora nodded as she ducked down the hallway Vesper had pointed out. "I will go find him now."

It wasn't until Lyren and Vesper were out of sight that Elora realized she had no idea how to get to the kitchen wing. She'd have to explore the castle more. Since Brannick did have a good plan for winning the tournament, it was probably best if she turned around now while she still remembered how she had gotten to that spot. Otherwise, she might get lost.

When she turned on her heel, she stood face to face with another fae. One whose face she would have preferred to never see again.

Ansel rubbed his hands together as he glanced over her with his yellow eyes. "Prince Brannick lets you roam the castle on your own, does he? Interesting." His eyes narrowed as he looked her over once again.

Her hand instinctively reached for the sword at her hip. But grabbing it—even while it was invisible—could give everything away. Instead, she curled her hand into a fist.

Seeing the fist, Ansel let out a chuckle. "Are you preparing to fight me, mortal? How quaint. I can assure you, if I decided I wanted you, nothing would stop me."

She bristled at his words, but she wouldn't allow them to dig too deep. He had wanted her father, hadn't he? And yet he lost that bargain. Besides, she knew very well that he *did* want her. If he hadn't made a move yet, it was probably because he couldn't. Maybe Brannick had put some sort enchantment on the castle that protected her while inside its walls.

That only made her feel slightly less vulnerable.

Ansel brought a hand to his chin, stroking it a little too hard. "I heard your speech caused quite the reaction from High King Romany. He is rarely affected in such a way."

Every response that came to her mind felt like something he could twist for his benefit. Keeping her mouth shut was probably the best option.

The continued silence caused him to huff. He waved a hand flippantly. "That does not matter. I just wanted to let you know that I have thought about taking your brother as a pet instead."

Her mind spun in circles. She didn't have a brother. But then she remembered Vesper. But... could a fae be taken as a pet? That didn't seem likely.

Ansel narrowed his yellow eyes. "No." He waved his hand again. "I did not mean brother. So silly of me, I just misspoke. I meant I might take your sister as my pet."

In an instant, her body chilled. Every muscle inside her held in place except her eyes. She glanced toward him. If her face didn't speak of her fear, it didn't matter because it hung in the very air around them.

"Ah." Ansel's lips curled in a smile. "You *do* have a sister then. Interesting. And is she still in the mortal realm?"

Again, any answer Elora gave would only put her sisters in danger, but maybe not answering would be just as bad. She spun on her heels, eager to sprint in the other direction. When she turned, another fae stood in her way. He was tall with crooked teeth and white-blond hair.

Her heart squeezed in her chest. If she knew how to fly without help, she could have escaped them both easily. But she couldn't.

She was trapped.

CHAPTER 22

Even with a sword at her hip, Elora had never felt so vulnerable. She vowed to practice flying if she ever managed to get out of this mess. Her skills with the sword were the best, but she could use her fists if it came to that.

Ansel's grin widened as he twisted an orange gem attached to the lapel of his coat.

"Elora."

A squeaky voice sounded from down the hall. She had to lean to the side to see past the blond-haired fae in front of her. "Fifer?"

As the rabbit-sized creature moved toward them, Ansel folded his arms over his chest. "What are you doing here, brownie?"

Considering how large Fifer's eyes were, it was impressive that he could narrow them so tight. His flappy ears bounced as he tilted his head at Ansel. "I might ask you the same question, seeing as how I live here, and you do not."

Ansel responded with a snarl.

Fifer hardly seemed to notice the expression at all. He gestured forward. "Make way. Elora and I need to pass."

"You think I will answer to a brownie so easily?" Ansel's jaw flexed as he glared down at the creature.

Raising one hand, Fifer arranged his fingers as if to snap. "You forget that Bitter Thorn Castle is my home."

The mere sight of the hand was enough to make Ansel suck in a breath. He stepped out of the way with his eyes turned downward.

When Fifer began scurrying down the hallway, Elora darted after him. Once they turned down a new hallway, she glanced down at the small creature.

"Why does it matter that Bitter Thorn Castle is your home?"

Fifer let out a snicker that shook his short, squat nose. "A residence and a home are different. Home is where you feel safe. Where you *want* to live. Brownies have strong magic when they are inside their home." Now he shuddered. "Some fae who keep brownies make their living conditions miserable, so they cannot call that place their home. They do it to keep the brownies weak and unable to escape."

Elora touched a hand to her chest. "That's horrifying."

With a shrug, Fifer continued onward. "Most brownies are able to escape anyway."

After a few more turns, Elora swallowed the ache in her throat. She slowed her steps until the brownie turned to look at her. "You saved me."

Fifer's ears flapped as he shook his head. "No. Ansel cannot harm you while you are within the walls of the castle. The most he can do is intimidate you."

Not wanting to completely brush away his contribution, Elora tried again. "Still, your timing was perfect."

"Timing?" Fifer tilted his head while narrowing one eye. "That is a mortal word, but you mean that I came to your aid right when you needed it?"

She nodded eagerly.

He shrugged again. "That is the way Faerie works. I was coming to find you anyway. Prince Brannick asked about your hideous purple skirt."

She snickered to herself at his complete lack of regard at using the word *hideous*.

The brownie's ears continued to bounce with each step. "The prince said your skirt has been damaged and asked if I could repair it."

Her breath caught in her throat for half a moment. "Can you?"

His nose wrinkled as he glanced up at her. "I cannot make it look any better than it did when you first arrived in Faerie."

A chuckle escaped her. "That's all right. I would love if you could make it look exactly like it did when I first arrived."

He let out a sigh as he pushed open the door to her bedroom. "Then I will see what I can do." He retrieved the skirt from her wardrobe and disappeared through the door once again.

The moment he left, Elora forced herself to take a long, calming breath. When that wasn't enough, she took two more.

Finally, her eyes drifted upward. As she hoped, a small pink sparkle floated among the glowing green lights near her ceiling.

She took in another deep breath. "Tansy, I want to try flying again."

The sprite zoomed down in a flash, hovering right in front of Elora's face. Her green eyebrows raised up high. "Are you sure?"

Instead of answering, Elora pushed the wings out of her back. She curled her hands into fists. Jumping off the ground, she flapped her wings. Urging them to lift her off the ground did nothing. After jumping, she only landed back on the ground again.

Gritting her teeth, Elora jumped again. She willed her wings to flap harder. This time, they did lift her off the ground. But the motion came jerky. She slammed sideways into the stone floor only a moment later.

Tansy clutched her belly, but at least she was trying to hide her laughter.

Desperate, Elora asked, "What am I doing wrong?"

It took another moment before the sprite could smother her laughter completely. Even then, she giggled over a few of her words. "You have to fly like you're flying, not like you are walking or running."

That didn't help much, but Elora's thoughts turned back to when she flew across the lake with Tansy's help. She remembered that feeling, at least a little bit. Was that how flying was supposed to feel?

Preparing to try again, she clenched her fists only to relax them again. When flying across the lake, her wings flapped hard and free without the fear of failure inhibiting them.

That meant no muscle inside her body could tense up. Elora had to be completely relaxed. Completely unafraid. She glanced upward.

It couldn't be about escaping the ground. It had to be about embracing the air.

When she moved her wings this time, she put as much force into them as she could. She gave everything she had until they beat hard. And free.

Her feet lifted off the ground. First only her heels rose, but then the balls of her feet followed. Soon, even her toes dangled above the mossy stone. She didn't get any higher, but she managed to hover for a few moments.

When she started falling, she merely lowered down to the ground until her feet stepped lightly on the surface.

Tansy's eyes filled with light. She grinned. "Finally. Now you can work on strength. The muscles you need to fly are still weak. You will need to train for several days until you can get higher off the ground."

"Okay." Elora tried to hide how winded she was when she answered. "Build up strength. I can do that. I'll continue to train until I can fly as high as my tree without losing my breath."

CHAPTER

23

In a peaceful slumber, claws scratched against wood. Elora jerked herself awake, sitting up with a start. Had it been a dream? But the scratching continued. Her muscles groaned as she forced herself out of bed. They screamed when she pulled her sheath and sword out from under her bed.

The decision to spend an entire afternoon and evening in wing training didn't seem as smart anymore. Even buckling the clasp on her belt took effort, and not because it was invisible.

She wore a thick dress in a rich brown color. It would keep her warm in the halls, but she donned her boots anyway.

When she tore her bedroom door open, Blaz wasn't the only one panting. Her muscles continued to protest her every movement. And after all that practice, she had only managed to fly herself halfway up the height of the room.

She expected it, but it still hurt to see Blaz standing there alone. He grabbed onto her brown dress, pulling her out of the room. His black-furred ears stood up straight.

Fear trickled into her spine. She made no attempt to stop it. "I can't help like last time, Blaz. I'm too tired."

Either the wolf couldn't understand her words, or he refused to believe them. With the hem of her dress still between his teeth, he continued pulling her toward the hallway.

Even with her statement to the wolf, she didn't hesitate to follow after him. Walking sent knives into her sore muscles. Her panting got worse with every turn.

Soon, they arrived in the hallway with the door she assumed led to the throne room. It wouldn't be long now. Brannick's room was just around the corner.

But as she stepped past the two large doors, Blaz let out a yip. He jerked his head toward the large doors and whimpered.

"In here?" she asked.

The urge to suck in a breath came without any real reason. When she pushed open the doors to the throne room, it came even stronger, quickly turning into a gasp.

Huge trees with thick trunks and intertwining branches lined the walkway up to the throne. At one time, they were probably filled with lush green leaves that would flutter at the slightest breeze. Instead, briars had choked any semblance of life out of the trees.

A throne stood at the head of the room. As she had guessed, it merged stone and tree just like the throne in the council room. Except this one was at least four times bigger than the other. Thorns dug into almost every part of the trunk and branches, yet this tree still had a little life left in it. Only a handful of leaves hung onto the branches, but they were as lush and as magical as Faerie itself.

If Blaz hadn't yanked her away, she could have admired the throne room for much longer. She noticed a chandelier similar to the other was hanging from the ceiling. It was even more magnificent than the first. Blaz pulled her away. He led her to an open door off one side of the throne room.

Even before reaching the room, Brannick's voice erupted from it. Or rather, his grunts.

Her heart squeezed just enough that she found the strength to run, despite the aching in her muscles.

He stood in the center of the room, shirtless again. The room was larger than she had expected. Along the edges of it, weapons, trinkets, and other various items sat in tall piles.

Brannick stood with his back to the door. His hands clenched at his sides while every vein in his arms bulged. His light brown skin turned red, shaking from the effort. But then he panted, and his arms shot forward.

His feet stepped across the stone floor with jerky, awkward movements, as if trying to keep himself from moving forward. The effort failed. After reaching one of the piles, he plucked a cylindrical kettle off it. Steam sizzled off his fingers the moment he touched the metal. But of course it didn't end there. He then pressed the kettle against his bare chest, which immediately sparked and sizzled even harder.

"Is that iron?"

Brannick spun on his heel at the sound of her voice. Despite the kettle burning his bare chest and arms, he let out a long sigh of relief at the sight of her. "Yes."

Her chin quivered as she stomped forward. "You have to fight it, Brannick. I tried to tell Blaz, but I can't help like I did last time. I spent the entire day yesterday strengthening my flying muscles. I'm sore and weak."

Light left his eyes as he sucked in a tiny breath. In almost the same moment, he gave a smirk that wasn't convincing in the slightest. "I only have to make it until day dawns."

By then, she had reached him. She gripped the handle of the kettle harder than she had gripped anything. When she tried to yank it from his grip, he held on tighter. Setting her feet in a stronger stance, she glanced at a corner of the room. Her face twisted, but she couldn't see it to know if it gave the expression of interest like she intended.

Luckily, Brannick's gaze immediately turned to the corner where she looked. In that same moment, she yanked the iron kettle out of his grip. He blinked before he realized it was gone.

Hot welts were seared over the prince's chest where the kettle had been moments earlier.

He moved toward the piles again. This time, he reached for a large, circular shield. He lifted it with one hand. Before his other could touch it, she forced her body between him and the shield.

Using both hands, she ripped the shield from his grip before the iron could touch him anywhere else. She succeeded, but it came with a cost.

Though the iron shield only touched one of his hands for a brief moment, her back had leaned right into the prince's chest. Even part of her arm brushed against his. Gasping, she pulled herself away from him. The clatter of the shield as it fell onto a pile of objects was nothing as she stared at Brannick.

His entire being flickered. It wasn't until Blaz came to his side that he finally came back into focus.

They stared at each other. Both gulped at the same moment.

Elora rubbed one temple. "This is going to be difficult, isn't it?"

His face stayed completely still when he answered. "Nothing is easy where Queen Alessandra is concerned."

By the time he finished speaking, he was already reaching for another object. Drawing her sword, Elora batted the iron cup out of his hand. Her sword left a scratch and droplets of blood along one of his fingers."

"Oh no." She pressed a finger to her lips at the sight of the blood.

The prince merely chuckled. "No need to worry, look." He wiped the blood onto his pants. His finger appeared to have already healed. "Fae heal faster than humans. Now that you have a sword that is made without iron, it is far less dangerous to me than any of these objects."

When he reached for an iron knob of some sort, she slapped her sword against his wrist to prevent him from properly gripping the object.

Her arms dropped to her sides immediately, aching more than ever. "Why do you have a room full of iron objects anyway?"

He reached for the kettle again. His grip was tight, but once she slid her sword through the handle, she was able to yank it away.

Using his still-sizzling hand, he gestured toward the items. "We used to confiscate iron from mortals as soon as they entered Bitter Thorn. This room is where we kept everything."

When the prince reached for a dagger, she had to cut a large gash in his palm just to loosen his grip. Each time he touched something new, the welts on his hands turned a brighter red. And each time she cut him, it took a little longer to heal.

Kneading a particularly sore muscle in her arm, she glared at the piles. "How does Queen Alessandra know you have iron lying around your castle?"

Elora was not prepared for how the prince's look stabbed her in the gut.

His eyes dulled to an almost mortal-looking gray. The smile he attempted looked even more forced than his earlier one. "Perhaps she asked someone."

A chill shook across Elora's shoulders. "But you said she does not trust others."

"True." Brannick nodded as he reached for a metal rod.

Her sword clashed against the rod to knock it out of his hands. "So, it's not that. She remembered more, didn't she? She knows everything now."

When the metal finally clattered to the ground. Brannick let out a sigh and stared at his sizzling red palms. "Most likely."

He reached for the shield again. Her muscles groaned as she lifted her sword. If time didn't exist in Faerie, couldn't morning come whenever they needed it to?

Because they needed it soon. Sooner than soon. They needed it now.

Beads of sweat trickled down her forehead while she tried to beat the shield out of the prince's grip. Despite her effort, he still managed to hold it tight against his chest. Blaz jumped up, forcing his body between the shield and the prince. Even with their combined effort, it still took several hard blows to force the shield away.

Tears joined the sweat slipping down her cheeks. "I can't do this. You need someone else. Blaz, go find Soren. Or Vesper. Or anyone. Even Fifer might be able to help."

While her arms shook at her sides, more tears pooled in her eyes. She'd never been the weepy type, but after holding back her emotions for so long, apparently anything could set off tears now.

Before Blaz could leave, Brannick's arms fell. He didn't clench them tight like he had before. The veins in his arms rested inside without added tension.

Elora reached for one of the feathers in her hair. "Is it dawn?"

No words left the prince's lips, but he didn't need any. One look sent needles into her heart. Maybe Queen Alessandra had rescinded the order to touch iron, but another one was clearly coming.

He closed his eyes.

"Don't do it." Elora chewed on her bottom lip. "Whatever she just ordered you to do, don't do it."

When he swallowed, his throat bulged against the beaded necklace around his throat. "I cannot stop myself. I must follow the order." He raised one hand into the air and clicked his tongue three times.

A pit dropped in Elora's stomach. It felt like every bit of blood in her arms drained in that one moment. When a glowing green light flew down to the prince, dread was already turning her body to stone. She had a good guess about where that sprite was about to be sent.

That's when she noticed a pink sparkle inside the glowing green light.

"No." Her voice came out breathless. "Not you, Tansy. Can't one of the other sprites…"

But Tansy dropped onto the prince's palm anyway. She twirled her sparkly pink dress, awaiting the message.

Brannick's face continued to stay still as he reached into his pocket. He pulled a single flower bud from inside it. The purple petals closed over the center, but Elora could still see that it was the same as the purple wildflowers Brannick had conjured for her on several occasions.

His voice came out heavy, gravelly. "I have a message for Queen Alessandra of Fairfrost Court."

The twirling of Tansy's dress stopped at once. Her arms fell to her sides. Maybe it was Elora's imagination, but the little sprite seemed to physically shrink at the sound of those words. Even her arms looked frailer than before.

Brannick swallowed. "This is the message from me, Prince Brannick of Bitter Thorn." He probably tried to hide it, but his shoulders gave the smallest shudder. "You control me with your every order."

Armed with her shorter stature and frailer limbs, Tansy floated toward the ceiling. She moved slower than usual.

"Don't go." Elora pressed her palms together and held them tight against her lips. "Once you enter Fairfrost, Queen Alessandra will capture you and never let you go. Don't deliver the message."

"She must go." Brannick's arms hung at his side. "A sprite always delivers its message, no matter the cost."

Though Tansy flew slower than normal, she did not stop. She continued on, even knowing it would be her doom. Her tiny sparkle of pink disappeared through the doorway, snuffing out the last dregs of hope in the room.

Elora dropped to her knees, hugging her arms against her stomach. "Why?" Her chin trembled. "Why did she have to go?"

Dropping to his own knees, Brannick stared at her. His eyes followed the movement when tears dripped off her chin and onto the stone floor. When she re-adjusted and settled her legs into a crisscross position, he did the same.

A hard sob shook through her, causing her to wrap her arms around her stomach yet again.

It was only a subtle movement, but she saw how his hand flicked toward her. Had he been ready to reach out to her? Did he intend to touch her before he remembered he couldn't? After a beat of silence, he glanced at his wolf.

Blaz dipped his head at the prince and then padded up to Elora's side. He nuzzled his snout under one of her arms. When she rested her cheek on top of his head, he set a paw on her lap. She smiled and stroked the fur on his back.

The comfort caused her to cry harder. Blaz turned himself so he still snuggled at her side, but he could look forward at the prince as well.

Her hand continued to stroke his black fur. "Can't the queen just order you to reveal the weapon you're going to use in the tournament?"

Brannick stared at Elora's stroking hand for a moment before he met her gaze. "No. I had Kaia enchant me so that I am unable to speak about my plans for the tournament to anyone except you, Kaia, or Soren."

Elora sniffed. "An enchantment is stronger than a bargain?"

"Hopefully." Brannick shrugged. "Only Faerie can decide. If she asks, hopefully I will be able to say that an enchantment prevents me from answering the question directly."

Nodding, Elora rested one hand on the stone floor while her other hand continued to stroke Blaz's fur.

As if entranced, Brannick stared at her hand. Was he trying to memorize it?

He moved himself forward and then he reached. His hand slid across the stone floor, slowing as it neared hers. But it didn't stop.

He continued moving until his fingers were only a breath away from hers, not quite touching but still close enough to feel. While holding the position, he glanced into her eyes.

Her chest filled with a skittering she had never felt before. It warmed her. Filled her. Taking a deep breath, she kept her gaze steadily on him. "There has to be a way we can end the bargain you have with Queen Alessandra."

"Maybe." His fingers twitched, moving another hair's breadth closer to hers.

She leaned forward. "If there is a way, I'm going to find it."

CHAPTER

24

The castle walls blended together as Elora roamed them. She ducked into every room she could find, reaching for her sword hilt every few seconds. Some of the doors had enchantments, making it impossible to enter them. Those she left, but the others she entered and glanced around.

Finally, she entered a room and found exactly who she sought. "Vesper."

He stood over a desk, rubbing his thumb across his chin. At the sound of her voice, he turned. "Were you looking for me?"

"Yes." Her eyes darted around the rest of the room, confirming that it stood empty except for him. The bed in the corner indicated this was his bedroom, but she didn't look around long enough to notice anything else. Shutting the door behind her, she stepped toward him. "You have traveled to every court in Faerie, right?"

He glanced down at a paper on his desk before nodding.

She took in a deep breath. It couldn't hurt to stand a little taller. "I need you to open a door to Fairfrost for me."

After the shock wore off, he pinched his eyebrows together. "That is not a good idea."

Her spine straightened another degree. When the urge to grab her sword hilt came, she ignored it. "The door needs to take me just outside Fairfrost Palace."

He let out a scoff. "Fairfrost is the most dangerous court in Faerie. Are you going to offer me something in return for opening a door there?"

"No."

His head tilted to the side. "Then why would I help you?"

The straightness in her spine relaxed as she clasped her hands behind her back. She blinked twice before answering. "I'm your sister."

With both eyebrows lowering, his mouth pinched in a knot. "You ask for a favor so soon?" He shook his head. "It is too dangerous. I will not do it."

She let out a wistful sigh, eyeing the door behind her. "Fine, then I'll ask someone else. I might have to enter a deadly bargain, but if that is what must be, then so be it."

Vesper glared back at her. "You are infecting me with your mortal guilt again."

"Is it working?" A smile played on her lips as she leaned forward.

He continued to glare, but a gleam appeared in his eyes. With a wave of one hand, he opened a door. She recognized his fog-and-mist-filled door from when he opened a door to Dustdune long ago. Knowing that he had been banished from his court of Noble Rose, she could understand why the roses popping out from the edges of the tunnel were blurry. And now the other swirling colors made sense too. Green, orange, blue, and gray. Colors from the other courts in Faerie but not from his own. Just like before, his door smelled like adventure.

As she stepped forward, he eyed her carefully. "I am coming with you." When she opened her mouth to protest, he held up a hand to stop it. "Do not argue with me. Who else will open a door to help you return to Bitter Thorn?"

She immediately nodded, grateful that she wouldn't have to face Fairfrost alone. But she would have to be even more careful than ever to not reach for her sword hilt.

Freezing wind blasted into her face the moment she stepped through the door. A magical snowy landscape probably stretched out around her, but the icy wind made her eager to step inside the palace as soon as possible.

Once inside, warmth spread everywhere, but it didn't quite reach into her bones. A servant wearing a worn coat stopped her at once. Elora stood as tall as she could. "Take me to Queen Alessandra. I need to speak with her."

The servant nodded at the words and beckoned her and Vesper forward. Meanwhile, Vesper's eyebrows rose almost into his hairline. Elora did her best to ignore him.

They went down a long hallway adorned with a thick rug of red and gold. Paintings hung on the white marble walls of the castle. Wide golden frames outlined beautiful landscapes of sparkly ice trees.

At the end of the hallway, the servant stopped them. "I will tell the queen of your presence."

The moment he disappeared, Vesper tapped his toe and threw Elora a warning look. "This is a bad idea."

While they waited, several servants weaved in and out of the hallways and through doors. They moved so silently their presence would have been impossible to detect without seeing them.

At one point, a nearby door swung open, and glowing green light poured out of it. Her body jerked toward it at once.

The sprites.

An unassuming servant toddled out of the room, scurrying down the hallway immediately. Elora's breath caught in her throat. She could free the sprites. Right now. If she moved quickly, she could do it and still have time to speak to Queen Alessandra.

"The queen will see you now."

Elora's heart dropped at the sound of the servant's voice. She turned and noticed the same servant from before, beckoning her inside a nearby room. Her heart wouldn't settle though. It continued to long for a daring rescue.

Later.

She made that promise to herself. If she attempted to rescue the sprites now, she'd never be allowed an audience with Queen Alessandra. But at least she knew where to find the sprites now. She would still save them. It would just have to happen later.

Vesper gave her one last warning look before she stepped into the small room. The servant stopped Vesper, stating that only one person at a time could stand in the queen's presence. Elora assured him she would be back soon. With one last thought on her sword, she entered.

Queen Alessandra sat atop a plush velvet chair. She held a goblet full of thick red liquid in one hand. With the other, she strummed her fingers on the arm of the chair.

"Interesting." Her white crown gave off glints of every color while she spoke. "I thought it would be Prince Brannick who came to beg me to break his bargain." She shrugged. "But I suppose your presence is not wholly unexpected."

It took a moment for Elora to catch her breath. "You know about…"

Queen Alessandra let out a sharp laugh. "Yes, I know about the bargain. It took great skill from a fae who magicks in blood, but I finally have my memory restored. In fact," she leaned forward, narrowing her eyes at Elora, "never mind." She waved her previously strumming fingers. "You look similar to a servant I once had."

No response seemed appropriate for that, so Elora decided to get straight to it. "Revoke the bargain."

The queen took a long swig from her goblet before answering. "It is not that simple. It is a strong bargain. It will require something strong to break it."

Elora's fingers itched to grab her sword at her side. She curled her hand into a fist instead. "King Huron made a bargain with the sprites. It ended upon his death. Why don't I just kill you to end the bargain?"

Queen Alessandra leaned back in her chair, relaxing even more than before. "I am afraid you will be disappointed if you try that."

"I doubt it."

An eyebrow quirked upward on the queen's forehead. "I proposed the part of the bargain that requires Prince Brannick to follow my every order."

Folding her arms over her chest, Elora nodded. "I know."

The goblet moved to the queen's lips again while she took an even longer drink. A frightening grin passed over her lips when she spoke again. "But Prince Brannick proposed the part of the bargain that prevents him from touching anyone he loves." The grin twisted into a smirk. "I assume that part of the bargain is the part you are most eager to end."

Elora's jaw flexed against her will. "Why does it matter who proposed the different parts of the bargain?"

Queen Alessandra sat forward. "Since Prince Brannick willingly proposed that part of the bargain himself, it will continue even after my death."

Stillness filled the room, but it suddenly felt colder. Elora's throat thickened. "I don't believe you."

A cutting laugh burst from the queen's lips. "Kill me then. Once I am dead, there will be no way to break that part of the bargain. Do you dare try it? Could you bear the regret?"

The necklace around Elora's neck buzzed with energy. Someone, probably the queen, was attempting to enchant her. But Brannick's ward necklace kept her safe. Her fist curled again. "What will it take to break the bargain?"

The queen raised an eyebrow. "You think I will simply tell you?" She took a sip from her goblet. "I have all the power now. I can order Prince Brannick to purposefully lose the tournament. Why would I give that up?"

"There must be something you want." Elora raised both her eyebrows as she stepped forward. "Your heart's greatest desire, perhaps. You already have a good chance of winning the tournament anyway. I've heard how strong your magic is. But maybe there's something else that's just out of reach."

Squishing her mouth to one side, the queen began strumming her fingers on the arm of her chair again. "I admit. I am intrigued by that suggestion."

"Tell me what you want, and I'll get it for you. I'll do any task."

Sharp delight filled the queen's eyes. "This is your bargain? You will do anything for me?"

"No." Elora placed a hand on her hip. "Tell me what you want, and I will decide if that price is worth breaking the bargain you have with Prince Brannick."

Queen Alessandra nodded, but she stared across the room with unfocused eyes. "There *is* something I desire." Now her gaze sharpened. "The item is inside the throne room of Bitter Thorn Castle, but I am certain you do not even know how to find that room."

Elora narrowed her eyes. "I know where the throne room is."

The queen glanced toward the ceiling as she leaned back in her chair. "Your word means nothing to me, mortal. Tell me what hangs from the ceiling in the throne room, and I might believe you."

"A chandelier. It gives off its own light."

After sitting up fast, the queen nearly lost her grip on the goblet. "Interesting. And advantageous to me." She took a sip of the thick liquid. "The item I want is a stone. It is small enough to fit in the palm of the hand, and it gives off a magical energy."

Nodding, Elora asked, "What color is it?"

"I do not know. But it once sat at the front of the crown High Queen Winola used to wear. The stone is still in the throne room somewhere, I am certain of it."

"I can find it."

The frightening grin on the queen's face returned. "Then I propose a bargain. Bring me the stone from the Bitter Thorn throne room. If you do, I will reveal how to break the bargain Prince Brannick has with me."

"*Reveal* how to break the bargain?" Elora raised an eyebrow. "You must *break* the bargain, not just reveal how to break it."

Queen Alessandra glanced at her fingernails. "I cannot break the bargain myself. As I already explained, Prince Brannick willingly added to the bargain. Breaking it will require something from *him*."

It seemed incredibly convenient that Queen Alessandra couldn't break the bargain herself, but fae couldn't lie. Unfortunately, the meant she spoke the truth.

Letting out a huff, Elora nodded. "Fine." Her head tilted to one side while she considered the queen's other words. Now she glanced toward the queen again. "When will you reveal how to break the bargain? As soon as I give you the stone?"

Swirling around the liquid in her goblet, Queen Alessandra shook her head. "Pesky mortals with your sense of time."

But Elora knew she had found a loophole in the bargain or the queen wouldn't have been so upset. "Say you'll reveal how to break the bargain as soon as I give you the stone."

"And what if I have not learned how to do it by then?"

Elora managed a casual shrug. "Then I will keep the stone for myself."

A very un-queenlike huff escaped Queen Alessandra's nostrils. "I will reveal how to break the bargain on the day of the tournament. I will not do it sooner. If you insist, then we have no bargain."

It didn't seem likely that the queen would give up her most powerful bargaining chip in the tournament. Brannick would have to find some other way around that. But this was about breaking his bargain with Queen Alessandra. Even if it happened after the tournament, that was better than nothing.

Glancing back at the queen, Elora tapped a hand against her leg. "You must reveal how to break the bargain before night falls on the day of the tournament." Her head tilted again. "On the day of the testing tournament. High King Romany's testing."

The queen winced at those words. "Very well. You are surprisingly good at finding loopholes." She let out a sigh. "I propose a bargain. If you bring me the stone from the Bitter Thorn throne room, I will reveal how to break my bargain with Prince Brannick before night falls on the third phase of High King Romany's testing."

Elora considered every word of the bargain at least three times before she finally took a deep breath. "I accept."

With two words, she bound herself to another fae. Yet again. But this time she didn't do it for a pair of wings she didn't even think were real. This time, she did it to save her beloved.

Though being bound by a bargain twisted her insides, she could only feel gratitude. No matter what happened with the testing, at least Brannick would be free of the Fairfrost queen. Elora just had to find that stone.

CHAPTER 25

The moment Elora stepped back onto the stone floor of Bitter Thorn Castle, the lecturing began. Vesper shook his head so many times, she almost feared his curls would tumble right off his head.

"You made a bargain with Queen Alessandra? That is one of the worst things you could have done. Only dying would be worse—*slightly*."

He had taken them back to the hallway with his room. It took Elora a few moments to re-orient herself. She hadn't explored that part of the castle as often.

Vesper dug both hands through his hair while he followed after her. "I never should have taken you to Fairfrost. She probably asked for something that would sabotage Prince Brannick's chance in the tournament."

"All she wants is a stone." One more hallway, and they'd get to the throne room.

Smacking his forehead, Vesper huffed. "I do not care if she wants a speck of dirt. If she asked for it, something about it will make her more powerful."

As much as Elora missed her parents, the lecturing was one thing she'd never miss. She pushed open the doors to the throne room, desperate for a way to distract her companion. An idea struck her almost at once.

"Tell me about your wife." She even clasped both hands in front her chest to give off a great sense of eagerness.

His eyes went misty as a soft smile overtook him. He leaned into the closed doors of the throne room. "My Cosette. She is lovely. Her cheeks are pink in the cold and golden in the sun. Her hair is the color of ripened apples. Some of our children got her hair color, but not all of them. I do not know if it continued through the generations, since you do not have it."

Elora had already reached the throne at the back of the room. She dug through the thorns around it, attempting to find any glimpse of a stone. "You have children? Not just one child?"

Even Vesper's voice sounded like a grin. "We had four children before High King Romany found me out. My youngest was just a baby, still waking in the night."

Though he started wistful and happy, his final words came out strained. His mouth had fallen into a frown.

Shaking her head, Elora turned back to look at the base of the throne. "My youngest sister has red hair."

"Then the hair color *did* continue through the generations. How wonderful." Only some of the earlier happiness returned. "Cosette would be delighted to find out."

Just as Elora reached to pull away another handful of briars, her fingers grabbed onto something that didn't feel like briars at all. It felt like a crown.

Sucking in a breath, she pulled the item closer to herself. As she moved it away from the throne, a glamour fell away. Now a crown made of obsidian and branches sat on her hands. At the front, a large circle sat where it was clear a stone had once laid.

Vesper moved across the throne room with impossible speed. His face drained of color as he stared at the crown. "Whatever Queen Alessandra asked for, you cannot give it to her. If she has any part of the Bitter Thorn crown, she will be unstoppable."

Of course, the piece Alessandra wanted wasn't even attached to the crown. The empty spot for the stone pulsed all the same. Elora held her breath as she stared.

The crystal in her pocket. The one that held Brannick's essence.

She couldn't explain it, but she knew her green crystal had once belonged in the empty spot on the crown. She could *feel* it.

Without a word, she tucked the crown back against the bottom edge of the throne. The glamour returned, blending it in with its surroundings. Even still, she used her boots to push the briars and thorns back to where they had been covering the crown.

Her heart thundered in her chest. She couldn't give the crystal to Queen Alessandra. She wouldn't even consider it. But perhaps the bargain didn't have to be lost. She glanced to her side. "The words to a bargain are everything, right?"

Vesper looked ready to scold her again. "Yes."

Elora tapped her chin as she walked down the length of the room. She had to remember the exact words to the bargain, without any room at all for error. Queen Alessandra had asked for *the stone from the Bitter Thorn throne room*. She never specified that it had to be the stone that had once been inside High Queen Winola's crown. Just that it had to be the stone from the Bitter Thorn throne room.

A grin danced over Elora's lips. She hadn't even found the crystal with Brannick's essence inside the throne room. It wouldn't satisfy the bargain anyway. Her eyes danced over the ground. Now she just had to find something that would.

"I need you to help me find a stone."

Vesper folded his arms over his chest. "What stone?"

She waved a hand at him while moving toward the edge of the room. "It doesn't matter. Any stone. It just needs to fit in the palm of the hand."

Queen Alessandra also said the stone gave off energy, but hopefully Faerie was magical enough that any stone would give off some kind of energy.

Finding a wicker table, Elora pulled away the thorns to check under and over it for a stone of some sort. Vesper huffed and shot her glares, but he still helped her look.

They found a few loose stones, but most of them were gray and utterly unmagical. They kept one in case they didn't find anything else.

But then Vesper spied a pretty turquoise stone that had been smoothed and polished. She dropped it into her palm at once. The size was a little bigger than the crystal in her pocket. If she tried to place it in the empty spot on the crown, it most likely wouldn't fit. But Queen Alessandra said she didn't know what it looked like. Surely, she'd never know.

And the turquoise stone did buzz with energy. That could have been good or bad, but since the options were limited, it would have to do.

Elora carefully placed it into the pocket holding Lyren's shell and bag of salt. Once she secured the turquoise, she placed a heavy hand on Vesper's shoulder. A sigh left her lips before she spoke. "You should know, your wife is dead."

His face lost its color as he stepped back.

Looking down at the ground, Elora continued. "I come from many generations after Cosette, remember? If I am here, that means she is gone."

He let out a sigh of relief as he touched a hand to his chest. "She is not gone. She is both alive *and* dead."

Elora attempted the kindest, but firmest tone she could. "That's not possible."

"It is possible." His blue and gray eyes turned bright. "There are many, many places in the mortal realm where my Cosette is dead. But there are also places where she is alive."

After blinking three times the words finally settled in. "I forgot, fae can travel to any place in the mortal realm, but you can travel to any *time* as well."

"Yes." He swallowed as his gaze turned downward. "Even after High King Romany's death, my banishment from Noble Rose will continue. I will still be cursed to not be able to open or step through any door that leads to the mortal realm. But another High Ruler of Faerie can revoke my banishment and lift my curse."

Her mouth hung open for a moment before she could speak again. "That's why you want Prince Brannick to become High King. So that you can be with your beloved again."

His mouth turned up in a tender smile. "Yes. I have been waiting and waiting to get back to her, but hopefully she will not have to wait for me at all. I just have to return to the right place."

The touching story should have held Elora's attention more, but she was suddenly overcome with an entirely new thought. A new idea that could change everything.

Vesper couldn't help because he couldn't get to the mortal realm. Brannick might refuse for a number of ridiculous reasons. But Lyren owed Elora a debt.

And she finally knew what to ask for.

CHAPTER

26

On the return to Fairfrost, Elora's mind was too occupied to be frightened. Her thoughts spun while she tried to remember how to walk properly. Vesper kept shooting her glares, which she ignored.

The Fairfrost servant led them down the halls of the palace, but Vesper simply lowered his voice to a whisper. "What did you ask Lyren to do for you?"

"Nothing."

He raised an eyebrow at her. "Just because you have the ability to lie does not mean you should use it."

Elora's boots stumbled over the ground. She tried to hold her breath, but that didn't help at all. She couldn't say it. Saying it would make it real. It was better to wait until Lyren returned.

Waving a hand, Elora shook her head. "It's just a little thing."

It was nothing more than asking Lyren to pull her parents' living bodies from a burning cottage before they were engulfed by flames. And if the fae happened to glamour some charred logs to look like her dead parents, that would be even better.

Lyren just had to travel to the right place in the mortal realm. *And* the right time.

Warmth blossomed in Elora's chest as she continued down the halls of Fairfrost Palace. She had spent all that effort keeping herself from mourning her parents' deaths. But maybe there was a reason for it. Maybe they had never really died at all.

Soon, Lyren would bring them to Faerie, completely unscathed.

Vesper's eyes narrowed to tiny slits. "I do not like you when you are being mysterious."

Elora shrugged. "Brothers and sisters cannot possibly like each other all the time. This is normal."

Though his face contorted with a glare, he didn't quite hide the amusement in his eyes. This time, they didn't wait at all for the queen. Elora was ushered inside while Vesper had to wait in the hallway once again.

At once, sweat pooled in her palms. Her mind had been too focused on her parents to consider what she was about to do, but it hit her with full force now. What if the stone in her pocket didn't work? What if the bargain recognized the turquoise wasn't the stone Queen Alessandra wanted?

Going by the words of the bargain alone, the turquoise should work. But Elora knew all too well that Faerie made it impossible to go against a bargain. What if the bargain forced her to give the crystal instead?

"Back already?" Queen Alessandra had traded her goblet for an opal-encrusted axe with a rounded edge. She used a sharpening stick and slid it across the edge. It gave off a zing every time her sharpening stick moved over the blade.

"I found the stone." Elora held her hands in tight fists so the queen wouldn't notice them shaking.

A smile as bright as the sun spread across Queen Alessandra's cheeks. She held her hand out expectantly.

Taking in a short breath, Elora reached into her pocket. Her mind raced with a thousand thoughts in the span of a single moment. Had she reached into the right pocket? She couldn't give Alessandra the green crystal. She couldn't.

But even as her heart thundered against her chest, she rubbed a thumb over the stone in her hand. Smooth. Polished. She had grabbed the turquoise as intended.

Maybe it would look strange to hold her breath, but she couldn't help it. Her fingers gripped the turquoise tight to hide the trembling in her hands. When she dropped the turquoise stone into the queen's palm, Elora tensed every muscle inside her body.

"Excellent." Queen Alessandra brought the stone right up to her nose, examining it carefully. She didn't even seem to notice the heavy breaths huffing out of Elora's nose.

With her eyes still on the turquoise stone, the queen set the axe with the rounded edge onto her lap. Then, she reached into a pocket inside her heavy white dress. When her hand emerged from her pocket, she held a long marble box big enough to hold a bow and several arrows.

The queen's gaze turned toward the box as she lifted the lid.

Before Elora could let out any breath of relief, a long piece of metal inside the box stole her breath away entirely. A glinting blade, a strong cross guard, a leather-wrapped hilt. She knew the weapon as well as she knew the harp.

That was *her* sword. The one from her father that she had lost when Queen Alessandra stole the piece away from Bitter Thorn Castle. It hadn't been destroyed after all.

"You like this?"

The queen must have noticed her staring. Using her delicate hands, Queen Alessandra lifted the sword by touching the leather on the hilt. On the very top of the pommel was the shield and chevron symbol with the star inside that her father left on his personal weapons. The symbol further confirmed the identity of the sword.

Queen Alessandra ran a finger along the leather hilt. "I managed to acquire this during my last visit to Bitter Thorn. Ansel, another fae, was most jealous when he saw it." Now she hovered her finger over the mark on the pommel. "I had to take it, at least for a little while. For revenge."

The queen had gone on long enough to allow Elora to catch her breath again. She even managed to relax the tightened fists at her sides. Now she looked up with an expression that hopefully looked curious but not too curious. "Revenge? Did someone injure you with that sword?"

Of course she knew the answer was no. The only creature who got injured from that sword was a troll, and even it had gotten away with only a small puncture under his arm.

Setting the sword back into the marble box, Queen Alessandra sat up straighter. "No, I was not injured, but this sword belonged to Theobald, a great mortal swordsman. He killed one of my trolls."

The words rocked around in Elora's mind. Killed? She had merely injured the troll. It hardly suffered at all from her strikes.

Queen Alessandra ran a finger over the opal embedded in her axe. "I already took Theobald's life, but I thought it fitting that I should take his sword as well. I have no idea how it ended up in Bitter Thorn."

Acid crawled up Elora's throat, keeping her from speaking at once. When the words finally came, she almost had to cough them out. "You killed him?"

Nodding, the queen began pushing back her cuticles. "Yes, him and his wife. I would have frozen them to death, but the season was not right. I had to settle for a fire instead or the mortals would have been suspicious."

Burning heat filled every part of Elora's skin. Her fingernails dug so deep in her palms, little half moons would linger there for a while. When she let out a huff, the queen lifted her eyes toward her.

"My, you are very upset. He is only a mortal."

Elora's jaw clenched tight. "I am a mortal too."

Queen Alessandra shrugged off the words.

Forcing herself to take a deep breath, Elora asked the greatest question plaguing her mind. "Did you *see* Theobald kill your troll? Are you certain the injury was great enough to kill the creature?"

The queen clasped her hands together and leaned forward. "The troll had a dagger stabbed deep in the only place where trolls are weak. The dagger had Theobald's mark on the end of it, the same exact mark as this sword."

"A dagger?" Maybe it wasn't the troll Elora had fought at the castle then. Maybe Queen Alessandra was talking about an entirely different troll altogether. Her father had been in Faerie before. He must have killed a troll during that visit.

With a nod, the queen lounged back in her chair. "I am certain that Theobald killed my troll, which is why I killed him." She gestured toward the marble box. "Do you wish to admire his sword?"

Elora spoke through her teeth. "I would rather use it."

"And kill me?" The queen let out a tittering laugh. "What about breaking Prince Brannick's bargain with me? He will still be bound by the bargain if you kill me now."

If there hadn't been two guards flanking the queen, Elora might have tried to steal the sword right then. Even still, her hands twitched at her sides. But Queen Alessandra snapped the lid closed and stuffed it into her magical pocket before Elora got the chance.

With fists curled tight, she took a step closer to the queen. "You will wish you had never done such a thing."

The queen snickered as she lifted her axe and sharpening stick once again. "You are this upset over the deaths of two mortals? Many more than that have died at my hands."

After a hard swallow, Elora marched out of the room and demanded Vesper open a door to Bitter Thorn Castle immediately.

When Vesper tried to speak, she only glared at him. The moment her feet touched the mossy stone, Elora sprinted toward Lyren's room.

Her fingers pulsed. Her muscles twitched. Her whole body was on fire. It didn't matter if her parents were really dead or not. Queen Alessandra had at least attempted to kill them. Elora and her sisters had endured too much because of it.

She wanted revenge.

Her fist slammed against Lyren's door, hitting too hard to truly sound like a knock. Vesper arrived right as Lyren opened the door.

There were no silver bursts in her eyes. Her black curls hung loose.

"Where are they?" Elora swallowed as soon as the question left her lips.

Lyren reached for the sea flower in her hair. It wasn't there. "I…" She shook her head, turning her eyes to the ground.

Elora took a step closer. "You did it, right? You owed me a debt."

"I still owe you." Lyren choked over the words.

Vesper looked from Lyren to Elora and back again. "What is it? What did you do?"

They both ignored him. Elora's chin quivered while she tried to swallow. "But you promised."

"I tried." Lyren shook her head, pinching one of her curls. "I found the right place, but there was magic there. Your cottage had a protective enchantment surrounding it. I could not get past it. If the fire had been natural, it would have been easy. I tried everything. No fae, not even Prince Brannick, would have succeeded. The fire came too fast."

Elora reached an arm over her stomach, feeling the need to release its contents. Not again. How was she losing them *again?*

Why had she allowed herself even the smallest moment of hope?

Her fist slammed against the door frame. It only made her sicker.

But Lyren had to be wrong. Maybe she wasn't strong enough to get past the enchantment, but surely Prince Brannick would be. If she begged him to save her parents, he couldn't possibly refuse.

CHAPTER 27

Despite instructing her feet to do otherwise, Elora ended up in her bedroom. She curled onto her bed, pulling her knees up to her chest. Tears burned against her cheeks. It wasn't over yet. She'd still go to Brannick. She just had to rest first.

When morning came, she continued to huddle under her blanket unable to move. She would. Eventually. But the blanket was so warm.

And what if Brannick refused to help? She couldn't take it. She couldn't accept her parents' death a third time. It was better to stay in bed and believe they still might be saved.

Glowing green lights danced near the ceiling, but the sight of them only sent a yank through Elora's insides. No pink sparkle twirled among glowing lights. Tansy was in Fairfrost now. Captured.

Elora pulled the blanket up her chin. She had been to Fairfrost Palace twice. She even knew where to find the captured sprites. But she hadn't saved them.

Deep inside, she knew it wouldn't be so simple to save the sprites. Surely there were guards keeping the sprites imprisoned. Surely there were enchantments or magic keeping others out. Even if she *had* tried to free them, she probably would have been captured herself. But logic had no place in her mind now.

Once guilt wriggled in, she could only feed it, not remove it.

Now she buried her face under the blanket entirely. It wasn't as productive, but it certainly felt better to hide in her room where nothing bad could happen to her.

As soon as she had that thought, the door to her room swung open. She sucked in a gasp as she jolted upward. An even breath came out when a rabbit-sized creature entered.

"You look terrible." Fifer held a folded length of fabric in his arms. Purple fabric.

She wrapped the blanket tighter around her shoulders. "Is that my skirt?"

He wrinkled his nose at it as he moved across the floor. "It was badly damaged. I could not make it look exactly as it did before."

As he moved closer, she could see what he meant. The rich purple dye had faded to a light lavender. Fifer had done something to make the lavender a magnificent, layered color. But it still wasn't right.

"Would you like to wear it?" He held it out to her.

Her fingers merely brushed across the surface of the fabric before they burned. Just like when she tried to touch the ribbon from Chloe. Elora jerked her hand back and tucked her still-tingling fingers under the blanket with the rest of herself. "Maybe tomorrow."

By tomorrow, her parents would be in Faerie, safe from the fire.

Fifer tugged at her blanket until he could drop a tray of food onto her lap. A clear broth with herbs and another corn muffin sat on the smooth wooden tray.

Her mouth tasted like sand when she stared at it. "I'm not hungry."

Instead of arguing with her, Fifer used his spindly fingers to force part of the corn muffin into her mouth. Fighting him off would take too much effort. She allowed him to continue until half the soup and the entire corn muffin were gone.

But now the brownie stared at her with his big eyes. Even without showing emotion, she could still feel his concern. Getting away moved higher on her priority list than moping in bed.

She gestured toward a corner of the room. "I dropped one of my soaps last night. I think it fell over there and maybe made a mess."

While Fifer turned his head, she snuck a hand under her mattress to retrieve her glamoured sword and sheath. By the time he turned back again, she had already buckled them around her waist.

His eyes narrowed. "I will see if I can find it."

He probably didn't believe her story, but it didn't matter. She just waved and ducked into the hallway outside her room.

She ran straight into Soren. The gnome grumbled as he bent to pluck his pointed hat from off the ground. After putting it back on his head, he brushed his white pointed beard.

How had she spent so many days roaming the halls of the castle, but the moment she wanted to be alone, suddenly every creature in the castle was there?

Soren gestured toward the hallway, blinking his all-black eyes.

She threw him a look before starting down the hallway. "I haven't seen you in a while."

The gnome's beard shook as he twisted his mouth up. "We are preparing for battle."

Her feet stopped mid-step as she looked at him.

He cleared his throat and continued onward. "In case Prince Brannick does not win the testing. Battle may soon come to Bitter Thorn."

His voice was a gruff as ever, but the grumbling and complaints that usually accompanied his words were absent. Nothing but seriousness drifted off him now. He flicked his eyes toward her. "The prince asked me to escort you to the armory, but I have much to do. Can you get there by yourself?"

A nod came without hesitation. Finally, she'd have the peace she sought. If Fifer hadn't been in her room still, she probably would have crawled back into bed.

But if Brannick was waiting for her in the armory, then no time would be better than this to convince him to save her parents. She'd find a way to convince him. She had to.

An ache stung in her throat as she turned a corner. It might have evolved into a burn, but an unexpected sight stole her attention away from it.

Ansel stood before her, twisting a yellow gem attached to his coat's lapel. The same blond-haired fae with the crooked teeth that had accompanied him before stood at his side.

Elora pinned them both with a glare. But mostly Ansel. "I know you cannot injure me inside the castle walls."

When she moved to stomp past him, Ansel innocently blinked his bright yellow eyes. "Why would I want to injure you?"

She shuddered at the sound of his voice. His scheming was palpable. She could feel it. Taste it.

As she moved past them, the blond fae grabbed her by the wrist. She immediately attempted to jerk her hand away, but he held on fast.

"Let go of me." She gritted her teeth through the words.

When the blond fae continued to hold on tight, she slammed her heel onto the top of his foot. The shock of the pain gave her just enough time to yank her hand away. Without thinking, she sprinted down the hallway, closer to the armory.

But fae could move faster than mortals. Both Ansel and the blond fae caught up to her when she turned a corner.

Her wings.

She still wasn't great with flying, but she had greatly improved. Maybe it would be enough to help her get away.

Before she could release the wings, the blond fae grabbed her wrist again. He immediately yanked it to one side, causing her entire body to slam into the castle wall.

Pain stabbed into her shoulder and hip as they met the mossy stone. Her fists curled. "Stop it. Get away from me." She raised her voice as she spoke, hoping someone might hear.

Ansel glanced over her before turning to the blond fae. "Harder."

She sucked in a breath. "But you can't injure me."

The corner of Ansel's mouth tipped upward, his eyes flashing a brighter yellow. "I did not even touch you. The castle wall is what injured you."

With a nod, the blond fae yanked her arm again. This time, her forehead hit the stone hard enough to draw blood. She could feel it trickle down her forehead.

"Perfect." Ansel swooped in close, using one finger to wipe the blood off her forehead.

She pushed him away and stepped to the side. But it wasn't fast enough to stop him from wiping away some of the blood.

Ansel stared at the red drip on his finger. Smiled at it. His eyes closed as he brought her trickle of blood to his nose. He sniffed long and hard, as if no other activity could bring him greater pleasure.

If she hadn't been hit with the urge to vomit, she would have sprinted away. Right then, the blond fae stepped to her side, blocking the path anyway.

With his eyes still closed, Ansel touched the tip of his tongue to his finger, licking the blood there as slowly as possible. "Fae blood," he crooned.

He sniffed it again, somehow looking even sicker than he had the first time. "But there is something else I recognize." One last sniff and his eyes widened. And then they widened even more.

"Theobald's daughter." Ansel moved in closer, blocking her off from her escape even more. "Now I know exactly where to look to find your sister."

Her stomach flipped. It folded in on itself. Her heart refused to beat.

His grin turned sickly. "Still, I must have *you* for my collection too."

She reached for her sword. It didn't matter what the consequences might be. She looked Ansel in the eye while gripping her sword tight. "Get away from me." It came out even louder than the last time she spoke.

To her great surprise, he did. He stepped back and even gestured that the blond fae should make room for her too. Perhaps it was the enchantment Fifer said protected her, but truthfully, she didn't care. She just wanted to leave as quickly as her legs could carry her.

The moment she began moving, footsteps sounded behind her. One hand still gripped her sword tight as she glanced over one shoulder. The blond fae charged toward her. His fae speed closed in too fast. In a blink, he'd be there.

But he wasn't just running toward her. He carried a weapon too. A long sword with a black blade was raised high above his head.

She only registered that she had pulled her own sword from its sheath when she swung it upward to meet the fae's blade.

It was visible now. No part of her sword touched her sheath, which meant both Ansel and the blond fae could see it.

When her weapon met the fae's black blade, no clash filled the hallway. His sword only rippled away into nothing.

A glamour. The black sword hadn't been there at all.

But of course, her sword *was* real. Its sharp edge sliced through the blond fae's chest, releasing a splattering of blood along with it. The blood poured onto her arms as the fae nearly landed on top of her. Then he sank to the ground.

Blood pooled around the blond fae while one last breath left his body.

Her entire body froze at the sight. She couldn't even breathe.

She'd killed him.

Chuckling, Ansel stepped toward her. "You have Theobald's blood, but it appears you have his sword skill too. How interesting."

From the corner of her eye, she could see how he tilted his head to the side.

"You demonstrated your skills with the harp, but you hid your skills with the sword." He leaned in closer to her while his yellow eyes pulsed. "Now who might benefit from a secret like that?"

He stroked her cheek with cold fingers. It might have caused a reaction, but she was still staring at the dead fae whose blood soaked her clothes and hair.

"You must come with me." He whispered the words.

The ward necklace from Brannick tingled as he spoke. She shuddered.

He opened his mouth again. But instead of speaking, he took a step backward.

The frenzy inside Elora's chest calmed a single degree. Brannick had appeared. He stood too far behind for her to see, but she didn't need to see. She could feel his presence. And she could hear the snarling and spitting coming from Blaz's mouth.

When they moved to her side, Blaz growled at Ansel, snapping his teeth along with it.

Ansel's shoulders hunched forward. He glanced down at the ground, but then met the prince's gaze again.

Brannick squared his shoulders, standing to his highest height. "Leave. Now."

CHAPTER 28

A Faerie door of green and brown swirls twirled in front of Elora, but she couldn't move. She held her palms up, staring at the blood dripping all over them. The blood was so dark it was almost black. The thick liquid splattered all over her dress, her hands. Her hair.

Even when Blaz nudged her from behind the leg, she still did not move forward. She could only stare. Breathe. Or attempt to breathe, anyway.

"Soren will take care of this mess. Come with me, and you can clean yourself off."

The prince's words grounded her. She vaguely recognized how he sent a message to his captain of the guard explaining there was a dead body that needed to be moved and the castle floor cleaned.

When Blaz nudged against the back of her legs again, she finally stepped into the door. Her head was spun when she arrived on the other side. Brannick's room.

He moved toward the corner that was hidden by a wall of vines.

She tried to wipe a splatter of blood away from her arm, but it only smudged the blood across more skin. It left a sticky, dark trail behind. Her breath stilled. "I have never killed anyone before. I've trained with the sword nearly all my life, but…"

Her arms curled around her stomach. Bile rose before she could stop it. When she bent over, Brannick rushed to her side carrying a wooden bucket. The bits of breakfast Fifer had forced her to eat now sat at the bottom of the bucket.

Blaz nudged the back her legs again, leading her behind the wall of vines. Brannick stood at the edge of the large stone basin he used as a bath. He filled it with steaming water, then gestured that she should stick her arms inside.

She used her fingernails to scrub the blood away, but the color still stained her skin. While she worked, the prince retrieved soft white cloths from his wardrobe. He soaked them in soaps that smelled of wild berries before handing them to her.

Those finally washed away the stains on her arms. Next, she dipped her hair in the water, soaking the ends until all the blood had washed away.

Under his direction, she scrubbed her face and neck. He must have discovered the gash in her forehead from where the blond fae had caused her to bleed, but the prince said nothing about it. When he declared her face and neck clean, she stepped away from the basin.

Water soaked her dress around the stomach, but blood was still splattered over the length of it.

With the wave of a hand, the prince conjured a new dress. Black.

She sniffed, hoping it might stay the tears in her eyes. It only made them fall faster instead. Never had she been so overcome with the desire to fall into Brannick's arms and cry on his shoulder. Her father had caught many of her tears on his shoulder. She once assumed that no one besides her father could comfort her in that way. But maybe that was still true because she had finally found someone she trusted enough, and she could not even touch him.

She stared at him instead. With her lip trembling.

He glanced away. "Once you change, I can dispose of the other clothes." He set the black dress on a clean table and disappeared behind the hanging wall of vines.

At least she hadn't been wearing the clothes from her mother when she killed someone. At least she hadn't used her father's sword. What would they think of her if they knew? She could claim it was in self-defense, but it wasn't really. The blond fae didn't even have a sword. And now he was dead.

Tears spilled over her cheeks, stinging her insides and outsides at the same time. After shrugging off her blood splattered clothes, she reached for the dress Brannick had conjured.

It was fitted at the top with a full skirt at the bottom. The shape was similar to the dress and corset she wore when she first entered Faerie. Delicate sleeves adorned her shoulders. Geometric designs were embroidered along the hem with green and silver threads.

Once dressed, she cleaned the blood off her sword and then dropped it into its sheath. She buckled it over the black dress, gaining strength in her fingers with every breath.

By the time she joined Brannick on the other side of the hanging vines, her tears had stopped. Her heart beat with a steady rhythm. She opened her mouth at once.

"We have to go back to the mortal realm and get my sisters."

The prince sat atop the trunk at the end of his bed. The bear skin rug lay under his feet. He gazed at her for a long moment before answering. "No."

It took everything in her to not shudder when she spoke again. "Ansel smelled and tasted my blood." She gestured toward the small gash in her forehead.

Brannick reached an arm over his stomach, while the lightest tinge of green colored his light brown skin.

Elora stepped closer to him. "Ansel knows I am Theobald's daughter. He knows where to find my sisters."

But the moment of nausea had disappeared from the prince's face. His eyebrows lowered tightly together. "You said you would stay in Faerie until the testing is finished. The tournament is coming soon."

She reached for one of the feathers in her hair. The feather from Soren protected her from accidental danger. Why could the feather tell that the attack in the hallway was not accidental, but the enchantment in the castle could not? She swallowed. "Ansel knows where my sisters are. He'll take them both as pets if he finds them. We have to leave now. Before he can get there."

Brannick leaned back, draping an arm on the bed behind him. "I can return you to the exact moment you left the mortal realm. Even if Ansel is in the mortal realm right now, it does not matter. You can still return to your sisters before he gets there."

She blinked once before shaking her head. "Right." When she spoke again, her eyes roamed over to the nearby wardrobe just so she wouldn't have to meet the prince's eyes. "I also need you to save my parents from the fire that killed them." Her shoulders bunched as she took in a breath. "I need you to get there before the cottage burns."

"I cannot." A strain stretched through his words.

She tried not to groan *too* loudly. "Because of the protective enchantment?"

He had been glancing at the wardrobe too, but now he looked straight into her eyes. "The what?"

It took a sniff and a swallow before she could speak again. "Queen Alessandra put a protective enchantment over the cottage. But you have stronger magic than her, don't you? I'm sure you can get through if you try. You have to at least try."

Scooting forward on the trunk, he looked at her more carefully. "How do you know Queen Alessandra put an enchantment on your cottage?"

Elora knew what he was really asking, but she gave an answer she hoped might distract him. "Lyren tried to save my parents already, but she couldn't get past the enchantment."

His eyes narrowed. "But how do you know Queen Alessandra did it?"

So much for distracting him. Elora rubbed a hand over her arm as she stared at the mossy floor. "The queen told me herself that she killed them. She doesn't know they were my parents." Her head dropped to her chest. "But she is friends with Ansel, so maybe she knows now."

Brannick stood from the trunk, trying to catch her eye. "When did you speak to Queen Alessandra?"

A gulp passed through Elora's throat before she could answer. "When I went to Fairfrost."

His eyes widened as he took a step forward. "How did you get there?"

Her head had to tilt upward to meet his gaze now. "Vesper took me."

His jaw dropped and then he let out a sigh. Now he massaged his forehead with one hand. "Did you make a bargain with her?"

"Yes."

He winced. "Did you conspire with her the way you did with King Huron?"

"No." She shook her head hard. "Of course not."

He stared at her for a beat before dropping his hand to his side. "Then what possessed you to travel to the most dangerous part of Faerie to speak to my greatest enemy?"

"I was going to kill her." That death wouldn't have caused even an inkling of guilt to linger inside Elora. "But she said that wouldn't break the part of your bargain that prevents you from touching... me." She bit into her bottom lip. "So, I made a bargain with her instead. She is going to reveal what you have to do in order to break your bargain with her."

His mouth hung open again. His eyes went wild with movement. The muscles in his face didn't move, but she detected several emotions bursting in his magical eyes. Exasperation, anger, but maybe a little excitement too. Of course, he tried to suppress all of them, but she still caught glimpses.

He spun on his heel and began marching toward his desk. "Get your sword. We need to train for the tournament." Before he finished speaking, he had reached the desk and plucked his own sword off the top of it.

Blaz jumped onto the bed and settled near the end of it with his head resting on his paws.

Grateful for something to focus on, she tore her now-clean sword from its sheath. After two strikes against Brannick's blade, she decided to press the issue further. "I need you to save my parents."

One eyebrow twitched on the prince's forehead as he jabbed his sword forward. "I cannot."

A grunt left her lips as she slammed her sword against his in a complicated block. "But you might be the only one with magic strong enough to get past the enchantment. You have to try."

His jaw flexed now that *he* was the one having to block blows. "I cannot do it. I am already in that place in the mortal realm. I am watching you watch a tournament. I was hoping to see your sword skill before I brought you to Faerie."

Her grip held the sword too tight, but she swung it anyway. "But you said you could travel to any place in the mortal realm."

Stepping back, he dropped his sword to his side. "I am already *in* that place. I cannot be there twice." Now his eyes turned toward his wolf. "I already would have saved them if I could."

Her own sword landed next to her leg with a soft pat. "Oh."

Silence strung around them, but apparently, Brannick was eager to smother it. He raised his sword high and charged her again. It took a strong arm and perfect footwork to block his blow.

She raised an eyebrow. "Your skill has improved."

He nodded before charging again. "I have been practicing on my own, which is not as helpful. But at least then I can avoid…"

"Me?" Her eyebrow rose even higher on her forehead.

After spinning his sword around hers and shoving it backward, he took a step back to reset his stance. "I find your presence distracting."

The corner of her mouth twitched with a smile. Her heart fluttered in her chest while warmth trickled through her body.

At that exact moment, Blaz bounded off the bed and out the door of the room.

"Where are you going?" The prince's sword fell to his side as he stared after his wolf.

When she turned to see the wolf's movement, she also noticed the sprites near the ceiling were behaving strangely. The glow around them gave off a slightly different light, as if they had all turned their backs and were now staring at the ceiling.

Were they purposefully ignoring Elora and Brannick's conversation?

She glanced back toward the door, which had been closed again. "Is Blaz okay?"

"Yes, he just left to go hunting." Brannick rubbed the back of his neck. "Although, he usually does that early in the morning while I am still sleeping."

The silence had returned. She rubbed her thumb over the hilt of her sword, wishing it was the leather hilt on the sword from her father. "Queen Alessandra most likely knows by now that you plan to choose swords as the weapon for the tournament."

"I am well aware." He lifted his sword again, swallowing before he stepped forward.

Elora managed a short shrug before she had to parry his blow. "At least she doesn't have much time to train for it."

Brannick slashed his sword down with greater force than he usually used. "This is your fault." He huffed as he lifted his sword again. "I knew you would be trouble, and yet I brought you to Faerie anyway. Why did I do that?"

"Were you too entranced by my beauty?" Her sword clanged against his, forcing it back. "Or was it the way I failed at climbing a tree that you couldn't resist?"

When he huffed again, the smallest grunt came out along with it. He sent another blow toward her. "I did not want to fall in love."

She blocked the blow with almost no effort at all. "Neither did I."

He sent her a single, piercing glance before swiping his sword down for another blow. "Well, mortal, we—"

Her sword blocked his much sooner than he expected, cutting him off short. The swords hovered, pressing against each other just under their chins. It allowed them perfect eye contact.

Gritting her teeth together, she held his gaze. "I have a name."

His eyes narrowed.

The conversation died altogether when he ripped his sword away and slashed it again. Another clash, another parry. Then he had to block instead of strike. They fought harder with each swipe. Brannick's eyes burst with more colors on every blow.

He pushed forward at every chance. She kept having to step back to reset her stance. But then her heels touched the wall at her back.

Swiping his weapon upward, he caught her blade. Her arm flew upward as he pinned her sword against the wall. He didn't stop there. One of his shoulders pressed against the wall at her side. Heat surged off his skin, mostly due to the physical activity sword fighting required. But feeling the heat from his skin stirred her heart. Spun it. Tangled it into a mess that she never wanted to sort.

"Elora." He whispered it, his breath fluttering through her hair. And then he said it again louder. Every light and every color burst in his eyes, which made her skin sizzle.

He leaned in close. Too close. So close she could hear his heart beat. Or maybe that was hers. His nose nuzzled next to hers, not quite touching it. Her cheeks warmed. It took everything in her to keep from licking her lips.

But she couldn't.

If she did, she would certainly touch him. Because his lips were right there. Hovering just over hers. Even knowing the consequences, her willpower was draining fast.

Breath from his nose heated her skin.

And then his sword clattered to the ground. He pushed himself away from the wall. Leaving both his sword and her, he left the room.

It took a moment to catch her breath. She lowered her hand to her side, then used her other hand to place a single finger against her lips. She smiled then. Unable to stop herself even if she tried.

She sunk to the floor as the smile grew, wishing she could hold onto the feeling forever.

CHAPTER 29

Black fabric swished around Elora's ankles as she marched into the hallway outside of Brannick's bedroom. He had left the room some time ago, but her heart still sank when she didn't see him anywhere in the halls.

No matter. It would just take longer to find him than she anticipated.

After turning a corner, she nearly ran into a group of three fae with their heads huddled together. When they looked up at Elora, they shared identical expressions of relief. Vesper, Lyren, and Quintus stepped away, giving just enough room for her to join their conversation.

Vesper raised his brow. "We were just discussing the tournament."

Using one finger, Lyren traced the chain on her seashell necklace. "It is coming soon. I can feel it."

Quintus sketched idly in his notebook as he shook his head. "Brannick has not said a word to any of us about it."

For once, Elora knew exactly what to do. Maybe she had caused a mess, but she could clean it up too. She leaned in toward the others. "I have an idea. Quintus, you go find Soren. Lyren, you get Kaia. Vesper, you need to find Prince Brannick. Meet me in the council room, and I will explain everything."

The others vanished through Faerie doors, leaving Elora to walk the rest of the way. She didn't mind. It gave her time to think through every crook and cranny of her plan. When she entered the room, she merely lowered herself into one of the chairs and continued to poke holes through all her ideas until they were solid.

Stomping footsteps sounded behind Elora's chair. She glanced toward the doorway, but she already knew whose feet they belonged to.

Soren stomped forward, narrowing his eyes as he moved toward the table. "You are getting very bold. Now we are being summoned to the council room by a…" His voice faltered. He cleared his throat, then started speaking with the same syllable he had ended with. Except he tilted it, so it sounded like a new word. "Uh, Elora."

He had most certainly been about to say *a mortal*. Realizing that only made her grin.

Quintus entered the room next, pulling out his sketchpad as soon as he sat down.

Lyren and Kaia came after. They both sat without a word. The dryad took the seat next to Soren. Kaia's brown and green eyes were magical as she stroked her emerald hair. Her gaze pierced Elora like never before.

"Prince Brannick said you traveled to Fairfrost."

"Yes." Elora nodded.

"Did…" Kaia swallowed. "Did anything strange happen while you were there?"

Elora raised her eyebrow at the oddity of the question. "I found out Queen Alessandra killed my parents."

"What?" Vesper had just entered the room, and now his mouth hung open.

Frowning, Elora turned back to the dryad. "She said it was revenge because my father killed one of her trolls. She didn't see it happen though. She just found a dagger with my father's symbol on it deep inside of a troll."

When Kaia swallowed again, her dark brown skin turned dull. Her eyes even dimmed.

Elora wanted to ask why.

Instead, Vesper spoke as he sat down. "Ansel never said anything about Theobald traveling to Fairfrost. He always told the story as if Theobald stayed in Mistmount the entire time."

Kaia snapped her head toward the other end of the table. "Ansel often leaves out any part of a story that does not suit him."

Elora had never heard the dryad speak with such a bitter tone. The raised eyebrows in the room indicated the others hadn't often heard it either.

Finally, Vesper bent his head. "That is true."

When Brannick entered the room, Blaz came in at his side. The wolf then bounded forward to nuzzle Elora's leg while the prince lowered himself onto his throne.

Even with him much farther apart than they had gotten in his bedroom, she was almost afraid to look at him. Her cheeks grew warm as she stood from her chair. "I have an idea for the tournament."

Everyone moved forward on their seats.

She gestured across the table. "Soren, you once gave me a feather that protects me from accidental injury." She bit her lip. "Can you give Prince Brannick a feather that will protect him from harming himself?"

The gnome blinked his black, bug-like eyes twice. But then a light gleamed inside them as understanding took hold. His beard ruffled as he nodded. "Yes."

She spared the tiniest glance toward the prince. His own eyes also gleamed when he responded. "Smart."

Standing a little taller, Elora spoke again. "An enchantment is stronger than a bargain, right?"

"Usually." Soren's voice came out gruff. He steepled his fingers under his chin. "How does that help?"

Elora immediately turned her gaze to the dryad.

Kaia only stared for a moment before she tapped a finger to her chin. "I can enchant Prince Brannick." Her eyes narrowed for another moment before they opened wide again. "I will enchant him that he must try his hardest to win the tournament."

Brannick sat so far forward in his throne, he nearly toppled out of it. "If I am ordered to lose, Kaia's enchantment would compel me to win."

The scratching of Quintus's pencil on his pad stopped. "Ordered?"

Vesper narrowed his blue and gray eyes. "You spoke to Elora about the tournament but not to us?"

Sitting back in his throne again, the prince shrugged. "I did everything to make my success most likely."

Lyren waved a flippant hand through the air. "It does not matter what secrets Prince Brannick kept. It only matters if he wins. The tournament is coming soon. I can feel it."

Brannick nodded, staring across the table with his jaw flexed. "The tournament will begin when day dawns tomorrow. I just received word from High King Romany before I got here."

Elora's heart leapt at those words. "Good." She reached for a feather in her hair, giving herself another moment to breathe. And then she stared across the table once again. "Kaia, I have one more enchantment you need to place over Prince Brannick."

CHAPTER

30

The day of the tournament had arrived. After gathering in the council room, Elora, Brannick, Lyren, Vesper, and Quintus stepped through a door to the Court of Noble Rose. Instead of landing in the throne room, the door led to a space outside Noble Rose Castle. Perhaps that was the only reason Vesper was allowed to go.

Turrets rose high into the air with stone of brown, white, and cream. A large portcullis heralded the entrance to the castle. It stood tall. Arrow slits and a few larger windows covered the surface.

Though the castle was a sight to behold, the area around it had even more beauty. Rolling hills covered the landscape. Two different gardens stood on either side of the castle. They featured highly manicured flower bushes and trees with delightful paths running through them. Quaint benches and trellises covered in flowers dotted the gardens. Roses showed up frequently, but there were also lilacs, lilies, orchids, and a number of flowers Elora had never seen before.

Right in front of them, a large open field had been marked off with a white picket fence. The field would almost certainly be used as the tournament grounds for the final phase of the testing. Rows of chairs surrounded the outside of the fence. Behind those chairs, there was a mound which allowed for another row of chairs that sat taller than the first. And behind that, there was a third row even taller than the others.

A large throne of red velvet and gold sat in front of the field. Its high back stood nearly as tall as a tree. Three much smaller thrones were situated next to the large one.

High King Romany sat in the largest throne. Or rather, he crumpled in it. His head sank low while he leaned as far back as he could. Every time he let out a cough, his entire body shuddered. Even from the distance Elora stood away from him, she could still make out wrinkles in his forehead that had never been there before.

Queen Noelani and King Jackory sat on two of the other thrones. They spoke to each other quietly. A fae with dark hair that grew down to her knees sat in the last throne. She wore golden ornaments in her hair.

Brannick used his chin to point toward the throne. "That is Princess Nerissa of Dustdune. They finally located King Huron's daughter, but she has not had an official coronation to make her queen of Dustdune yet."

Elora nodded, but she couldn't help note that the princess wore a silk and crystal encrusted crown much like the one King Huron had worn while he still lived. Queen Noelani wore her silver and seashell crown, King Jackory wore his crown of braided silver and gold, and of course, High King Romany still wore his red velvet and golden crown.

But Prince Brannick's head wore nothing but his glossy, shoulder-length black hair. If the princess of Dustdune wore a crown, then his lack of crown had nothing to do with his title as prince. Perhaps it was a personal choice, but it seemed more likely to be a result of the curse on his court.

In the moments while Elora waited with Brannick and the others, the chairs around the blocked-off area filled. Fae appeared through Faerie doors and took seats on all three levels of chairs.

Everyone wore fighting clothes. Prince Brannick and his council, including Elora, all wore suede pants and shirts with brown leather armor on top. Everyone carried weapons too, though Brannick had explained that the clothes and weapons of the spectators were just for show.

Soon, High King Romany waved a hand from his throne. His fingers immediately gripped the arms of the throne while he tried to sit up straighter. His back still arched over, but the crowd silenced all the same.

"Welcome. The third and final phase of my testing has begun. Prince Brannick and Queen Alessandra, come forward."

From the other side of the field, Queen Alessandra marched forward. Her white crown shimmered in the light while the white beads dangled over her forehead. Soft wool clothing wrapped tight around each of her limbs. Thin plates of armor covered her, giving off multicolored opalescence. She carried the opal-encrusted axe she had been sharpening during Elora's visit. Two guards in thick wool coats followed behind the queen.

Elora marched forward with the rest of her group as they followed Prince Brannick to the high king's throne.

Once they arrived, everyone had to wait for High King Romany to finish coughing into his golden handkerchief. At last, he tilted his head upward. "Prince Brannick. Since you won the second phase of testing, you may choose the weapon to be used in the tournament."

Elora's heart leapt as she sucked in a breath. They had schemed and trained, but now it came time to see how High King Romany would react to their plan.

Brannick rolled his shoulders back, looking more regal than anyone, even without a crown. "I am afraid I cannot do that."

Gasps sounded throughout the crowd. Even Queen Alessandra took a step back before she could stop herself. She managed to blink away her surprise, but her posture still suffered.

Brannick continued. "I have been enchanted that I cannot lift a weapon until a new day dawns."

The high king dabbed a speckle of blood from the corner of his lips as he narrowed his eyes. "Then you lose the tournament."

Even gripping the sword at her hip didn't bring Elora any sort of comfort. It couldn't be over just like that.

From a smaller throne, the princess of Dustdune sat up taller. "Or we could reschedule the tournament until the enchantment has faded away."

High King Romany whipped toward her with a sneer, but so did Queen Noelani and King Jackory. Apparently, they did not approve of her suggestion. Or perhaps they simply didn't approve of her *offering* a suggestion.

The moment ended quickly, and High King Romany glanced toward the prince once again. "You should not have allowed yourself to be enchanted."

A tiny smirk adorned Brannick's face as he let out a sigh. "Alas, it is done. But fae throughout all of Faerie have come to watch this tournament. We cannot leave them without some spectacle to enjoy."

One of High King Romany's eyes squinted. "I assume you an alternative to suggest."

"Indeed." Brannick swept one arm outward, gesturing toward the tournament grounds. "The tournament will proceed as usual with one minor change. Instead of fighting for myself, I will choose someone to fight in my place."

If Elora could have bottled the expression of rage and surprise that Queen Alessandra showed, it could have fueled her through anything. She wanted to wear it like a crown.

On the large throne, High King Romany nodded as he dabbed speckles of blood off his lips. "A tournament by proxy. Intriguing. Of course, Queen Alessandra would also have to choose someone to fight in her place."

The smallest sigh left Elora's lips. The tournament would have been *so* much more fun if Queen Alessandra were forced to fight. But at least the high king was considering the idea.

Each time High King Romany nodded to himself, a little more of Queen Alessandra's face contorted.

Whether High King Romany noticed her distress or not, he did not react to it. He gave a final nod. "Yes, this is an acceptable plan."

He opened his mouth as if to continue, but Queen Alessandra stepped forward. The twitching in her face had relaxed. She wore nothing but grace now. "I have an alternative suggestion as well."

High King Romany raised an eyebrow. "Go on."

Tension rocked and strained as Elora tried to keep her expression even.

Queen Alessandra tilted the pink lips that matched her pink cheeks up in a smile. "Prince Brannick has only been enchanted that he cannot lift a weapon."

The high king's face remained passive as he waited for further explanation.

Raising both eyebrows, Queen Alessandra continued. "But he can still use magic to fight, can he not? Why not allow Prince Brannick to fight for himself in the tournament but require that the weapon must be magic?"

Several coughs sputtered from High King Romany's lips before he could answer. "Another intriguing idea."

The tension in Elora's gut curled into a snake that slithered along her every limb. She held her breath, even knowing that wouldn't help.

High King Romany rubbed a hand across his forehead before he finally shook his head. "But Prince Brannick did win the speech phase of testing. He should still be allowed a chance to choose the weapon. And I quite like the idea of a tournament by proxy. I am curious to see who the prince trusts enough to fight in his stead."

Queen Alessandra's fists clenched tight, but Elora could finally breathe. She glanced toward Blaz who relaxed his ears that had been pointing straight.

But then the high king's face twisted in a way that didn't look promising at all. He sat forward on his throne. "We will do both suggestions. We will first have a tournament by proxy with a weapon of Prince Brannick's choice. And then we will have a tournament with magic where Prince Brannick and Queen Alessandra will fight each other."

Brannick tilted his head to the side. "But what if there are two different victors in the two different tournaments?"

The high king shrugged. "It does not matter. The phases only *help* me decide who to choose. The final decision is my choice alone."

In a matter of a few words, the hint of hope Elora had allowed herself got snuffed out. Two tournaments. Her expert sword skill gave them a good chance of winning the first one, but the second? Queen Alessandra merely had to order Prince Brannick to lose.

Soren had given the prince a feather that would prevent him from harming himself. And Kaia had enchanted him that he must try his hardest to win. But everyone knew those would only help so much. And anyway, Queen Alessandra's magic was great. She only needed the smallest advantage to win.

Cold trickled through Elora's shoulders. She tried to ignore how this turn of events pained her. The queen of Fairfrost stole magic from Swiftsea. She hurt and tortured Brannick without any regard for how it affected him. Worst of all, she murdered Elora's parents.

And now she was going to win the testing too.

It wasn't over, but their chances of winning had just greatly diminished.

High King Romany took a deep breath. "We will begin with the tournament by proxy. Prince Brannick and Queen Alessandra, you may have a moment with your council to discuss your strategies. But only a moment, mind you. And then the tournament will begin."

Elora followed the prince as he stepped out of ear shot of the throne. He gestured that Lyren, Vesper, and Quintus should keep walking. When he turned to glance at Elora, she felt his gaze down to her toes.

He swallowed. "There may come a point during my tournament that I need your help."

"I can help you?" Her eyebrows trailed up her forehead. "With my sword?"

"No." The prince pursed his lips before continuing. "Queen Alessandra's greatest magic is in emotion. If she cannot order me through our bargain, she will attempt to manipulate me through emotion. It could alter my essence."

Elora set her stance to keep her knees from shaking. "What am I supposed to do against something like that?"

A smirk curled across his lips. "You have a piece of my pure, unaltered essence."

"The crystal?"

He gave a slow nod. "Do you have it with you?"

She patted a hand over both of her pockets, which wasn't strictly necessary. The green crystal with Brannick's essence sat in one pocket. The shell and bag of salt from Swiftsea sat in the other. Letting her hand linger over the pocket holding the crystal, she leaned forward. "What should I do if she tries to manipulate you? Should I throw you the crystal in the middle of the tournament?"

"No." The answer came with a shudder through his shoulders. "Do *not* let anyone see that you have it, *especially* not Queen Alessandra. Keep it in your pocket."

"And?"

His shoulder relaxed. "Just touch it and think of me, the *real* me."

Now a smirk adorned her own face. "The *fun* you? The one who climbs trees and tosses clay pots and dances while glamoured to look like a bear?"

The smile that overtook his lips was even more enchanting than his eyes. "Exactly. While you draw on my essence, I will draw on yours, which will then lead to mine. It will help me resist Queen Alessandra's magic."

Reaching for a feather in her hair, Elora tried to hide her hard swallow. "Do you think it will be enough to help you win?"

He turned his gaze toward the others. "We must go. I would like to speak to my council before the tournament begins."

His refusal to answer her question was not reassuring. But before they even got to the others, the high king called them forward once again.

CHAPTER

31

Scratchy dryness crawled down Elora's throat when High King Romany waved his scepter. He had not been exaggerating about them only having a moment to discuss strategy. Prince Brannick never even got to speak to his council before they were all called forward once again.

At least the proxy tournament would be first. Hopefully that would give Brannick and the others some time to think of an advantage that might help the prince during his magic tournament with Queen Alessandra.

High King Romany clutched his stomach as he dabbed his lips with the golden handkerchief. "Before we begin, let us review the rules. First, do not kill your opponent or your victory will be forfeit."

A whisper fluttered into Elora's ear.

"That is the most important rule. Do not forget it." Brannick had moved to her side, but Blaz stood between them.

Her chin dipped in a short nod. Hopefully the movement was subtle enough that Brannick would see it but no one else in the chairs around them would notice.

The high king continued. "The tournament has several possible ways to end. One, a competitor yields. Two, a competitor is too weak to continue. Three, a competitor loses consciousness. And finally, four, a competitor receives an injury that is not fatal but must be attended to immediately in order to heal."

Brannick whispered again. "Do *not* attempt the last one. Fae heal more quickly than mortals. You may assume an injury might be close to fatal, but it probably won't be. But if you injure too much, the opponent might die and then we will forfeit victory. It is much better to weaken or tire your opponent."

As Elora nodded, she realized that though she had now killed, she had never once trained specifically to tire or cause her opponent to go unconscious. It would take a whole new set of techniques she had never considered.

With each word that left the high king's mouth, the moment drew nearer. Anticipation swallowed up her fear, but both still curdled in her gut.

"Prince Brannick." A coughing fit ensued before High King Romany could continue. "Choose your weapon."

Brannick glanced back at the crowd before taking a deep breath. "I choose swords."

Another fit of gasps rippled out through those seated around the tournament grounds. Even High King Romany and the other rulers raised their eyebrows.

But as they suspected, Queen Alessandra showed no indication of surprise. She even glanced at her fingernails.

They must have been correct in assuming Ansel had told her about his discovery inside Bitter Thorn Castle.

High King Romany nodded. "Prince Brannick, choose your proxy."

The prince stood even taller than ever. All around him, wind and magic crackled. He gestured to his side. "I choose Elora."

The quiet noises of whispers and shifting clothes stopped. Every fae in the crowd jerked their heads toward Prince Brannick. And then they looked at Elora. No, they didn't look. They gaped. Glared. Blinked, as though that would make them see it wasn't true.

Even the rulers on thrones sat with mouths open wide.

Queen Noelani's eyes dimmed as she whispered, "A mortal?"

Leaning toward the queen of Swiftsea, King Jackory spoke out the corner of his mouth. "I thought he wanted to win."

Disbelief intertwined with the queen's whispered response. "I need him to win. Why would he make such a dismal choice?"

After narrowing an eye at Elora, High King Romany looked back to the prince. "Are you sure?"

The question caused even more reaction in the crowd. Was his offering of another chance imprudent or improper in Faerie?

Brannick's eyes burst and shined with color. The energy around him continued to crackle until it silenced the crowd. "I am confident that the daughter of Theobald will act as a worthy proxy for me."

Fae were gasping again. Elora heard her father's name repeated throughout the crowd in both whispers and shouts.

Now Brannick smirked. "Her father trained her well."

High King Romany clapped his hands together. "You certainly know how to put on a show, Prince Brannick. I am more eager than ever to see this tournament." Now he turned to the queen of Fairfrost. "Queen Alessandra, choose your proxy."

Seeing the high king's delight brought a measure of victory through Elora. But it vanished once she saw the expression on Queen Alessandra's face.

The queen of Fairfrost smiled too wide. Too sweetly. "I thought a rematch of sorts would be most appropriate." Her smile grew. "I choose Ansel of Mistmount as my proxy."

Elora's teeth clenched. The news hit her like a ton of rocks, but really, she should have known it was coming. She should have guessed it would come to this. She assumed Queen Alessandra would have chosen one of her guards, or at least someone from Fairfrost. But then again, why would she? None of them used swords.

In Mistmount, however, swords and daggers were the weapon of choice. And Elora already knew Queen Alessandra and Ansel were friendly.

She should have known.

But all she could think about was how Ansel had tasted and smelled her blood. How he drew his fingers across her cheek and tried to enchant her.

"You can beat him." Brannick's whisper came out steady. His face was set, offering every reassurance both in his eyes and in his body language.

Still, Elora gulped. But what if she couldn't?

"It is in your blood." Vesper came to her other side, looking just as sure as Brannick.

It must have been easy for them to be so sure when they weren't the ones who had to fight. Reaching across her body, she pulled her sword from her sheath. The metal hilt still felt unfamiliar in her grip, but her sword skill was so automatic, she would be fine. Hopefully.

Commotion rippled through the crowd while Ansel descended from his place on the third row of chairs. He moved with the grace and speed of any fae. His pointed ears stuck out beneath his brown hair.

His yellow eyes flashed. "Before we begin, I request that I might use the sword Elora is carrying." The devious smirk on his face did not look promising.

Her fingers gripped tighter, instinctively pulling the sword closer to herself. "Then what would I fight with?"

The devious smirk on his face only grew. He glanced over the large crowd watching them as he stuck a hand inside of his magical fae pocket. When it emerged again, he carried a long marble box that Elora recognized at once.

She sucked in a breath.

He grinned wider.

Carefully tipping open the lid, he held the box out for all to see. "I have a sword made by Theobald himself. It may even be a sword that he made for his daughter, who stands with us now."

She wanted to sprint forward. Her toes itched with every step. Instead, she moved forward carefully. Methodically. Her eyes were trained on the sword the entire time. Was it a trick? Had he really brought her own sword? Would he really allow her to use it?

Perhaps it was a glamour, but something told her it wasn't. It looked like her sword.

But why would Ansel give her the exact sword she would have killed for?

His growing smirk spoke of mischief. Or maybe it was danger. Still, if she had a chance to take back her father's sword, nothing could stop her from doing it.

She reached out. Her fingers tingled even before they brushed against the leather-wrapped hilt. Her breath hitched while her fingers stretched.

And then she touched the sword.

The moment her fingers brushed the hilt, heat burned into her hand in a sharp burst. Gasping, she pulled her hand back at once. She studied her fingers, but they showed no sign of being burned. And now they felt fine.

It happened exactly the same as when she had attempted to touch the red ribbon from Chloe and the skirt from her mother. It burned her. But why?

Ansel snickered in a way that suggested he wasn't surprised in the least by this turn of events. "How amusing. The mortal has become so accustomed to Faerie that she cannot even abide her own token."

Elora's eyes flicked up to Ansel's. Token? Had her sword become a token?

The smirk on the fae's face confirmed it. "Even mortals will avoid the emotion a token gives off, which only proves how dangerous emotions are."

She could only blink. He smirked, looking much too proud of himself. "If you do not wish to use your sword, then I will. But I will not ever give you another chance to take it. Do you really want to be beaten with your own sword?"

Her blinking continued.

His eyelids dropped closed as he chuckled. "Go speak with your council if you must." He waved her off. "I will allow you a moment to decide."

Weight lined her insides as she dragged herself back to the others. Quintus spoke first, his eyes a little too bright. "Your father's sword is made with iron, is it not? It could give you an advantage over Ansel if you use it."

Vesper's nose wrinkled. "Not if she cannot even touch it. I know your father's skill was great, but Ansel is an expert swordsman." He tugged at his collar while his eyes turned downward. "I know women in the mortal realm do not have as much skill with weapons."

Flashing her teeth, Lyren jerked her head toward Vesper. "What does being a woman have to do with weapon skill?"

Vesper shook both hands in front of himself. "That is the way it is in that place in the mortal realm." He turned back to face Elora. "Ansel is just trying to get in your head. He does not care what sword he uses, but he knew you would not be able to touch your father's sword. He is trying to twist your thoughts so you cannot focus. He knows it will give himself an advantage during the fight."

Lyren managed one more side eye in Vesper's direction before turning to Elora. "Use the fae sword from Brannick."

Elora bit into her bottom lip as she stared at the others. It took her a moment to form her words, and even then, they didn't convey the storm inside her. "But it's my father's sword. If I do not take it now, I may never get it back."

Pinching his eyebrows together, Vesper leaned forward. "You cannot fight at all if you use a weapon you cannot even touch. Do you think you can touch your father's sword?"

Instead of answering, Elora dropped her chin to her chest. The sword had definitely burned her. It would burn her again if she tried to touch it. But it was her *father's* sword. It was the only thing she had left from him.

Lyren ran a hand over her seashell necklace. The silver and brown in her eyes tumbled together in bursts. "My entire court is dying from decay. If Prince Brannick does not become high king, my court may be lost forever." Her palms came together under her chin. "Use the fae sword and win."

When Elora glanced toward Brannick, everyone else did too. But surely no one else's eyes implored quite as strongly as hers did.

He glanced away almost immediately. "I cannot tell you what to do. You know how much you want your father's sword." He swallowed. "But you also know how badly I need to win."

The words cut into her, but it made the decision easier. She had to use the fae sword. She had cast away her mother's skirt and her sister's ribbon. She should have known she would cast away her father's sword as well.

Even with the decision made, her fingers still shook and yearned to reach for her father's sword, to allow herself the familiarity of the leather and weight of her favorite weapon. The sword had been there for her while others mocked her for sword fighting. It had been there for her when she snuck out to avoid harp lessons. It had been there for her when her father told her she would have to marry a stranger.

Coming to Ansel's side, he reached the box out again. "Are you certain you do not want it?"

How did he know? The gleam in his eye made it clear that he knew exactly how he tantalized her. Maybe this happened to any mortal who entered Faerie. Maybe they grew accustomed to the fewer emotions. Maybe others had tried to escape grief like she had.

Something sparked within her then. It wasn't a memory really, but it stirred her the same as one.

The sword only burned because she couldn't abide the emotion. Because she had spent so much time blocking it out. But hadn't she already realized her grief was a part of her now? She could ignore it and bottle it up, but it would never disappear completely.

Death would always be close to her now.

Trying to hide from that truth would never help. But she had good memories of her parents. Good emotions. Would those also diminish when she blocked out grief?

Her eyes flicked upward, staring Ansel straight in his yellow eyes. For the first time, his expression faltered.

No matter how much pain it brought, living without the grief was worse. There would be no joy if she blocked out the pain.

She threw the fae weapon at his feet and reached for her father's sword.

CHAPTER

32

Heat stung into Elora's fingertips. It surged and burned like pulsing daggers. She curled her fingers over the leather-wrapped hilt of her father's sword. The burning grew. If it hadn't been right in front of her eyes, she would have sworn her hand was on fire.

It took a deep breath for her to grip her other hand around the hilt along with the first. Doing so forced a gasp from her lips.

She hadn't caught her breath before Ansel swung his first blow toward her. After years of sword training, her movements came automatically. She parried the blow but lost her footing at once.

Taking several steps back, she attempted to catch her breath before she was forced to block another blow. But how could she catch her breath when her fingers were on fire?

It felt as though needle-like flames sliced into her skin. The fire surged deeper as she held the hilt. Then, her grip loosened to ease the pain.

Another blow hurled toward her.

She set her feet, but nearly lost her sword when she blocked Ansel's blade. Once her grip tightened back up, she had to clutch her stomach to keep from crumpling to the ground.

Why?

The question littered her thoughts as she urged her body to stand up straight. It ignored her.

Why had she done something so stupid? She *knew* touching her father's sword would hurt. Maybe she didn't want to lose it, but had it really been worth it for this?

Ansel laughed as he slapped the flat side of his sword against her leg.

Pain possessed her every movement, her every thought.

The tiny slap of Ansel's sword was enough to send her sprawling toward the ground. He swung his sword toward her again, which she blocked at the last moment. But only just.

With her father's sword in one hand, she heaved herself off the ground. Her feet could barely choose where to rest while her hands continued to burn. To melt.

Why had she believed this would be better than losing her father's sword forever? She didn't want Ansel to have it, but this was too much. Too much pain.

Maybe it only hurt because she had blocked it away for too long, but it didn't matter.

Feeling nothing was better than feeling this horrible.

Ansel's sword sliced toward her stomach. She couldn't even swing her sword to block it. Instead, her feet stumbled backward until she fell onto her back. She intended to stand back up again. She didn't intend to give up completely.

But then Ansel kicked her father's sword out of her hand.

Sweet relief cooled against her burning palms. She could breathe again.

No more pain.

When Ansel's boots crunched over the tournament grounds, her fingers twitched. Instinct kicked in. She had to retrieve her sword. She couldn't lose.

Her shoulders lifted off the ground while she stretched one hand outward. The fae continued to approach, but she still had time.

Just a little closer.

The moment her fingers made contact with her hilt, the burning pierced her again. It licked into her palms, sparking through every nerve. She gasped and pulled her hand back to her body.

Away from the sword.

It was too much.

Ansel's sword came crashing down toward her. She made no effort to block it. Her knees curled toward her chest as she rolled out of the way instead. Dirt and pebbles burst into the air from the force of Ansel's sword as it hit the ground.

Burning still worked through her fingers, suffocating each pore. But she wasn't even touching the sword anymore. And her hands showed no sign of being injured. Still the pain continued. Growing. Writhing.

A breath escaped her as she fell onto her back once again. Ansel strutted forward, wearing a smirk. She should have jumped up. She should have reached for her sword. She should have attempted to trip him or trick him. She should have done *something*.

She didn't.

Her body didn't move at all. She simply lay there waiting for it to end.

He reeled his arms back, giving a pointed look at her neck before he swung. And then his sword fell, sending a whistle through the air.

She didn't move.

Her eyes even fluttered closed. Why watch her impending doom? Wasn't feeling it enough?

But when the sword met her neck, the blade only hovered lightly against her skin.

Peeling one eyelid opened, she checked to see that she hadn't imagined the whole thing. Ansel's sword sat against her neck as she thought it did. His muscles shook. But he hadn't killed her.

Why not?

The answer came as soon as she considered it. The only rule was that neither of them could kill the other. If they did so, their victory would be forfeit.

Fire burned in Ansel's eyes as he glared down at her. "If you are too weak to continue, then I win the tournament."

The *tournament*.

The word stuck inside her, wriggling along the edges of her mind. It stirred and twisted. And then it grew.

That used to be her only goal in life, to compete in a tournament. Faerie had so many distractions, she had nearly forgotten how tangible that goal had once been. She had let go of her dream. Forgotten it entirely.

Blocking out pain caused her to lose her family, but she had lost herself too.

Was feeling nothing better than feeling pain? Because feeling nothing meant being nothing too.

She didn't want to be nothing. Her fingers twitched while a new sensation stirred within her. She wanted to fight. And she didn't just want to compete in the tournament. She wanted to win.

Ansel's sword swung toward her leg this time. An injury on that part of her body would incapacitate her, but it wouldn't kill her. He wouldn't stay this blow.

But she didn't need him to.

Just as his sword clashed down, the heel of her boot shot up to meet it. The sword cut a gash into the soles of her boot, but it left no injury.

His eyes widened. He swung his sword again.

This time, she rolled to the side before he could strike her. The move brought her close enough to retrieve her own sword. He barreled toward her, but she allowed herself to take in a breath.

One last breath.

And then she snatched her father's sword from off the ground.

It. *Burned.*

Scorching pain ripped away whatever feeling she had left in her hands. But this time, the pain didn't stop her.

For the first time, she swung her sword in an attack instead of a block. Ansel parried it easily.

She gripped the leather hilt of her sword even tighter. The burning slithered up to her arms. She swung her sword again.

The pain didn't hurt any less. She just stopped treating it like an obstacle. It wasn't a physical pain anyway. Not really.

It didn't really burn in her hands, no matter how she wanted to believe it did.

In truth, the pain came from her heart. She held her father's sword. And her father was dead.

Forever.

Ansel's jaw flexed as he sent a series of strikes toward her. It took skill and practiced footwork, but she avoided every one. Now her own sword sliced toward him. He jumped away just in time.

Her father couldn't be saved. Not ever.

That would always hurt, but her life didn't have to end because of it.

When her sword swiped again a second time, it left a slice across Ansel's shoulder. He flashed his teeth as sizzling steam erupted from his skin. Gritting his teeth together, he stepped back.

In the moment he spent out of her reach, the sizzling stopped.

It wasn't fair that fae could heal so quickly.

Charging forward, she left another slice, on his leg this time.

He let out a hiss while stepping backward even farther away from her. The second gash went deeper than the first. Crackles accompanied the sizzling steam.

Yellow flashed in his eyes as he sprinted toward her. He wanted blood. And he got it.

His sword sliced into her arm, just above the elbow.

It cut deeper than any injury she had ever received from her father. She glanced at it before she turned her eyes upward. She donned a devious smirk. Just like any fae.

"Perfect. Now I'll have a scar to help me remember my first tournament."

The confidence in his stance faltered the moment she moved forward again. A shiver passed through his shoulders as he flicked his eyes toward the cut in his leg.

Burning surged through her arms and chest. It hurt. But it also gave fuel to her fight. Now *she* sent a series of strikes toward her enemy. He could not block all of them.

Two more minor cuts sliced under his ear and across the back of his hand.

A shadow of fear passed through Ansel's yellow eyes.

The tournament ended in that moment. Of course they still traded several blows, but they were inconsequential. It wasn't a question of who would win anymore. It was a question of how many iron-filled injuries she could deliver before Ansel finally gave up.

When the tip of her sword sliced across his cheek, he dropped his sword at her feet and raised his hands.

He had never been fighting for himself the way she had. He had been fighting for Queen Alessandra. And apparently, the Fairfrost queen wasn't worth slices from an iron sword.

Ansel snarled before he finally opened his mouth. "I yield."

When he ducked his head, Elora could have jumped off a cliff and flown with only that feeling to hold her. She glanced over her shoulder at the council.

Quintus raised a fist into the air. Lyren held a hand to her chest while her eyes glistened with actual tears. Vesper beamed with cheeks stretched wide in a smile.

Blaz repeatedly tapped his paws on the ground while he let out happy yips.

But Brannick's face was the best of all. He smirked. Not because he was proud of her or impressed, although he was probably both of those things as well. But the half-smile on his face said one thing.

He'd known she would win. And now she had.

She slipped her father's sword into the sheath on her hip, which turned it invisible right away. Ansel inched closer to her, slowly, while they both turned toward the large throne.

Queen Alessandra sent an icy glare toward Ansel, which only gave Elora extra reason to stand tall.

High King Romany let out a breathy chuckle. It immediately turned into a raucous cough. By the time he had stopped coughing, Ansel stood close enough to Elora that their shoulders were nearly touching. *Why* was he standing so close?

She could suppress her shudder because the victory she had just earned was too sweet.

After nodding, High King Romany tilted his chin upward. "The mortal wins, which means Prince Brannick is victor for the first tournament. You two may leave the tournament grounds."

While cheers erupted through the crowd, a tight arm wrapped around Elora's waist. Ansel's arm. He yanked her backward without warning. She couldn't stop it; she could only react.

She lifted a foot to pull away, but his grip tightened. He yanked her backward even harder. She lost her balance.

Before she knew it, she was tumbling backward through a rocky, gray Faerie door while the tournament grounds disappeared from view.

CHAPTER 33

Jerking her limbs in every direction, Elora tried to escape her captor. She had never been a coward. Her automatic response to fear had always been to fight. That was one reason the sword always appealed to her.

But even as she squirmed and punched and shouted, the rocky Faerie door surrounding her continued to hurtle her forward. The arm still held fast to her waist.

Her shoulder landed with a thud on a polished wooden floor. Only an arm's length away, a white fur rug laid over the wood. Long wooden beams stretched across the high ceiling. Clear, crystal light fixtures hung from the ceiling from a blackened metal rod, though it probably wasn't iron like it looked. The entire room smelled of fresh mountain air and snow. But something darker laced through it. Rot, or even more likely, blood.

A kidnapping rated high on the list of worst possible outcomes for the tournament. Once the second tournament began, Brannick would be susceptible to Queen Alessandra's manipulation. If Elora wasn't there with the crystal, he'd have no hope against his opponent.

After landing, Elora finally had her bearings enough to dig her fingernails deep into the arm around her waist. When Ansel didn't release her, she dug harder, clawing across his arm. It wasn't until she drew blood, but his arm finally released her.

Lunging for the other side of the room, she drew her sword at once.

He faced her, though his attention was fixed on the gashes she had dug into his arm. Hovering one hand over them, the gashes began closing up with magical puffs twirling above them.

Her jaw clenched. She marched forward. She meant to stab her sword straight through Ansel's heart, but he leapt away at the last moment. The tiniest smirk lit on his face as he jumped onto a nearby wooden table decorated with clear, crystal candlesticks and gray ceramic dishes.

She continued to stomp forward. "I have no reason not to kill you now."

His carefree chuckle sent her stomach tumbling. He leapt from the table to a sofa made of navy blue plaid fabric. "The third phase of testing is not over yet. If you kill me, your victory will be forfeit."

"Even if we aren't on tournament grounds? Even if we aren't in Noble Rose?"

"Yes." Ansel's yellow eyes pulsed with a glow. "There is magic surrounding us both. High King Romany will know if you kill me."

She growled, wishing Ansel happened to be the one fae who could lie and that he was lying now. But of course, such a wish was only a child's dream.

He landed in front of a wooden bookcase with glass doors over parts of the shelves.

She charged him, despite what he had said. Even if she couldn't kill him, she did have an iron weapon that could inflict great damage. Considering she most likely stood inside his own house, she wasn't eager to keep him standing. With the right threat, he'd certainly open a door and bring her back to the tournament before it ended.

Her feet flew over the white fur rug. Ansel grinned and flicked over a wooden bird figurine that sat on the bookcase.

At that exact moment, the fur rug at her feet shot upward. It changed from a rug into a net made of rope, and it strung her up where she could no longer reach the ground.

Huffing, she sat crisscross inside the net. At least she had kept a steady grip on her sword. "How long do you expect this to hold me?" She glared at the net while beginning to saw her sword across a piece of the rope.

Ansel only chuckled again. "Mortal minds are always so restricted by the limitations of the mortal realm."

She raised an eyebrow at his statement but didn't stop sawing. Her arms yanked back and forth, pulling her blade across the rope. Soon, heat emanated from the rope and into her sword. But the rope never bristled, never changed. Even after sawing hard, no cut had been made.

Whether through an enchantment or some other magic, the truth became clear. Her sword would have no effect on the net entrapping her.

From in front of the bookcase, Ansel eyed her far too intensely for her liking. "In answer to your question, I expect it to hold you until you have learned your place."

Setting the sword in her lap, she turned her eyes upward. "It will hold me until I die then because I will never accept whatever place you think I should have."

His eyes narrowed, intensifying his gaze even more. "So be it."

The words slithered across her, sending a shiver down her spine. With the sword still in her lap, she curled her hands into fists. "Take me back to the tournament."

He smirked, leaning back against his bookcase.

Now she grabbed tight onto the net holding her. Her knuckles turned white. "Take me back now."

He adjusted the purple gem on his lapel. "Why would I do that now that I finally have what I want?"

A blood-curdling scream burst from her lips. When he stood unaffected, she screamed even louder. Longer. He continued to stand with no reaction at all.

Narrowing her eyes, she leaned her head closer to the net. "You will not get away with this."

A cruel smirk twitched at his lips. "And who is going to stop me? Prince Brannick? He will not leave in the middle of his tournament. By the time the third phase of testing is over, I will have you glamoured to appear as someone else. And by then, you will not want to leave."

"It does not matter." Elora leaned back. "Prince Brannick will not give up until he rescues me."

Raising one eyebrow, Ansel's smirk grew. "If you were fae, you could not speak those words."

A weight dropped in her stomach. "Why not?"

Ansel's smile grew, but his yellow eyes pulsed thick like blood. "Because you are lying. You want to believe Prince Brannick would do everything to rescue you, but you know he may not. You just won the tournament for him. Is that not why he brought you to Faerie? You think he cares for you enough to be bothered by your absence?"

Elora had to tip her chin upward to hide its quivering. "Yes, I think he does."

Ansel narrowed one eye. "How bothered?"

When no words came to her lips, she gulped.

He chuckled before speaking again. "You are a mere mortal, and he is the prince of Bitter Thorn. You do not belong with him."

The weight in her stomach bulged. Gnarled. Her throat stung while she tried to convince herself Ansel was wrong. But was he? Brannick liked to remind her that fae were selfish.

But what about the crystal?

It buzzed inside her pocket even now. His essence was there with her even while they were apart. Hadn't he said it meant his heart was tied to hers?

But then her stomach dropped. Down. Too far down.

No. He had only said it meant *her* heart was tied to his. That *she* loved him. But not that he loved her. He couldn't touch her, which proved he had romantic feelings for her. But were those feelings as deep as hers?

Nodding at her once, Ansel opened one of the glass doors on his bookcase. He retrieved a gray ceramic plate and mug. A small chunk of light yellow cheese sat on one side of the plate. In the middle, there was a pie that smelled of potatoes, cream, and herbs. The mug held a thick red liquid.

With a wave of his hand, a little wooden table near the sofa flew toward him. He set the plate and mug on top of it. After waving his hand again, the table flew upward until it hovered just outside the net, right in front of Elora.

He gestured toward the table. "Eat and drink that. You will feel better after you do."

She folded her arms over her chest. "And what if I refuse?"

His jaw flexed before he answered. "It will simply make you more agreeable. It will not harm you."

Her head tipped to the side. "Why do I have the feeling that agreeing with you will eventually harm me?"

Now he kneaded his temples. "I remember your father was defiant, but you may be even more so. Just eat and drink what I have given you."

"No."

A murderous gleam sparked in his eye. "Then I will kill your sister as soon as I find her."

She rolled her eyes. "You do not even know where my sister is. If you did, you would have captured her already."

One eyebrow twitched above Ansel's eye. "And are you certain I will never find her? Not ever?" His mouth twisted up in a wicked grin. "I vow to you that if you do not eat and drink what I have given you, then I will kill your sister as soon as I find her."

Cold chills dug into Elora's shoulders. A vow like that probably had the same magic as a bargain. That meant Ansel couldn't break the vow, even if he wanted to. She sneered at the fae below her, but she reached for the mug all the same.

Herself she could doom. But her sister? It didn't matter which one Ansel found first, she wouldn't put either of her sisters in danger.

But as she brought the mug closer to her lips, the ward necklace around her neck began to buzz. The drink held an enchantment. She never expected anything less, but the confirmation still twisted her stomach into knots.

What if by *agreeable*, Ansel meant that the food and drink would force her to follow his every suggestion? What if eating and drinking the food meant she could never escape?

She brought the mug straight to her lips, and even breathed in the scent of the liquid. It had that same rotting smell she noticed before. Luckily, she knew exactly what to do about the enchantment.

Ansel grinned at the sight of the mug at her lips. He turned back toward his bookcase to shut the glass door it had come from.

The moment he turned his back, she dug deep into her pocket for the shell and bag of salt from Lyren. Ansel turned back to face her quickly, so she simply dropped the shell into the mug.

Did it need time to work?

He narrowed his eyes and took a step forward. "Are you really drinking that?"

She gave an eager nod before knocking the mug back. The liquid felt thick in her mouth like a gravy, but it tasted as sweet as honey. She made a show of drinking every last drop, mostly so he wouldn't try to glance inside the mug and then see the shell from Lyren.

It took a bit of fidgeting with her hunk of cheese and the potato pie before Ansel turned around again. When he did, she quickly sprinkled the Swiftsea salt over every bit of the food.

By the time he faced her again, she was already chewing a chunk off the cheese. "It is even better than I expected." She spoke with eagerness, trying to seem more agreeable than she felt.

It seemed to please him.

While the cheese actually had been delicious, the potato pie had an unexpected sourness in the creamy sauce. Perhaps it was only because of the salt she added, but she had to choke down every bite. But of course, her lips grinned wider with each chew. She nodded and complimented the food like every morsel was the sweetest thing she had ever tasted.

He eyed her greedily, spinning the gem on his lapel. "You are more fun than I expected. I will enjoy you greatly."

She giggled at his words, which might have been overkill. But he didn't seem to mind.

When she swallowed the last of the food, he waved his hand. The table floated down to the ground once again. After another hand wave, the net lowered from the ceiling. When it touched the floor, it opened wide and transformed back into the white fur rug once again.

Ansel stepped forward and stroked her cheek with a single finger. "You must stay in my house. You must not try to leave. Escape is bad. And you must not speak to anyone else anymore. You must only speak to me unless I tell you otherwise."

She bounced her head up and down and giggled again. "That sounds delightful."

With a grin, he reached into his pocket. He pulled out a polished blue gem on a hairpin and fastened part of her hair up with it. When he touched her, she noticed her hands shifted, taking on a slightly different shape and color. Even her clothes changed. Now she wore a full maroon skirt and soft gray slippers.

A glamour. She could still feel her suede fighting clothes and leather armor around her limbs. But now they looked like a skirt and blouse. Since her hands had changed, her face probably looked different too.

Ansel nodded at the sight of her. "Very good. Now do not get into any trouble. I will be back once the testing is over. I will tell you all about it when I return."

She clapped her hands together to hide the grin on her face. "Don't be gone too long."

He soon disappeared through a swirling gray door.

Now her escape could begin.

CHAPTER 34

Slipping her sword into its sheath, Elora trailed around the edge of the room. She had already retrieved her magical shell from the mug. Now she just had to get out of there. Once she found an exit, she'd be free from Ansel's home. Getting back to Noble Rose before Brannick was manipulated by Queen Alessandra would be more difficult. Would she have to make another bargain to get out of this court?

Thoughts spun inside her. So many of them tumbled, she almost didn't realize she had walked around the entire room. Shaking her head, she glanced over one shoulder.

But where was the door?

Her head shook as she stomped around the edge of the room again. Every room had an exit of some kind. She simply must have missed it the first time.

The second jaunt around the room only confirmed her first finding. The room had no exit. A grunt huffed from her lips as she kicked the wall.

Even if fae could create magical swirling doors to get them places, it still seemed like a significant design flaw to have no exit in a room. But maybe that was the point.

One eyebrow quirked up as she glanced through the room once again. Maybe it didn't have a door, but the room *did* have windows. The large panes of glass let in clear light from the mountainous landscape outside.

Unsheathing her sword, she slammed the pommel into the nearest window. The pommel instantly bounced back, throwing her onto the floor. Never one to back down, she charged the window again. She threw even more weight behind her pommel this time.

It bounced off the window again. The glass didn't suffer a single crack.

She grunted. Some enchantment must be protecting the window.

With her sword still drawn, she sliced a long gash across the length of the plaid sofa. Stuffing spilled out of the gash. Now a smile played at the corner of her mouth.

Good. The plaid looked terrible anyway.

Unfortunately, the destruction didn't get her any closer to escaping.

Stretching her fingers over the leather hilt of her sword, she glanced down. The sword didn't burn anymore. Or maybe it had burned so much she just couldn't feel it anymore. Either way, it felt nice to use her favorite sword without consequence.

She dropped it into the sheath as she tapped one toe. Maybe things would look different from another perspective.

Her wings popped out of her back with only the barest urging. Using them would be another matter.

Holding her breath, she tensed the muscles to send her wings beating. Her body jerked hard to one side, nearly knocking her over. Relaxing her wings, she wrinkled her nose.

Why did she always feel the need to hold her breath before flying? She should have known by now that it only made things worse.

This time, she took in a deep breath and let it out slowly. Relaxing every muscle she could, she sent her wings beating again. Now they moved freely. She only had to welcome the air.

Her feet slowly lifted off the ground. Sucking in a steady breath, she eased herself higher into the air.

It took effort, but she managed to rise higher than she had been while inside the net. Everything still looked the same, even from above.

But when she moved just a little higher, something flickered near the ceiling. She beat her wings and flew just high enough for a glamour to fall away.

Near the ceiling, there was a loft that had been hidden by the glamour. A huge loft. It was big enough to hold a crowd and even led into a long hallway with several doors. Even better, several fae lingered in the loft. Their pointed ears peeked out through their hair. Most of them sat on thin cushions on the ground, but some of them stood.

The little excitement Elora had at discovering others quickly faded. Their eyes all looked dead. Even stranger, they all looked exactly the same.

There were at least a dozen young women in the loft, but each of them wore the same maroon skirt, white blouse, and gray slippers as Elora. Their faces were the same, their hands, everything. It looked like the same fae a dozen times.

If Ansel had glamoured Elora to look like someone else, he must have glamoured these others too. But why glamour them with the same face?

There were men too. They had the same deadened expression in their eyes. They also had white-blond hair and crooked teeth. They looked exactly the same as a fae she had already met.

The fae she had killed.

But maybe that blond-haired fae had been wearing a glamour too. Maybe the man she killed looked different than she thought.

Either way, at least a dozen identical iterations of the blond-haired man stood in the loft. They stared at the ground or at their hands. Not one of them seemed to know what to do.

"Hey!" Elora gestured toward a pile of folded blankets on the loft. "Someone lower one of those blankets down and pull me up. I can't fly high enough to get up there."

Blinks rippled across every face before her. Most of them kept their heads in place, but a few did turn in her direction. Slowly.

Aches tightened in her shoulders with each beat of her wings. "Someone help me. There's no door down here. I cannot escape."

One of the young women jumped up from her cushion and stumbled backward. Her hands were clasped over her mouth. Several of the others, both men and women, gasped. A few touched a hand to their chests.

Elora felt her body sink. The glamour over the loft went back up until she managed to fly just a little bit higher once again. "Can you help me get out of here?"

A man placed his head in his hands and shook it back and forth. "I do not wish to escape. Escape is bad."

Half a dozen of the people stepped backward away from Elora. When they reached the hallway, they disappeared through it. The others just sat there, as if nothing had changed at all. As if Elora didn't exist.

With her shoulders aching even more, Elora lowered herself back to the ground. So much for that idea. But the second tournament had probably already started by now. She needed to get back soon if Brannick had any chance of winning.

When her feet touched the ground again, a little creature wearing a stained burlap tunic scurried across the white fur rug. The creature had big eyes and spindly fingers just like Fifer, but this brownie's body was thin and frail. Stringy blonde hair fell over her forehead in a way that resembled rotting straw.

The brownie did not look up at Elora. Her large eyes barely blinked as she dragged herself across the rug until she reached the table with the ceramic plate and mug.

Dropping to her knees, Elora looked into the brownie's eyes. "Can you help me?"

The brownie's big eyes grew even bigger. She glanced at the plate and mug, which were both empty. When she turned back to Elora, one of her eyes narrowed. She glanced toward the empty plate and mug once more.

Letting out a sigh, Elora tilted her head toward the brownie. "Can you help me escape? You have magic, right?"

"Not here." The words croaked out of the brownie's mouth, as if it was the first time she had spoken in years.

Elora frowned. "Because this is not your home. Is that right?"

The brownie blinked back, her eyes growing wider each time. Finally, she jerked her head away. "I have no home." Then the brownie whisked the ceramic plate and mug off the table and scurried away.

It seemed best to just let her go. But then Elora jumped to her feet.

Where had the brownie come from? If it had no magic, then it must have entered the room through an entrance or exit of some sort.

She chased after the small brownie, ignoring how it sprinted faster with each step. At the edge of the room, the creature lifted a black fur rug and jumped down through a hole.

A *small* hole.

Screwing her mouth into a knot, Elora reached for the hole. It was smaller than a shield. The brownie had jumped through with ease, but it would take much more effort for Elora to squeeze her body through.

She shrugged and pushed her feet down anyway. At least she was wearing pants and not a skirt. She had to wriggle her hips through, but then she began falling down a much greater distance than she had anticipated.

Her wings popped out, catching her just before she slammed against the ground. This room didn't look any better than the first. In fact, it looked much worse. It was dark and dingy and cold as ice. The wall had been built with cobblestones. No glowing sprites flew anywhere nearby. The rotting smell she smelled upstairs was much stronger down here.

The scent alone churned her stomach. She would have gone right back up to where she started, except the tiny hole looked too far away. Her amateur wing skills couldn't fly her up that high. She'd just have to explore instead.

After a few steps, she found the brownie. The creature scrubbed the ceramic plate and mug in a metal tub of water. Off to the side, there were stacks of clean dishes. And on the other side, there was a dingy pile of straw that looked suspiciously like a bed. Not a nice one.

Shuddering, Elora moved on. She marched down the entire length of the dingy room, but only found clothes, blankets, and laundering supplies. And of course, there were no exits at all.

It seemed like a good time to slice her sword through something.

Before she could reach for her hilt, she got to the end of the room. A young woman who looked like all the others stood in a darkened corner. Her face held no expression. Her hands were clasped in front of herself.

Elora raised an eyebrow. Would this one also be frightened off if Elora spoke to her?

The sound of splashing water filled the area, but not a drop of water could be seen anywhere.

Narrowing her eyes, Elora took a step closer to the young woman. Though her arms and upper body didn't move, the young woman did move her lower half in strange, fluid motions. Her legs jerked to one side and another splash sounded against the ground.

This time, a few splatters of ice-cold liquid fell onto Elora's clothes. Thinking back to when Ansel made her own appearance change, she glanced straight at the young woman's hair.

Just as she suspected, a hairpin with a blue gem had been neatly tucked above the ear.

"I know this seems strange," Elora whispered as she moved closer to the young woman. "But…"

When she plucked the hairpin away, the familiar young woman with the maroon skirt melted away only to be replaced by a mermaid sitting in a large bucket of water. Her dark skin was tinged with blue. Bruises formed around her wrists where her hands were tied to the bucket with a thick rope. Another rope was tied over her mouth, gagging her.

Drawing her sword, Elora immediately cut the bonds away. Standing closer now, she nearly gasped as the rope fell away. She knew this mermaid. She had met Lyren's friend on her first trip to Swiftsea.

"Waverly?"

The mermaid merely shuddered, which sent her mane of blue and green hair flipping behind her back.

Elora's eyes flew up to her forehead. "You're a fae. Can you open a door to get us out of here?"

Shivering, Waverly shook her head. "Not with that iron close by."

Pulling her sword from its sheath where the mermaid could see it, Elora raised an eyebrow. "My sword?"

"No." The mermaid winced as she jerked her hand toward a nearby stool. "That."

A talisman sat on top of the stool. It looked exactly the same as the talisman Elora had removed from the island in Swiftsea.

With her face wincing, Waverly sneered at the talisman. "It has been enchanted to fill the room with iron. It grows smaller every moment while bits of it float into the air."

After moving toward it, Elora stuffed the talisman into her pocket. She specifically chose the opposite pocket from the one that held Brannick's crystal. Glancing back at the mermaid, she asked, "Is it better now?"

Waverly's blue and green hair flapped around her as she shook her head. "No. You have to put it up there." She gestured toward the small hole in the ceiling. "Put it inside the bookcase with the glass doors. That is the only place that is safe."

Elora gulped. "But I cannot get up there."

The mermaid's expression fell as she sank deeper into her bucket. "Then we are doomed."

Pulling the talisman from her pocket, Elora took a step toward the hole. It would be hard. Exhausting. But she hadn't done all that wing training just to give up now.

She squeezed the talisman tight and then popped out her wings from her back again.

CHAPTER

35

When faced with an impossible task, Elora had always tried a little harder than before. She had the desire to do more than others expected. More than others thought possible. And so many times that had served her well.

She checked the talisman in her pocket once more before attempting to fly herself off the ground. The determination that always fueled her sent her wings beating. She set her jaw, ready to push herself harder than ever.

But that was the thing about flying. Pushing harder only hindered her progress. Whenever she tensed her wings like she was ready for a fight, they only curled and refused to beat properly.

Being driven had helped her a lot in life, but she was learning, sometimes she just had to let go and *feel*.

No wonder flying had been so difficult for her to learn, especially lately.

Instead of tensing her muscles, this time she focused on her thoughts instead. With beating wings at her back, she remembered Tansy. Her sprite friend was stuck in Fairfrost. For a second time.

Elora clenched her first and made a promise to herself.

If I can escape this dreadful house, I swear I'll help Tansy escape from Fairfrost.

The words simmered inside her mind, but they weren't enough. She needed Faerie itself to know her decision. This time she spoke out loud.

"If I manage to escape this dreadful house, I—" Her mouth froze for a moment before she continued. "I *vow* that I will help Tansy and the other sprites escape from Fairfrost."

From the edge of the room, Waverly raised an eyebrow. "Vows mean nothing when spoken by a mortal."

Whipping around to face her, Elora narrowed her eyes. "It means something to me."

And then she let her wings go. She released all power and feeling into them. Wherever they took her, she trusted them to do it safely.

They did.

It started with a gentle flutter and soon the wings beat hard on her back. They lifted her upward toward the ceiling. Each flap made her feel more deeply. For a moment, her wings burned just like her father's sword had. But she didn't stop. She didn't attempt to shove the emotion away or explain it. She just *felt* it.

Soon, the pain trickled away on its own.

As her body rose into the air, her wings had to fight to bring her higher. It was still hard, despite her recent revelations.

Maybe it would always be hard.

But some of the best things in life were.

With one last burst of flapping, she grabbed onto the side of the hole that led into the room she had first entered. She had to retract her wings to get through. Getting out of the hole took more effort than it had to get in.

Once through it, she sprinted straight for the bookcase and tucked the iron talisman inside one of the glass doors.

Her stomach flipped as she thought of the tournament. Had it started it already? Probably. Had it ended? Her body shuddered.

Brannick had the enchantments and the feather that would help him in his fight against Queen Alessandra, but even those wouldn't be enough. He needed the essence from her crystal. And he needed her to be there to feel it.

When she ran back to the hole that led downward, her legs ached for how fast she ran. She forced herself through the hole, caring little for how it bruised her hips.

Waverly already had a swirling Faerie door open in front of her. The edges were made with foaming sea water that gave off sparkles. The mermaid raised her hands above her head, as if ready to dive into the door.

"Wait." Elora didn't even pop out her wings until she had fallen halfway to the floor because she was so focused on calling out.

A shiver passed through Waverly's shoulders, but that didn't stop her from nearly diving into the door.

Elora clenched a fist at her side as her wings helped her flutter softly to the ground. "You have to wait for me. I helped you escape. You owe me."

The mermaid finally paused, wincing as she did.

Once she landed, Elora glanced toward the other edge of the room. "And we're taking that brownie with us too."

The brownie had been staring at them with wide eyes from behind a pillar. At the mention of her, she jumped and tried to look away.

Elora glared at the brownie and then she glared at Waverly. "No arguing. The brownie is coming with us. We're all getting out of here."

Shuddering again, the mermaid gave a stiff nod. "Fine, but we must hurry."

If they had more time, Elora might have insisted they try to rescue the others who were in the loft. That might have been a lost cause anyway, though. None of them seemed like they *wanted* to be rescued. And with the tournament going on, Elora didn't have time to try.

From behind the pillar, the brownie shivered. Her eyes gleamed when she looked at the mermaid's door, but she didn't move.

In the end, Elora had to pick the little creature up before diving into the door herself.

Her clothes soaked through with seawater the moment she entered the swirling tunnel. It made sense that a mermaid would have a door made of water, but it still came as a shock. Strands of wet hair clung to her face while she tried to kick her legs to keep afloat.

On the other side of the door, they arrived in a large lake. At least they landed above the water's surface instead of far underneath it. Pushing her hands forward, Waverly sent some kind of magic that pushed Elora toward the shore.

Black goo covered the crusty, textured sand. The palm trees nearby had blackened leaves that looked as though they had recently been on fire. Even the seawater stuck to Elora's clothes, a little thicker than it should have been. The air smelled of salt and decay.

Elora recognized the shore at once. It was the same place Lyren had taken her on her first visit to Swiftsea. Elora's story had once fought off the decay in this area, but it was back again now. And even worse than before.

From inside the lake, Waverly shot glances every which way. Each time her eyes grew wider and her mouth twisted up in horror. "It is so much worse than when Ansel captured me."

Setting the brownie down, Elora took a deep breath. "I can help."

The brownie and mermaid both watched with rising eyebrows as Elora settled onto the crusty beach.

Waverly shook her head. "The land may not be able to heal after this much decay."

But Elora was unconcerned. She set both her hands into her lap. "I know a story that can do it."

An icy chill filled the air at the sound of her words. Or perhaps it was her heart itself that chilled. Elora took a deep breath. "One day, when I lived in the mortal realm, my sisters begged me to go with them into town. I did not want to go. I wanted to do more sword training. I wanted to steal my father's old clothes so I could sneak into a tournament."

A lump had already settled itself deep in her throat. "But I rarely got what I wanted. Not then."

Reaching for her sword hilt, she began stroking a thumb over it. "So, I went into town with my sisters. They had fun while I waited. On the way home, we watched part of a tournament."

Her eyelids fluttered closed as she stretched her fingers over the hilt. "It only served as a reminder of how much I couldn't have."

With one hand on her sword, she reached the other up for a wet strand of hair. "But when you want something new, sometimes it's easy to forget what you already have. And sometimes you only realize what you have when you lose it."

The tears came now. Slow and steady and stinging. The sword hilt burned at her fingertips, but so did everything around her. Even her toes and the top of her head burned. It tore away every last defense she had. Her throat choked as she tried to speak, but she forced the words out anyway.

"My parents died in a fire. If my sisters and I had been home, the fire would have killed us too. They are gone forever now." Her fingers squeezed over the lock of her hair. "Not even the most powerful fae in Faerie can save them."

Her tears dropped hard against the sand, each one falling heavy like a stone. She slammed her eyes shut. The burning inside her had shifted to more of a tingling sensation. "I cannot save my parents." She swallowed over the ever-growing lump in her throat. "But maybe losing them does not have to be the end. Maybe I can miss them but still move on."

The tears fell faster than before. Her eyes flickered open just long enough to see purple steam bloom above each tear drop. The steam burst in the shape of wildflowers before spreading outward over the decaying landscape.

Her eyes fell closed again. She clutched her sword hilt tight while her heart squeezed in her chest. She forced herself to breathe. To feel.

To remember.

It would always hurt.

But maybe like flying, she could learn a new way to live. A way that *included* the pain.

"Look." Waverly's voice came out breathless.

The little brownie gave out a squeak. "I have never seen such magic from a mortal."

Getting to her feet, Elora glanced around. Everything had changed. The water was clear and sparkling. Lush green leaves wafted at the top of the palm trees. The beach on the sand had turned soft and brown.

Warm air ruffled all around, sending pleasant scents of salty air and coconut across the waves.

But it wasn't just the area around them. The lush landscape stretched out even farther. As far as Elora could see, the decay had been eaten up by the flash of life.

While Waverly's dark skin sparkled with a tinge of blue, she suddenly clapped a hand over her mouth. "Queen Alessandra will be here soon to steal the creation magic."

The slightest smile played on Elora's lips. "No, she won't. She is busy at the moment."

The mermaid pinched her eyebrows together for only a moment before she let out a sigh of relief. "Then this magic will keep the decay at bay longer than anything else we have done. It has not solved the problem completely. But now we can search for the cause instead of having to constantly keep the decay at bay."

Elora mostly ignored the words. They would sink in later. But right now, she had something more important on her mind. "I helped you escape Ansel's house, and I helped heal your court. Now I need you to do something for me."

Waverly offered a solemn nod. "I vow to—"

"No." Elora shook her head with her lips pressed together. "I need something specific. I need you to open a door to Noble Rose. Open it right outside the castle. And I need you to do it now."

CHAPTER

36

Tumbling through a watery Faerie door was much easier the second time. It helped that Elora landed on a grassy hill instead of inside a lake. A shower of droplets fell down on her as her feet hit the ground.

The rolling hills and manicured gardens of Noble Rose looked back at her. She could see the tournament grounds and the fae crowd surrounding it. Now she just had to run.

Before her feet started moving, she pulled a pin from her pocket. It was the same hairpin with the blue gem that Ansel had glamoured her with. Since her hair was soaking wet, and since the entire crowd had just seen her be kidnapped by Ansel, maybe disguising herself would be a good idea.

She tucked the pin into her hair, watching her hands and clothes change at once.

The moment she began moving toward the tournament grounds, she could feel that something was wrong. Tense energy sizzled in the air. Every step she took closer to the tournament grounds, the energy tightened and twisted.

Blasts of colorful sparks shot into the air. Showers of dirt and twigs followed behind the sparks. Maybe the energy was simply the magic Brannick and Queen Alessandra used in their fight against each other. But maybe it was something more than that.

Reaching into her pocket, she found the crystal that held Brannick's essence. Tension radiated from it, even greater than that in the air. Her chest rose with a heavy breath as she squeezed the green stone.

Would he be able to tell? Would he know she was touching it even if he couldn't see her?

Whether he could or not, it seemed like a good moment to run. She sprinted toward the tournament grounds, ignoring the stinging in her side that grew with each step.

By the time she moved close enough for spectators to see, no one looked her way. Every eye was stuck on the tournament grounds.

Good.

It would help her get to the others faster if she didn't have anyone noticing—or worse, stopping—her along the way.

By the time she reached Brannick's council members, they didn't react to her presence. At least not until she tapped Lyren on the shoulder.

The sea fae whipped her dark curls as she threw a seething glare over her shoulder.

"It's me. Elora." She kept one hand in her pocket as she spoke.

Lyren clapped a hand over her mouth while a tiny gasp escaped. "You are alive. Why are you glamoured?"

Her hand landed on Elora's shoulder, only to shoot backward once again. "Why are you soaking wet?"

Vesper peeled his eyes away from the tournament grounds only to poke Elora on the shoulder. "How did you get back here?"

"Never mind that." Elora pushed past them both. "I need to see what is going on."

Quintus raised an eyebrow at her appearance, but his face still looked fallen. "You might prefer to not see."

Lyren gave a heavy nod. "Prince Brannick is going to lose. Queen Alessandra is just torturing him as much as she can before he loses consciousness."

Lowering his eyes to the ground, Vesper wrapped an arm over his stomach. "I have never seen a more painful fight."

Gritting her teeth, Elora tried to push past them again. "He is *not* going to lose. Now get out of my way."

When they finally moved, Elora didn't look straight toward the tournament grounds. Instead, her eyes flicked over to the side of the grounds where Queen Alessandra's council stood. As she suspected, Ansel stood among them, watching the tournament with flashing yellow eyes.

After positioning herself behind Vesper just enough, she made certain that Ansel could no longer see her. Only then did she remove the hairpin from her hair. The glamour disguising her fell away at once.

Finally, she looked toward the tournament grounds. She reached for the green crystal in her pocket once again.

Prince Brannick's skin had turned sallow. The copper undertone in his light brown skin was dulled to an almost green tinge. Dark circles shadowed under his eyes. His limbs shivered every time he moved. He didn't wave his hand the way he usually did when he used magic. Now he jerked it around in stiff, uncoordinated movements.

His eyes dimmed to a grayish hue. They looked colorless, but not in the magical way they usually did. When she removed the hairpin from her hair, the air around her shimmered before it fell away.

It was just enough of a change to attract Brannick's attention.

He glanced toward her. A blast of colored sparks hit him in the chest at the same moment. He dropped to the ground, but he hardly even seemed to notice the fall. His eyes had locked onto hers.

Surprised. Relieved.

It didn't matter which exact emotion it was because his eyes burst with colors again. A smile skipped across his lips.

She nodded toward him, squeezing the crystal all the while.

Maybe the tournament had gone badly so far, but she and the prince knew something none of the other spectators did.

This wasn't over yet.

CHAPTER 37

New energy radiated from the crystal in Elora's hands. She held it tight, letting the energy wash through her. That moment when Brannick smiled? That changed everything. Now the crystal pulsed and sparked.

Remembering the prince's instruction, she thought back on the day he climbed the tree just outside her window. His eyes had never looked freer than in that moment. She had only ever seen tiny glimpses of his carefree attitude, but on that day, she experienced it.

The true Brannick.

She held onto that memory as tight as she could while he used dirt and twigs and even the ground itself to throw attacks toward the Fairfrost queen.

Vesper sidled up to Elora and whispered under his breath. "What are you doing?"

"Nothing." The answer came out rushed. She needed her concentration to stay on the crystal in her pocket, not on some unimportant conversation.

Apparently, her answer did not satisfy him. "Remember how I said that just because you *can* lie does not mean you should?"

"Be quiet, Vesper." Her jaw had clenched, forcing her to speak through her teeth.

Lyren came up on the other side, sniffing. "You smell like Swiftsea."

The crystal buzzed. Elora closed her eyes and took a deep breath before she nodded. "Yes. Waverly took me there."

Lyren probably wore some expression of shock, but Elora was too focused on the tournament grounds to see it. When Lyren did speak, her voice came out forlorn. "That is impossible. Waverly is gone."

"I know." Elora closed her eyes again. "I found her, and she took me to Swiftsea."

A new pair of footsteps moved closer. Even with her eyes closed, she knew it was Quintus.

"Your face is different now. It looks more like it did when you first arrived in Faerie."

Elora beamed at the words. Maybe the fae didn't know why, but she knew exactly the reason her face had changed.

Emotions. They were back again.

Her eyes shot open. The tournament grounds came into focus while the crystal in her hand buzzed. "Aren't any of you interested in the tournament?"

Lyren flinched as she turned away. "Does it not pain you to watch it?"

A smirk pricked at Elora's lips. "Not anymore."

The three fae stared at her before they braved a glance toward the tournament grounds.

Queen Alessandra stood frozen inside a mess of twigs and dirt. No matter how she flailed her arms and legs, the earth around her would not allow her to win.

Even better, her eyes drooped. She was tired from the effort of fighting against Brannick for so long.

Vesper let out a chuckle. "She should have beaten him while she had the chance. She spent all that time torturing him, but now she is too tired to fight."

After another moment, the queen's eyes fluttered closed and her limbs relaxed.

Brannick still looked weak, but at least his eyes glimmered the way they usually did. He held the queen in place just long enough to glance backward at the high king.

Atop his throne, High King Romany coughed into his golden handkerchief as he nodded. Once he finished coughing, he sat up straighter. "Prince Brannick is the victor for the second tournament."

At the sound of those words, Brannick released his magic on Queen Alessandra. She fell to the ground in a heap, but it only took a moment before she gained consciousness again. Her entire face burned a bright crimson as she clenched her hands into fists.

Before the queen could glance anywhere else, Elora tucked the hairpin back into her hair, glamouring herself once again.

High King Romany's arm shook as he gestured outward. "You two may leave the tournament grounds."

Barely a moment had passed before Brannick raced to Elora's side. He reached toward her glamoured face only to stop it just before touching her. But then he smiled. Such a smile would have stopped time, if it had existed in Faerie.

Indeed, perhaps that smile was the very reason time *didn't* exist in Faerie.

Movement pulsed in his eyes. "I should have known you would escape on your own."

Releasing the crystal, she pulled her hand from her pocket at last. She gave a little shrug. "I did have some help."

His grin grew wider with each word. "A mermaid from the smell of it."

With a nod, she glanced toward the thrones holding the other fae royalty.

As if anticipating her question, Brannick tilted his head toward the throne. "High King Romany will take some time to think before he officially declares the new High Ruler of Faerie."

Lyren clapped her hands under her chin as she gave a little jump into the air. "But Prince Brannick won the speech and he won both of the tournaments. His victory is inevitable."

"It is not over until it is over." Quintus raised both eyebrows as he spoke.

Letting out a sigh, Lyren nodded. "Fine. I should have said, Prince Brannick's victory is *nearly* inevitable."

"Uh, Prince Brannick." Vesper titled his chin upward. "Perhaps Soren needs to know—"

"Right." The prince touched a hand to his forehead as he gave it a tiny shake. He then pulled a cork stopper from his pocket. At the same time, he raised one arm and clicked his tongue three times.

A glowing green sprite flew down from above until it landed on the prince's palm. Brannick handed the cork stopper to the sprite before speaking again. "I have a message for Soren of Bitter Thorn. Tell him to hold back the troops. Elora is safe again."

The sprite zoomed off as soon as the message was given.

Tingles went through Elora's arms as she bit her bottom lip. "You were going to send an entire army to rescue me?"

Brannick took a step closer to her, keeping only the smallest distance between their shoulders. "I never did give you a gift of thanks after you helped me with the iron. Now I will still have to think of one."

Her cheeks warmed as she glanced toward the ground. But then her head shot up again. "Where is Blaz?"

The others all glanced at each other before turning toward the prince.

Wincing, Brannick frowned. "He is on his way to Mistmount. I would send a sprite after him, except they do not deliver messages to animals. And Blaz would not understand a message from a sprite anyway. But Blaz will be fine. He knows how to take care of himself."

High King Romany hit his scepter on the ground three times. He stood from his throne, though his entire body shook from the effort. "The time has come for me to choose my successor. Prince Brannick and Queen Alessandra, come forward."

CHAPTER

38

Crackles of energy sparked in the air. The fae stood from their chairs, and the chairs vanished in clouds of red dust. Roses bloomed above every head, appearing from thin air. Once the flowers went from bud to full bloom, they dropped to the ground. Each one burst into a large shower of red dust and golden sparkles. Higher in the sky, colorful sparks shimmered all around.

Elora stepped forward to get a better view of the magical sight. When she did, she caught a glimpse of the fae who had tried to capture her. Ansel.

Though her fists curled tight, she still shrank back out of his sight. Another promise danced around in her mind. Maybe it wasn't an actual vow yet, but she wanted it to be. If she ever got the chance, she'd kill him.

Prince Brannick and Queen Alessandra moved toward the throne at the same time. With each of their steps, their clothing transformed. Brannick's suede fighting clothes and leather armor glimmered and changed into regal clothes. The fabric of his coat and pants was almost dark enough to be black, but hints of forest green still shone through. His long hair was slicked back, showing off his pointed ears.

Queen Alessandra's tight fighting clothes changed into an opulent white dress with even more iridescence than she normally wore. The thick beading down the front of her dress must have been heavy. The pins that held her hair in a tight bun fell away. Long brown curls tumbled down her back.

The transformation was likely nothing more than a glamour, but it was spectacular all the same. Both Brannick and Queen Alessandra looked more regal than ever.

Despite the incredible sight, Elora's stomach still writhed as she watched them both move forward. She tried to shake the feeling away. Hadn't Lyren already said Prince Brannick's victory was inevitable?

Elora had no reason at all to worry.

And yet, her muscles tensed. At her sides, she could feel even more tension drift into the air around. Lyren, Vesper, and Quintus all wore expressions that were not quite confident. Each of them stood tall, but fear shimmered in their eyes as they looked ahead.

Shaking her head, Elora tried to take a deep breath. Maybe victory was inevitable, but waiting for it certainly wasn't pleasant.

Queen Alessandra's nose wrinkled as she glanced to her side. She turned just enough that Elora could see a curved axe in the queen's hand. The opal-encrusted handle glinted in the light. Elora jolted at the sight of it.

She tried to shrug the fear away. Since Brannick was holding two white feathers and a large stone, the queen's axe was probably ceremonial or symbolic in some way.

But then the queen stood taller. Calmer.

Why wasn't she angrier?

Tingles pricked at Elora's fingertips.

High King Romany sat higher on his throne. He raised a hand to silence the crowd, but still, he did not speak. He sat and stared. He even swallowed a few times. Was he trying to make everyone in Faerie go mad with waiting? Or perhaps his sickness prevented him from speaking right away.

When he finally did speak, his voice came out croaking. "In all three stages of the testing, Prince Brannick proved himself worthy of becoming High King of Faerie."

The words were too perfect. Elora held her breath, waiting for the high king to add a *but* to the end of his sentence.

He didn't. "Prince Brannick's mother, High Queen Winola, once created the portal that allows us to enter the mortal realm. Her actions gave us mortal emotions, which we still suffer from."

Tension pulled across Elora's shoulders while she tried to stand without collapsing. High King Romany clearly still had disdain for what Brannick's mother did long ago. But he *couldn't* keep the victory from Brannick because of it. Brannick didn't have any control over what his mother had done. It wasn't his fault.

Now the high king shifted in his seat. His grip got tighter on the scepter in his hand. "But Prince Brannick has not followed after his mother's actions. He will lead Faerie as a true fae." The high king stood from his throne, gripping tight to his scepter. "I choose—"

"Wait." Queen Alessandra barely raised her voice, but it sliced through the air for all to hear. Her face was neutral, but her voice definitely sounded like a smile.

High King Romany let out a grunt as he collapsed back onto his throne once again. Blood splattered from his lips as he tried to get his golden handkerchief up to his mouth in time. When he glared at Queen Alessandra, the look could have killed. "You dare interrupt me while I choose my successor?"

Even with the neutral expression on her face, she still managed to give off the impression of a grin. "What I have to say is pertinent. You will be glad to hear it."

His nose twitched at the words, looking very skeptical indeed. The silence that surrounded them only moments earlier was now replaced by hurried whispers and speculations.

There were too many gasps to count. Too many raised eyebrows.

The energy around Elora and the others in Brannick's council curled into a writhing tangle. She could feel it in her gut. They all held their breath.

It was a good thing Prince Brannick stood near the throne because Elora might have reached for his hand. She might have grabbed onto it, trying to offer comfort at the same time as taking it. But touching him would have killed him. So it was better that he stood far away.

Turning to her side, Queen Alessandra lifted her chin. "Prince Brannick, kneel before me."

Elora sucked in a breath at the words. Waited. Her skin prickled.

But Brannick did not move. He stared straight ahead at the high king, not even acknowledging the queen's words.

Was it the crystal? Elora reached into her pocket to squeeze it once again.

Maybe the other enchantments that were only supposed to help during the tournament were somehow helping him now. Didn't everyone say Faerie magic was unpredictable? Maybe Faerie itself was helping Prince Brannick in this moment.

High King Romany pinched the bridge of his nose. "This does not appear to be pertinent in any way. If—"

The queen raised a hand, her grin turning cruel. "Prince Brannick, I *order* you to kneel before me."

Brannick's knees jerked. His fists clenched, and his face grew red. He stood still for a few moments, but of course, it wasn't enough. Soon, he dropped to the ground, bowing his head at the queen.

From his throne, High King Romany raised both eyebrows high. Then he narrowed his eyes.

Queen Alessandra did nothing to hide her smile now. "Prince Brannick, I order you to tell the high king that I should be his successor. Not you."

Veins popped out across Brannick's chin as he clenched his jaw. The same redness filled his face, but again, it wasn't enough. With a burst, his lips parted. He barely glanced toward the throne as he spoke under his breath. "You should choose Queen Alessandra to become the next High Ruler of Faerie."

"You see?" The queen gestured toward the ground. "Prince Brannick entered a bargain with me long ago. He must follow my every order. And believe me, I will give him many, many orders. Whether I am chosen or not, I will be the true High Ruler of Faerie."

High King Romany touched a hand to his chin. "I see." He sat back farther into his chair while dabbing his handkerchief across his lips. "That does change things."

With a grunt, Brannick forced himself to his feet. "The bargain between us may not last forever."

The queen waved a flippant hand at the words. "It does not matter. Faerie needs a strong ruler, not someone who will bow to the command of another." She turned her gaze back to the high king. "You see that Prince Brannick is unfit to rule. Only I am strong enough to be High Ruler of Faerie."

Brannick gulped before he spoke again. "High King Romany."

Rising from his throne once again, the high king shook his head. "I have made my decision." While standing, he took in a deep breath. The ruby on top of his scepter glowed bright, sending magic up the high king's arms. The magic made the high king's limbs sturdier. His face turned brighter. Even the redness in his eyes vanished and his blue eyes sparkled. He stood taller. "I choose Queen Alessandra as my successor."

Elora sucked in a breath so fast, her stomach tightened.

The high king lifted the gold and red velvet crown off his head. When he did so, glowing golden magic emanated off it. The grand crown shrank to a more modest size. At the same time, the tines of Queen Alessandra's crown grew taller. Grander.

Little bells tinkled all around, as if welcoming in a new High Ruler of Faerie.

It didn't matter how much Elora's stomach sank, it still sank further with each new moment.

When the magic stopped, Queen Alessandra's face twisted. She raised her curved axe and shot a frightening glare toward the high king.

High King Romany still looked strong after drawing power from his scepter.

Gritting her teeth, Queen Alessandra lunged toward him with her axe swinging.

CHAPTER

39

Elora gripped her sword tight. On instinct, she moved to lunge right after the queen. Anything to stop her from plunging her axe in its target. But once Elora tried to lift her feet off the ground, two pairs of arms held her back.

Lyren hissed in her ear. "She will kill you if you try to stop her."

Vesper held her tight on the other side.

By the time Lyren finished speaking, the queen's opal-encrusted axe crushed High King Romany's chest, splattering blood everywhere. The life left his eyes before he could even crumple in his throne.

A laugh skittered off Queen Alessandra's lips. Blood dripped down her arms and face. With a wave of her hand, it was all glamoured away.

"I am High Queen of Faerie." Her hands raised high above her head. The air chilled.

Rising from his smaller throne, King Jackory of Mistmount stood. "You are not high queen until all other rulers swear fealty to you."

"Do it then." A smile twitched on her lips as her gaze fell on the newest ruler of Dustdune. "See what happens if you try to defy me."

Her grip tightened on her axe.

In her smaller throne, Princess Nerissa of Dustdune gulped. She jumped up. "I swear fealty to you, High Queen Alessandra."

The queen gave an approving nod. "Very good. I will remember that you were the first to do so." She threw a pointed look toward King Jackory and Queen Noelani of Swiftsea.

Neither of them moved.

Glancing down at her axe again, Queen Alessandra gave the slightest shrug. "Maybe Mistmount is ready for a new king then." Her gaze turned toward Ansel. "Someone who is not so defiant toward me, perhaps."

He cringed first, but King Jackory immediately yielded. "I swear fealty to you, High Queen Alessandra."

Queen Noelani continued to sit in her throne, gazing out at the landscape ahead. "What about Noble Rose? It has no leader now."

Sweeping a hand out over the land, Queen Alessandra said, "The Court of Noble Rose belongs to me now. I will rule this court, the Court of Fairfrost, and Faerie." Her eyes narrowed toward the Swiftsea queen. "I may choose to conquer other courts too, if I must."

A beat of silence filled the air as Queen Noelani's jaw clenched. At last, she stood. "I swear fealty to you, High Queen Alessandra."

Tipping her chin upward, Queen Alessandra turned toward Brannick. "That leaves just one other ruler."

Brannick stood on the tournament grounds. No part of his body moved. Not even his face.

Queen Alessandra's eyebrows fell low over her eyes. "I am waiting."

Still, Brannick did not move.

Vesper and Lyren held Elora fast by both arms. But maybe if she moved quickly enough, she could wriggle out of their grasp. It seemed like a good time to kill Queen Alessandra. Despite the consequences.

The longer Brannick stood without moving, Elora's urge to act grew. His defiance affected everyone around as well. Fae in the crowd began whispering to each other again. They looked to Queen Alessandra less with awe and more with anger. Even Vesper and Lyren reacted, but they only gripped Elora tighter.

Queen Alessandra stomped toward Brannick. Her voice came out shrill when she spoke again. "Swear fealty to me as High Queen."

Brannick kept his head high. "I will not."

"You will…" Queen Alessandra let out a breathy chuckle as her face contorted. "*What* did you say?"

Brannick folded his arms over his chest. "I will not swear fealty to you."

The laugh that erupted from Queen Alessandra had too much bite to bring humor. "You will not? Such defiance from someone who has no control at all."

When Brannick continued to stand motionless, she clenched a fist.

"You know what will happen if you refuse." The threat was clear in her tone, but Brannick did not react to it.

Flashing her teeth, the queen grew taller. It was probably just a glamour, but the sight of her growing was intimidating nonetheless. "Prince Brannick, I order you to swear fealty to me."

"I swear fealty to you, High Queen Alessandra." He spoke with no hesitation.

Her smile returned as she turned toward the crowd. "But."

The queen winced when Brannick spoke again.

He raised an eyebrow. "You and I know, everyone here knows, even Faerie itself knows that I only swore fealty to you because I was forced to do so." Now he smirked. "It is almost as if I did not even do it at all."

Her jaw clenched so tight, it bulged her veins. She spoke in a much lower voice this time. "I order you to go back to your castle."

Even though the queen appeared taller, Brannick still towered over her as he stared. He gave a simple turn and moved toward his council.

Vesper and Lyren pulled Elora far away from the crowd while Brannick moved toward them. She pulled the hairpin out of her hair as they moved, removing her glamour.

When Brannick drew near, he gestured that they should continue moving even farther away. It wasn't until they all stood far from the crowds that Brannick finally spoke again.

"Vesper, Lyren, and Quintus, you may go back to your homes, or you may go back to Bitter Thorn Castle. The choice is yours."

Lyren dropped her head in her hands. "We are doomed." She glanced up for a small moment before dropping her head again. "I would stay to help you, Prince Brannick, but what could I do?"

The confidence he displayed before the high queen had vanished now. His head hung. "I do not know. For now, we can only wait for her to make the first move."

With a quivering chin, Lyren nodded. "Then I will return to Swiftsea. If you call on me for help, I will return."

He gave a solemn nod before she disappeared through a Faerie door.

Quintus swallowed. "I will also return to my home. But I am a citizen of Bitter Thorn before anything else. Call on me if you need me."

Brannick nodded to that as well before Quintus went through his own door.

"I will stay in Bitter Thorn Castle." Vesper took a deep breath. "For now. I do not know when I may choose to travel again."

Brannick nodded again. "I will meet with you tomorrow."

When Vesper disappeared through a door, Elora got the strange feeling that everything would be different when she saw her fae brother again.

The prince turned to her now, which only made the feeling grow. "Elora."

She looked up at him through her eyelashes, trying to catch her breath after hearing her name on his lips. But how could she be calm when he made her name sound so magnificent? And when things had gone so wrong?

He leaned in closer. Though he stared at her with the same intensity as always, a new weight hung inside his eyes now. It looked even heavier than ever, and she guessed it would not vanish any time soon. He took a deep breath. Was he preparing to deliver bad news?

But then, he only said, "Come with me."

He offered no explanation when he opened a door and began to step through. She needed none to follow him.

The door took them back to Mistmount. She recognized the snowcapped peaks right away. A house with cobblestone walls and a black thatched roof stood before them. She shuddered at the sight of it.

"Why did you bring us here?" Strain worked through every one of her words.

Brannick only pointed in answer.

His wolf was nearby. Blaz growled and spat at the sight of the house, running toward it. The wolf hadn't noticed them yet.

"Blaz," Elora called to him, waving a hand to catch his attention.

In an instant, his sharp teeth and raised fur relaxed. Now he bounded forward with an air of excitement.

While the wolf ran toward them, she turned to the prince. "I thought the queen ordered you to go back to the castle. Don't you have to follow that order?"

He shrugged. "I will go back to the castle. I just had to find my wolf first."

She let out a sigh. "I suppose it should be encouraging that you can still defy her orders to some degree. Although, she could give so many orders it might not matter."

The prince did not respond. He just opened a new door. Once Blaz finally reached them, he stepped through it without even waiting to see if she followed.

CHAPTER 40

Inside the castle once again, Elora dropped onto a chair in the council room. She used part of her suede shirt to clean away the blood on her arm. With everything going on, she had nearly forgotten how Ansel cut her during their tournament. The blood had mostly stopped flowing by now, but some still seeped through.

The tiniest flinch passed over Brannick's face at the sight of it. Muttering under his breath, he reached into his pocket. "Mortals injure too easily." He handed her a clay pot. "You need to stop getting hurt."

She huffed while taking the pot from him. "I did not do it on purpose. Maybe if you didn't want me to be injured, you shouldn't have brought me to Faerie because of my sword skills."

A smirk or chuckle would have been nice. Instead, the prince just stared at her and began pacing across the council room floor.

The ointment inside the pot felt cool and thick like clay. She smothered it over her injury, trying to control her thoughts. She failed. When finished, her hand dropped onto Blaz's head, petting his fur.

Maybe that would give her strength.

But it only made things worse, because now both she and the wolf watched the prince as he paced back and forth on the council room floor.

Of course his own thoughts must have been harrowed and busy, but she could not wait a moment longer.

"Why did my father's sword burn me? Ansel said it was because it was a token. But you have the bear skin rug and the chandelier. They do not injure you."

Brannick stared at the ground as he paced across the room. "A token is only painful if it holds a painful memory."

Reaching for one of the feathers in her hair, she contemplated the words. "Your bear skin rug represents victory and escape, so it brings you those feelings instead of pain."

"Correct." He moved even faster over the stone floor.

Swallowing, she stepped right in front of him. He was forced to stop pacing immediately. She twisted her hands in front of herself. "We have to go get my sisters from the mortal realm. Ansel will…" Her body shivered hard. "We have to bring them here."

It took a moment before Brannick answered. His entire body went slack. Even his eyes drooped. "No."

Her eyebrows lowered. "But you came to Bitter Thorn Castle, right? You are here just like Queen Alessandra told you to do. Can you not leave now?"

"I can." He glanced at Blaz.

Elora twisted her hands, this time speaking more for herself than anyone. "I know Faerie is dangerous, but my sisters are not safe in the mortal realm either. Ansel knows where to find them. We must bring them here."

"I will not bring them to Faerie." Brannick clenched a fist before he turned away. "I will move them to another place in the mortal realm. Then Ansel will not know where to find them."

Digging both hands into her hair, Elora forced herself to nod. "Okay. Can we make sure they have food?"

Blaz let out a whimper. He lowered his nose, covering it with one paw.

Her eyebrows pinched together as she glanced at the wolf. "And can we make sure my sisters have a nice place to live?"

The wolf whimpered again, this time shaking his head. Her eyebrows drew together tighter. When she glanced toward the prince to see if he thought it strange, she found his expression matched the wolf's instead.

He stared at her, his face hardened in pain.

She gulped. "What is it?"

"You must go back to the mortal realm with your sisters."

She clapped a hand over her mouth, whispering through it. "No." When his face didn't waver, she took a step back. "No."

The fist at his side continued to clench as he turned his gaze away. "It is too dangerous for you here."

"I don't care." She folded her arms over her chest. "I have to save Tansy from Fairfrost. I want to rescue those other people Ansel has as well. And…" Her lip quivered. Instinct

311

tried to stop it, but she was done with smothering her emotions. She took a step toward him. "What about you? I couldn't leave you now."

His fist slammed against the nearest chair, toppling it onto its side. "What if she orders me to kill you?"

Setting her jaw, Elora stood taller. "Then we will fight through the night like we have already done before."

His jaw flexed. "I cannot protect you from everything." His eyes fell closed for a moment while he winced. "You do not belong in Faerie." His throat contracted with a swallow. "You do not belong with me."

She took a step back. The quivering in her chin continued, even worse than before. "How can you say that?"

But it only hurt because now she understood. He cared for her enough to send an army after her… but not enough to be with her.

Brannick scratched at a piece of his leather armor as he stared at the ground. "You do not understand how things will change with her in charge. I cannot keep you here any longer."

If her touch wasn't so dangerous to him, she might have slapped him across the face. He didn't even have the decency to look her in the eye. The urge to scream came hot and fast in her throat. It was almost enough to overpower the urge to sob.

Blaz whimpered again. He looked down, ashamed. Brannick stood with no expression at all. None of them moved while a fluttering breeze floated across the room.

But then a swirling door appeared at the head of the council room table. Glittery white tumbled around with an opal-like quality. It gave off a chill.

Before Queen Alessandra walked out of the door and into the council room, Brannick had stepped in front of Elora. His shoulders shook as he glared at the queen before him. He took another step to block Elora from the queen's view.

Queen Alessandra let out a chuckle. "You are always so dramatic. Does it not get exhausting?"

He did not answer.

Waving him off, the queen glanced around. "I did check for you in your throne room first, but it appears you prefer your council room these days."

Though Brannick spoke in an utterly calm voice, Elora could see how the muscles in his shoulders tensed. "Looking for my mother's crown again, were you?"

The queen let out a sigh as she dropped herself into the throne at the head of the table. "It would be so much easier if you just tell me where it is."

When the queen moved, so did Brannick. He kept stepping to keep himself between Elora and the queen. Elora had to tilt her head to see past him.

His fist clenched at his side. "I am surprised you opened a door inside my castle without an invitation. You know Faerie does not take kindly to such impoliteness."

"I had an invitation." Queen Alessandra twirled one of her curls around her finger. "Your mortal invited me here. I made a bargain with her."

Elora chose that moment to step out from behind Brannick. He would be angry about it, but she was angry at him anyway. "Did you come with the knowledge you promised?"

Brannick did indeed react to Elora's action, but at least he kept his mouth shut. Still, when she moved closer to the table, he walked as close to her as possible without touching.

The queen plucked a piece of lint from her sleeve. "As promised, I found a way for Prince Brannick to break our bargain."

313

He rolled his eyes before responding. "Do I even want to know it?"

She chuckled at that. "You probably guessed, but only a life sacrifice can break a bargain as strong as ours."

"A life sacrifice?" Elora flicked her eyes toward Brannick.

He sneered at the ground while answering. "That means the bargain will only be broken if I give my life to end it."

Elora reached an arm over her stomach and pinched her elbow. "But then you would be dead."

He raised an eyebrow. "Exactly."

Queen Alessandra settled herself back into the throne. "Actually, yours is not the only life that could be sacrificed. Due to the nature of our bargain, a life sacrifice from your beloved would also work."

Brannick rolled his eyes again. "Either way, one of us has to die, which means we cannot ever be together."

A smirk adorned the queen's face. "There is one other way." She leaned forward on the throne, steepling her fingers under her chin. "She could sacrifice her mortal life. That would break the bargain too."

"No!" Brannick nearly shouted the word.

Grinning, Queen Alessandra continued. "If she did it, you would be free of our bargain. You would not have to follow my orders. You could touch whoever you pleased."

He slammed a fist on the council room table. "Do not." Now he stepped between them again, blocking Elora's view. "Do *not* give her that choice. Leave now."

The queen settled back into the throne. "But it is not for you to decide."

With a growing smile, the queen reached into her pocket and pulled out a sparkling pink shard. She flicked it across the table until it stopped right in front of Elora. The balance shard left behind a glittery noise as it moved.

Queen Alessandra gestured toward it. "If the mortal plunges the shard into her heart, she will lose her mortal life and become a fae. Our bargain would be broken forever."

Brannick curled both hands into fists. "She will die. Everyone who uses a shard dies. No one can withstand the pain of living through the emotions of their whole life. And even if they could, the shard amplifies them." He shook his head. "You expect me to kill my beloved?"

The queen shrugged. "It is not for you to decide. If she wants to save you, she can."

He whirled around, pinning Elora with his gaze. "Do not let her guilt you into this. I found a way to evade her commands before. I will do it again. If you do this, it will break me, which is exactly what she wants."

"Brannick." Elora spoke in her softest tone. She glanced up at him. It was only a look, but hopefully her eyes conveyed how her heart beat and her stomach flopped.

A tender smile worked across his lips. He lifted a hand, as if to stroke her cheek, but he kept it just far enough away to keep himself from touching her.

She continued to stare into his eyes, hoping it would distract him from noticing how her hand moved. Once her hand curled, she finally spoke again.

"Save my sisters."

His head tilted at her statement for a single moment before she ripped her hand away from the table.

He shouted her name, begged her stop, but it didn't matter. She had already plunged the shard deep into her chest.

She was sick of running. Sick of hiding from the pain in her life.

If she couldn't live through it for the sake of her beloved, then what was the point of living anyway? And if she woke, he could not say she didn't belong. He could not say she was only mortal. She would be fae, and she could keep herself in Faerie no matter what he said.

But only *if* she survived.

Even while her eyes fluttered closed and her body shuddered in pain, she knew those thoughts might be her last forever.

THE STORY CONTINUES

Find out what happens to Elora and Brannick in book 3,
Crown of Bitter Thorn.

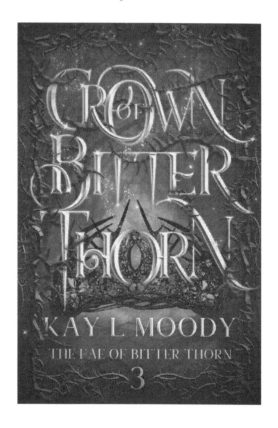

Faerie is forever changed.

Crown of Bitter Thorn is available now!

ACKNOWLEDGEMENTS

Thank you for reading my book! I don't think I can adequately express how grateful I am to readers like you who read and enjoy my writing. You keep me going when the writing gets hard. Thank you.

If you enjoyed the book, please consider leaving a review for it on goodreads or on the retailer where you bought it. Your review could help a fellow reader discover this story.

I am so extremely grateful for all my bookstagram friends. The book community on Instagram is so welcoming and positive. I am lucky to have a team of amazing bookstagrammers who work tirelessly to tell others about my books. To everyone on my team, thank you!

My editor, Justin Greer, deserves a huge heap of thanks. You always help me phrase things just right when my brain refuses to help. I am constantly learning more from your incredible expertise.

Angel Leya, my book cover designer, is so talented. I am honored to work with someone with such skill and an eye for design. Thank you for giving this series the book covers it deserved.

Queens of the Quill, you have been there for me through so much. Thank you for being the best author friends ever! Abby J. Reed, Alison Ingleby, Charlie N. Holmberg, Clarissa Gosling, Hanna Sandvig, Joanna Reeder, Kristin J. Dawson, Rose Garcia, Stacey Trombley, Tessonja Odette, and Valia Lind, you are awesome.

Last of all, thank you to my biggest supporter, my number one fan, and the best person I know, my husband. I am so grateful to have someone so perfect for me.

ABOUT THE AUTHOR

Kay L Moody is proud to be a young adult fantasy author. Her books feature exciting plots with a few magical elements. They have lots of adventure, compelling characters, and sweet romantic sub-plots. Most of her books have a dystopian flair. They include a variety of technology levels and lots of diversity.

Kay lives in the western United States with her husband and four sons. She enjoys summertime, learning new things, and doing her nails with fancy nail art.

MORE FROM KAY L. MOODY

Your Next Fantasy Binge Read!

She wasn't supposed to become so powerful.
She wasn't even supposed to survive.

Royalty, intrigue, and magic. This epic fantasy series will have you on the edge of your seat with all its twists and turns.

THE ELEMENTS OF KAMDARIA

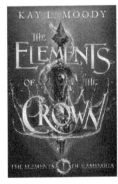  

GET THE PREQUEL NOVELLA FOR FREE

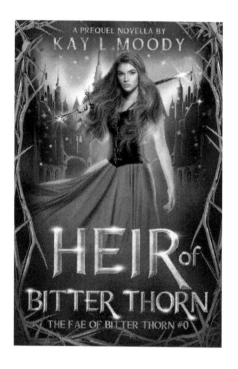

Visit kaylmoody.com/bitter for the complete prequel

Heir of Bitter Thorn is a prequel to The Fae of Bitter Thorn. Discover how Elora got the mysterious scar on her hand, how Prince Brannick escaped Fairfrost, and why the two of them don't remember their first meeting.

NEVER BARGAIN WITH A FAE.

Elora dreams of adventure.

With her unwanted marriage approaching, she is desperate to have some excitement before it arrives. A dryad appears and asks for help with saving a lost prince from the clutches of an evil queen. Believing it is nothing more than a dream, Elora agrees willingly.

But Faerie is more dangerous than she imagined. Alongside iridescent clouds and frosted beauty, it also has dangerous enchantments, scheming fae, and frightening trolls. Even with her experienced sword skills, the land challenges her courage and wit to their breaking points.

Unfortunately, she already broke the first rule of Faerie: Never enter a bargain.

Now she has no choice. She must save the prince… or die.

Visit kaylmoody.com/bitter for the complete prequel

Printed in Great Britain
by Amazon